Surprise Babies For My Billionaire Rancher
A Mistaken Identity Vacation Romance

Olivia Mack

Copyright © 2023 by Olivia Mack - All rights reserved.

In no way is it legal to reproduce, duplicate, or transmit any part of this document in either electronic means or in printed format. Recording of this publication is strictly prohibited and any storage of this document is not allowed unless with written permission from the publisher.

All rights reserved.

Respective author own all copyrights not held by the publisher.

Contents

1. Chapter one: Danielle — 1
2. Chapter Two: Adrian — 18
3. Chapter Three: Danielle — 27
4. Chapter Four: Danielle — 41
5. Chapter Five: Adrian — 60
6. Chapter Six: Danielle — 72
7. Chapter Seven: Danielle — 94
8. Chapter Eight: Adrian — 110
9. Chapter Nine: Danielle — 135
10. Chapter Ten: Adrian — 146
11. Chapter Eleven: Danielle — 161
12. Chapter Twelve: Adrian — 178
13. Chapter Thirteen: Danielle — 192

14. Chapter Fourteen: Danielle 209

15. Chapter Fifteen: Adrian 221

16. Chapter Sixteen: Danielle 234

17. Chapter Seventeen: Danielle 252

18. Chapter Eighteen: Danielle 264

19. Chapter Nineteen: Adrian 274

20. Chapter Twenty: Danielle 287

21. Chapter Twenty-One: Danielle 305

22. Chapter Twenty-Two: Danielle 322

23. Chapter Twenty-Three: Adrian 334

24. Chapter Twenty-Four: Danielle 351

25. Chapter Twenty-Five: Adrian 368

26. Chapter Twenty-Six: Danielle 380

27. Chapter Twenty-Seven: Adrian 398

28. Chapter Twenty-Eight: Danielle 427

29. Chapter Twenty-Nine: Danielle 439

30. Chapter Thirty: Sneak Peek 465

Chapter one: Danielle

"Excuse me, Miss? I need to pass."

I mutter something under my breath and ignore the soft voice that beckons me back to the land of the living.

Then someone touches my shoulder. I jolt awake, my vision swimming in and out of focus.

When it clears, I recognize the overhead compartments and the smell of airplane peanuts.

I blink, then I realize that the man sitting next to me is leaning sideways between us, an apologetic look on his face.

I rub a hand over my face and chase away the sleep. With a yawn I unfasten my seatbelt. Once I do, I stand up and move into the aisle between the seats.

With a smile, the older man with salt and pepper hair, and tight lines around his eyes, shimmies out of the seat next to me and into the aisle.

I sink back into my seat, and my hand moves to the drool collecting near the side of my mouth.

Hastily, I wipe it away with a cocktail napkin and squeeze my eyes shut. I hear another murmured voice.

When I open my eyes, I see the flight attendant in a black and white uniform two seats in front of me, a rehearsed smile in place.

Sighing, I sit up straighter and fold my hands in my lap.

I still have no idea what I'm doing on a plane or if going to this retreat is a good idea. Good idea or not, I know it's a little too late to change my mind.

After all, we're less than an hour away from our destination.

The plane gives a slight jolt, and I dig my nails into the armrests on either side of me.

Is this how I'm going to die? In an airplane owned by an airline whose name I can't remember? Before I even get the chance to make it to my retreat?

Stop being so negative. You're on vacation, remember? This is your chance to relax, unwind, and forget all about your life in the city. And about everything you've left behind.

Including an ex-husband who left me multiple messages before I got on the plane. And I already know I'll have many more when we land.

The thought leaves me with a bad taste in my mouth.

Ironic. This is from a guy who spent our entire three years of marriage ignoring me and only acknowledging me when he needed something. Now he won't leave me alone.

I can't deny the relief I feel at having finally plucked up the courage to leave him.

Being stuck in a loveless marriage has taken its toll on me. How I hate that I've wasted so much time on the wrong man.

As if I could've made Trevor into someone he wasn't.

You wasted too much time on that asshole. It's time to put him out of your mind. Kick him out of your heart once and for all.

The plane gives another jolt, and I press my lips together.

Then the fasten seatbelt sign comes on.

Out of the corner of my eye, I see several people return to their seats, wearing anxious expressions.

Moments later, I see the guy from the seat next to me coming back down the aisle.

Droplets of water slid down his face, and a furrow lies between his brows. I tuck my legs in closer and straighten my back.

When he squeezes past, I smell cheap soap and sweat mixed.

He pulls the seatbelt on and tilts his head in my direction. "You alright? You were really out of it."

I lick my dry lips. "Yeah, I'm fine. Sorry if it took you a while to wake me up. I didn't sleep much last night."

Or any night for the past three years.

I've been living off of coffee, anxiety, and the stress of my job for so long that I'm not sure I even remember how to be a functional adult.

Still, I have hope that it's not always going to be like this.

I have, after all, spent the past few months gluing myself back together and figuring out my next move.

Being at Savannah's felt good, particularly when I realized how stifled I felt. But I knew I couldn't hide in her apartment forever.

After weeks of moping around in my ratty old pajamas and eating soggy cereal and ice cream over the sink, it's time for me to start facing the outside world.

And with plenty of vacation days saved up, and nothing else to do with my time, I know that Savannah is right.

I do need a change of pace and scenery.

Which is why I'm hoping the Four Elements Ranch in Montana is exactly what the doctor ordered. Apparently, this ranch is a very unusual one.

According to Savannah, the owner of the ranch serves his guests personally.

And the ranch has a therapist and a psychiatrist who work with guests who need them and to overcome whatever they need to overcome.

I was quite intrigued. The on-site therapist, it definitely made it easier for me to decide to experience this unique therapeutic retreat for myself, up close and personal.

But still, I have my doubts.

With a sigh, I squeeze my eyes shut and roll back my shoulders.

The captain's voice comes on, low and soothing, but I can't make out what he says.

It isn't until the plane begins to shift and descend that my eyes fly open, and I stare at the other side of the aisle.

People are shifting anxiously in their seats. My stomach drops.

Finally, the plane touches the ground with a shudder. I hear the familiar screeching sound and brace myself for the plane to come to a halt.

When it does, a thin sheen of sweat covers my forehead, and I can't deny how relieved I am. I never liked this part of flying.

Shortly after, the seatbelt sign blinks off, and several people get out of their seats at once.

Luckily, my neighbor isn't one of them.

I study the people who retrieve their luggage from the overhead compartments. Then I fish my phone out of my pocket and take it off of airplane mode.

Predictably, several messages come in at once, all of them from a furious and pushy Trevor demanding to know where I am.

With a roll of my eyes, I ignore them all, pull up my contacts, and dial Savanna's number.

"Hey. How was the flight?"

"I slept through most of it," I reply. "The good news is that it's been a while since I've slept that deeply. The bad news is that I'm pretty sure I pulled something in my neck."

Savannah chuckles. "You always think you've pulled something. Just put a heat pack or an ice pack on it when you get there."

"That's if they have them." I shove my hair out of my face and peer out the window at the relatively empty runway, where the plane is still idling. "Remind me again why we thought it was a good idea for me to go to a ranch of all places."

"Because they have a good package. And you get the chance to work on your issues. Not just escape them."

I sigh. "I hate it when you're right."

"If it makes you feel any better, I miss you already," Savannah offers. "And so does Skittles. Right, baby?"

Skittles' familiar meow fills my ears, and a wave of longing hits me.

What am I even doing on this plane?

I'm not supposed to be in Montana, waiting to be cut off from the rest of the world for a whole month.

I want to be back home, in Savannah's apartment, with Skittles purring on my lap, a tub of half-eaten ice cream by my side, and a trashy TV playing in the background.

That's the kind of therapy and healing I need.

But I know if I fly back, Savannah will drag me here herself.

It's too late for me to change my mind, so I might as well see this through.

I clear my throat. "I miss you guys too. Don't watch The Voice without me, okay? Just record the episodes, and we'll watch them together when I get back."

"I don't know, Dee. That's a lot of episodes."

"What happened to being loyal?"

"It doesn't extend to TV shows," Savannah jokes before her voice drifts away then and comes back on. "Anyway, what's happening? Are you off the plane yet?"

"I'm getting off now. Let me call you right back."

Out of the corner of my eye, I spot a flash of movement, and the door to the plane opens. One by one, the other passengers trickle out, moving forward at a snail's pace.

When most of the plane has cleared, I stand up and retrieve my small bag.

Then I flash my neighbor a small smile and realize he's also on his phone, murmuring in a quiet voice.

As I make my way down the aisle, I take in the blankets thrown haphazardly, the empty wrappers thrown on seats, and the crumbs of food on the floor.

On my way off the plane, I give the flight attendants my best smile.

Despite the bags under their eyes, many of them smile back.

A blast of hot air hits me as I take the stairs two at a time. At the bottom, a bus is waiting. It whooshes open, and I breathe a sigh of relief when I realize it's got AC.

Smiling, I step in, wheeling my bag behind me. A few more people climb onto the bus, all of us standing and waiting.

After the last passenger climbs on, the doors whoosh to close, and it jerks to life.

I sit down and dial Savannah.

"I'm on the way to the terminal right now," I say when she picks up.

"Good, so how does everything look?"

"You do realize I'm not there yet, right?"

"Right, yeah."

"Sav, it's not too late to join me," I murmur, before patting my pockets for my earpiece. I place one in either ear and shove my phone into my pocket. "I did book a room with two beds in case you changed your mind."

"That's sweet, Dee, but you need to do this on your own. Besides, I'm buried under mountains of assignments. They're not going to correct themselves; you know."

"I'm sure no one would mind if you were a little late..."

Savannah snorts, and I hear the familiar beep of the microwave. "You've obviously never taught a day in your life. The second the students handed in the assignments, they started nagging me about when I'll post their grades."

My lips lift into a half smile. "Lucky for them it usually doesn't take you long. Since you don't have a life."

"Fuck you very much."

In the distance, the airport looms, a thick plume of heat shimmering around it.

The doors to the bus dart open, and I get off, wheeling the bag behind me. I'm already sweating in the few seconds it takes me to cross through the double doors.

A blast of cold air hits me, and I smile.

Then I follow the signs to the conveyor belt, the rest of the passengers trailing behind me.

"Hello? Sav?"

"....signal....phone....water...."

I roll my eyes. "Please don't tell me you dropped your phone in the sink again. I thought you were going to figure out a way to stop doing that."

With glass windows on either side of me overlooking a packed airport runway and several pulsing neon signs, I'm able to find my way easily.

I move from one auto-walk to the next, rushing past rows and rows of brightly colored shops on either side of me.

A few vendors even wave at me, but I ignore them all and make a beeline for the baggage claim area.

My shoes squeak against linoleum floors. I'm nervous when I round the corner and spot several conveyor belts.

Quickly, I study the screen and manage to figure out which one has my luggage. Then I wander over to it and shove a hand into my pocket.

"I didn't drop my phone in the water." Savanna's voice is finally back, and it's clearer than before. "Skittles pushed it into the sink."

I snort. "What did you do? Did you forget to pet her right?"

"I know you don't buy this because she normally behaves around you, but Skittles can actually be very mean. The other day she hissed at me because I tried to take her food bowl away."

"Maybe you shouldn't have taken the bowl away."

"She wasn't eating anymore, and you remember what the vet said about her weight."

As I wait for the conveyor belt to come to life, I shift from one foot to the other. "I'm sure she'll forgive you eventually."

Savannah sighs. "Or you'll come back home and discover my half-eaten body in the bathroom."

"You really need to stop listening to those true crime podcasts." I shake my head and stand up straighter. "All they do is freak you out and leave you paranoid."

"I can't help it. Besides, I'm not like you. I need to know what's happening in the world."

"I know what's happening in the world, thank you very much," I reply, a little too quickly. "I've just, you know, been busy."

"Babe, I know that pretending to be in love with Trevor must've been exhausting, but you know you don't have to make excuses anymore, right? That's part of what the retreat is for. I'm glad they actually have a few therapists on site."

I grimace. "Why did you have to remind me? I never should've let you convince me to do this."

Especially because I'm not comfortable talking to a stranger about how my marriage fell apart after only three years to boot.

I feel like a failure, and I have no idea how to come back from it.

Even though I still have a semi-successful career as a journalist, part of me wonders if that's going to fall apart too.

The rest of the world moved on while I was stuck in limbo.

When I was stuck trying to win the love of a man who can't love anyone but himself.

Why the fuck did I waste so much time on him?

Because you married him. And you don't like giving up. Even when you know you should.

"Babe, there's nothing wrong with going to therapy. You need someone to talk to."

"I've got you."

"I'm not a licensed therapist, and unless you start paying me—"

"I can do that."

"I was kidding," Savannah continues. I can hear the exasperation in her voice. "You do realize that even if you did pay me, it still won't work. I'm not supposed to be the one helping you."

"Then let me eat ice cream and binge-watch The Bachelorette. That's all the therapy I need."

"You can discuss that with your therapist. Anyway, look I've got to go. I've got leftover pizza to eat and a whole lot of assignments that need correcting. And I've got a pop quiz to prepare for."

"Alright, alright. Jeez, I get it."

"You're going to be fine. Message me when you've got your bag. Is someone picking you up?"

I stare at the bags spinning in a large circle and sigh. "Yeah, but I'm starting to think I should've sprung for something fancier. And fucking Trevor should've paid for this whole thing. He's the one who needs therapy."

"I agree. But unless you can figure out a way to forge his signature or something, it's all on you, girl."

I run a hand over my face. "I hate it when you make sense. Okay, I'll message you before I get into the car. Just remember that I won't be able to use my phone much. They have some policy about laptops and phones. We're only allowed to use them for like an hour a day."

"True! I forgot about that. In that case, I'm so glad I didn't come! Talk to you later, babe."

"Talk to you later."

When Savannah hangs up, I glance around at the cluster of people waiting. The knots in my stomach tighten.

I miss my best friend already. And I really hate that I'm out here on my own. Still, I try to convince myself that I'm doing the right thing.

Between the therapy and a near-total social media purge, I'm hoping this retreat delivers on everything it's promising.

Including rest and rejuvenation.

Because I desperately need to feel like I'm not floating around, aimless and lost.

A part of me can already hear Trevor's critical voice in my head. Dragging me through the mud like he always did.

Another part of me keeps reliving the day I woke up to his horrible mess.

When I saw Trevor in his den, leftover food and take-out boxes littering every surface, a pair of headphones pulled low over his head, something in me broke.

I realized that I'd had enough.

I'm still not sure what it was about seeing Trevor like that that made me snap.

All I know is that racing back up the stairs to pack my bag and message Savannah felt right.

Leaving my dead marriage was one of the best decisions I've ever made.

But I can't help but worry about what the future has in store for me.

And why it has to begin in Montana of all places.

Chapter Two: Adrian

"Where have you been? I sent you that note a while ago."

I glance over my shoulders, down both sides of the hallway, and step into the room. Then I let the door click shut behind me. "I was taking care of some new guests."

Brian uncrosses his leg and stands up. "You're supposed to be helping me."

"Brian, I am helping you." I walk over to him and give him a reassuring smile. "We've talked about this, remember? I can't be at your beck and call twenty-four seven."

Not while I'm running a successful business.

I love my brother, and there's very little I wouldn't do for him. But even I am beginning to wonder if bringing him here was a good idea.

He blows out a breath. "I know. I'm sorry. I'm just nervous. Are you sure no one knows I'm here?"

I nod and shove both hands into my pockets. "All of my staff are discreet. I have a zero-tolerance policy for anyone who gossips. So even if there is a leak which there won't be, I'll take care of it."

Brian wanders over to the curtain and pushes it aside. "It's only a matter of time before they find out. And when they do, they won't leave me alone."

"We'll cross that bridge when and if we get there." I study his room, taking in the large bed, the dresser with a TV mounted on top of it, and the mini fridge with a shelf above it.

When I glance at the bathroom, I notice it's damp, and there are some wet towels on the floor.

He must have just showered.

Staring at him from across the room is still a little jarring.

Since we were young, I've always found it unsettling to look at Brian. Unsettling to see my own features looking back at me.

Although we are twins, and physically identical, that is where our similarities end.

While I spent all of high school and college partnering up with friends and building an empire, Brian partied and fell in with the wrong crowd.

Despite my best attempts to steer him down another path, Brian never listened.

At least he's listening now. Fuck, Brian. How did you let things get so out of hand this far?

How did he go from a promising engineer to an alcoholic and drug user who lost everything?

Not to mention an occasional episode of hallucination due to his excessive drug and alcohol use, or it could be something more serious.

I don't know much, but all I know is that I have a big responsibility toward my only sibling and only immediate family, to make sure he is ok and well.

And if it wasn't for his neighbor—who found him passed out and nearly overdosed—he wouldn't be here today.

When I heard the news, I just knew I had to bring him here for treatment, even though I knew it's going to be very challenging.

For the life of me, I couldn't understand how he let things get so far.

Especially in his condition.

Brian has always been prone to anger issues and dark moods that left him locked up and isolated for weeks.

I've grown up alongside Brian, forced to familiarize myself with his every whim, mood, and trigger.

Another part of me knows it's not just his mood and anger to blame.

And now I hear that he's had some hallucination episodes, he believe that everyone is after him.

His violent streak and anger issues makes me think of our father.

A shadow of a man who darted in and out of our lives. Until the plane crash that claimed his life and mom's.

With a slight shake of my head, I turn my attention back to Brian. He has moved away from the window and is pacing the room. "I shouldn't have come here."

I take a step in his direction. "This is exactly where you need to be. Four Elements Ranch, with all its offerings, can help you overcome many things. I have read hundreds of guest testimonials. Brian, I'm not just saying things to make you feel better. Trust me when I tell you that it will help you. And you get to rest and relax with no one bothering you." I pause for a second and observe Brian, who's looking straight at me.

"You just have to do a few thing for me. Listen to me, follow the rules here, and don't do anything without talking to me first. Do not leave your room at anytime. I have a reputation to protect and a business to run. I can't jeopardize anything, including your sanity and safety." I pause and watch him again. He looks anxious.

"Your staff knows too much." Brian's hands curl into a fist at his side. "They're going to talk about me. They won't be able to help themselves."

"No, they won't. And you are not going to receive any special treatment or attention," I maintain, giving him a solemn look. "I've got everything worked out."

And all I need him to do is lie low and allow this place to work its magic.

Even Brian isn't immune to the healing nature of the Four Elements Ranch.

Or at least I hope he isn't.

Because the truth is I don't have any other way to be able to help my brother.

If the specialized diet, regimen of physical exercises, yoga, meditation, daily sessions with the therapist, and the serene environment of the ranch don't help, I have no idea where to turn next.

I hope that my brother is not beyond help.

Brian is like a fucking cat with nine lives. He's survived much worse, and he's going to be just fine.

Brian abruptly stops pacing and perches on the edge of the bed. "I wish I had your confidence."

"I'm going to go check on a few details, and I'll be back with a snack."

Without waiting for a response, I leave the room and step out into the hallway.

He's in a room connected to the main cabin, usually reserved for our VIP guests, so there's less chance of him getting into trouble.

Still, as I cross over to the main cabin and walk over to Maureen, my stomach is full of knots.

"How are preparations going for that guest we discussed?"

Maureen glances around and lowers her voice. "I've instructed everyone, Mr. Steele. As far as the guests are concerned, your brother is not on the premises. No one even knows or aware of such a guest here. I just mentioned to all that he's a very sensitive special guest and that no one is allowed to go to his room. And no one knows exactly what room he's in. Sir, I think it's best if you move him to the alpha cabin. He will have plenty of space to move around. He can even come out in the open and no one will see him. Since it's a restricted area."

"Ok, I will think about that. The only problem is that the alpha cabin is a little far, and it will take more time for me to visit him and more effort to watch over him. I can't leave him alone for long. And I don't think he needs that. That's a VIP cabin in high demand, and I rather keep that cabin available for our guests. Have you told the staff not to approach the special guest's room?"

"They will not approach the other Mr. Steele without your express permission. They don't even know what's going on. You did a great job, sir, of keeping things discrete."

"And if my brother asks for anything?"

"I handle it discreetly," Maureen replies, promptly. "And if there's any kind of leak, you'll be the first to know, Mr. Steele."

I straighten my spine. "Make sure that the rest of the staff knows what I will do if anyone breathes a word about us having a special guest on the premises. Not only will I terminate their contract, but I'll make it my personal mission to ensure they never work in the hospitality business again."

Without missing a beat, Maureen nods.

I like that she isn't fazed.

Out of all of the employees here, Maureen is the most professional. I know she can be counted on to keep my brother's presence under wraps.

Considering the extent of his bad reputation, and the number of people who have taken advantage of him over the years, I feel that the slightest thing could make him relapse.

Brian is here to rest and recover.

Not be hounded by the gossip and curiosity.

And I've made it my personal mission to ensure his stay here is smooth and uninterrupted.

After finishing my discussion with Maureen, I go back to my office, slam the door shut and press two fingers to my temples.

I can already tell it's going to be a long, long day.

Chapter Three: Danielle

A full half an hour has passed, and I'm still waiting for my bag.

Conversation rises and falls around me as I stand here. The smell of sweat and hand sanitizer fill the air.

Sighing, I go through Savanna's IG profile while I wait.

My lips lift into a half smile when I see her latest selfie, an apple laid out on top of a pile of papers, with Skittles dozing in the background.

Savannah's hair is piled on top of her head, and she's got an old t-shirt on. Despite the tightness around her eyes, she looks happy.

I briefly wonder if she's glad to have me out of her hair for a month.

Savannah and I are close. But still, I can't help but feel like she's sick of sharing her extra room with me while I mope.

With a slight shake of my head, I push the thought away and rummage through my carry-on.

After shoving a piece of gum into my mouth, I chew on it and tap my fingers against my thigh.

Sighing, I close the application and switch to the camera.

I take a few selfies, most of them with my head tilted and my lips pressed together.

Then I scroll through them and send a few to Savannah, who responds right away.

My fingers are moving quickly and without preamble when I spot a familiar bag.

Hastily, I tuck my phone away and step forward, pushing past the throngs of people forming a half-circle on either side of the conveyor belt.

When my bag finally rolls up, I hoist it up and grunt.

Pausing, I take my phone out again and take a picture with my bag, adding a quick caption to the bottom.

Savannah's response is instant, and I know she's procrastinating again.

My phone buzzes, and my heart skips a beat until I realize it's a work email sent to the entire staff.

I miss my office already.

And I know my boss was a little too eager to approve my time off.

Granted, I've spent far too much slouching over my desk and staring un-movingly at my screen, but a part of me had been counting on her refusal to give me the time off.

However, not only did she approve the entire month, but she was also nice enough to tell me it wouldn't affect my accountability or attendance.

I don't know if I'm relieved or worried.

After skimming through the email, a newsletter filled with pictures and anecdotes, I blow out a breath. Then I put my phone away and weave in and out of the people.

At one of the stores, I stop to buy myself a bottle of water and a hat. I pull it on and study the line of people gathered with signs held up to their chests.

I scan them carefully and grimace when I see my own name spelled out in cursive.

A short, dark-haired man in a brightly colored shirt and cargo shorts is waiting for me.

As I approach, I realize he's got pit stains under his arms, and his forehead is covered in sweat.

He takes out a pack of tissues and pauses to wipe his head. Then he offers me a bright smile and reaches for my bag.

"Welcome to Montana, Ms. Clark. I hope you've had a pleasant flight."

I nod and follow him. "I did, thanks. Is it always this hot? Mr. er...."

"Brady Horn." Without missing a beat, he wheels the two bags behind him, and I settle into a brusque pace to keep up with him. "We are experiencing one of the hottest summers in recorded history. But don't worry, the whole resort has central conditioning. And you'll find that the ranch occasionally gets a cool breeze."

"Occasionally?" We step outside, and I lift my hands up to shield my eyes from the sun.

Several cars are parked next to the curb, and I hear honks in the distance. Brady leads me to a small silver sedan parked on the far side of the street.

By the time we get there, my clothes are clinging to my skin, and I can smell myself.

Slowly, I wrench the back door open and watch Brady Horn as he places the bags in the trunk.

On his way past, he offers me a smile.

In the car, he rolls down the windows to let the hot air out and switches on the engine. "I'll take you straight to the ranch, Ms. Clark. Unless you want the more scenic route."

I shake my head and fan myself. "No, I think we can do that later. Right now, I just want a cold shower."

Brady chuckles and fiddles with the AC. "Understood. I'm the one you've been communicating with via email, Ms. Clark. And I've got everything set up for you, including some activities. And I placed an extra bed in your room."

I clear my throat. "Thanks. I'm not sure if my friend is going to be coming. But I figured better safe than sorry."

"That's no problem," Brady assures me. "We can have the bed removed anytime you want, Ms. Clark."

I stifle my disappointment and offer Brady a sigh. "Thank you. Is the ranch far from here?"

"Not at all." Brady settles back against his seat and sticks his arm out the window. A large white truck races past, nearly slicing his arm in half.

He doesn't seem fazed as he flips the driver off and rolls up the window. Then he fiddles with a knob, turning on the loud and intrusive AC.

But it's a welcome distraction from the heat. And being at the mercy of my thoughts.

You're a grown-ass woman, Danielle. You can handle being on vacation on your own. Besides, it's not Savannah's job to put you back together. She's already done enough.

And the last thing I want is to make her feel like I'm a burden.

I tell myself that I am not an insecure people pleaser who throws herself at the mercy of others.

And that if I am, the ranch is supposed to help me with that.

When we merge onto the highway, I press my face to the glass and study the world outside.

It rushes past in a blur of shapes and colors until Brady takes a right and butterflies onto a smaller, less worn-out path.

Soon, the metal buildings give way to smaller brick houses with lush greenery, and a few mountains in the distance.

I smile and trace the tops of those mountains with my fingers.

Brady clears his throat and places both hands on the wheel. "Are you sure I can't interest you in the scenic route? Montana's got some amazing mountains."

I turn away from the glass and meet his gaze in the rearview mirror. "I'm sure."

He nods and turns up the music.

Frowning, I settle back against my seat and take out my laptop. Then I take a look at the office newsletter and for the umpteenth time, wondering if I've made the right decision.

Most women whose marriages fall apart join a gym and go out for drinks when their friends. Some dye their hair outrageous colors, and others get a piercing or a tattoo.

I've considered all of those options and then some, but none of them felt right.

At least not to me.

Sure, I've considered getting extensions and going for purple streaks to liven up my brown hair, but the more I thought about it, the more ridiculous it sounded.

I'm not a teenager anymore. And I know that no matter how many glasses of wine I drink, gyms I join, or haircuts I get, nothing is going to fill the void that now exists in my chest.

My phone buzzes, and I smile at the selfie Savannah sent of herself with Skittles on her lap.

I send her another selfie, struggling to capture the scenic view in the background. Then I drop my phone in my lap and scrub a hand over my face.

When I blink, Brady is pulling to a stop outside a large two-story Victorian-style brick house with stretches of lush green land on either side of it.

In the distance, I can make out a few stables, a slew of brick cabins and a few tan-looking guests walking past the car.

All of them look relaxed and at ease with themselves. My stomach dips as I push the door open and pull my sunglasses down over my eyes.

Wordlessly, Brady opens the trunk of the car and takes my bags out.

Despite my protests, he carries them up the stairs and holds the door open for me. I duck inside, and I'm met with the smell of berry-scented air freshener and cool AC air.

Once my vision adjusts, I take in the large windows overlooking the scenery, a wooden desk in the center of the room, and a few chairs scattered on either side of me.

Behind the desk, three people in green and black uniforms are sitting and talking on their phones.

Brady leads me to the front desk, sets the bags down, and claps his hands together. "I will leave you in the capable hands of the Four Elements Ranch staff. I hope you enjoy your stay, Ms. Clark."

With a tilt of his head in my direction, Brady shoves both hands into his pockets and disappears behind one of the doors to my right.

When he comes back out, a few of the other guests wave at him, and he greets them by name. Then he disappears out the back door, and I am left leaning against the counter.

I open my mouth but before I can say anything, one of the employees, a blonde-haired woman, leaps to her feet and ends the call. "Hi, welcome to Four Elements ranch, Ms. Clark."

Without waiting for a response, she hands me a tall glass of water with a slice of cucumber and lemon wedge. "Your room is ready for you. Do you have any other requests?"

I shake my head and fish out my wallet. After I hand her my ID, her fingers move steadily over the keyboard. and I study the woman who is assisting me.

She has a high ponytail and a blindingly white smile. She holds herself with the grace and ease of someone who is comfortable in her own skin.

While I wait for her to check me in, I shift from one foot to the other and resist the urge to take out my phone.

A few moments pass. When nothing happens, I drift over to the nearest window and glance through the glass.

A family of four passes by, all of them on horseback and sporting identical elated looks. In the background, I see a group of hikers emerge, heat rising around them.

Smiling, I fish my phone out of my pocket and hold it up to the glass. After snapping a few pictures of the scenery, I send them to Savannah.

Shortly after I shove my phone back into my pocket, I wander back over to the main desk and pick up a pamphlet.

I skim through it, taking in the idyllic pictures of the ranch, the slew of photos of guests river rafting, sitting around a campfire, and posing on top of hills.

A few of the pictures even having couples lovingly gazing in each other's eyes against a scenic backdrop. I roll my eyes and pause at the paragraph underneath.

Did all of these couples really find love here?

A part of me figures it's a publicity stunt, meant to lure insecure and lonely women to the ranch.

But another part of me can't help but linger on that particular page, wondering what it would be like to form a real connection here.

With a shake of my head, I flip over to another page and skim over the paragraphs about the activities offered, wondering which of them would make a good fit.

I want to open myself up to everything the ranch has to offer.

When I leave here, I want to do so as a completely different person.

Clearing my throat, I flip to another page of the pamphlet and find myself reading about the ranch's owner and founder, Adrian Steele.

He sure sounds too good to be true. And with his suits, brown hair, and light skin, he looks like he walked off the cover of a major men's magazine.

Still, I study the pamphlet and tuck the information about him away in the back of my head.

The backdoor opens, and a large group comes. Everybody is covered in sweat, and a few have sunburned faces.

I grimace, but I'm unable to look away. Especially when a tall, broad-shouldered, tanned man in cargo shorts steps forward and says something to the receptionist.

He has on a cowboy hat and sun glasses. His sleeves are rolled up, showing off long and muscular forearms.

All of them laugh, and the women bat their eyes at him.

He flashes a smile at them, and I can almost hear their collective sighs.

With a shake of my head, I look away from him and focus on the teenage boy with too-large glasses and a few pimples scattered over his cheeks and nose.

He blushes when he notices me staring at him, so I avert my gaze and fix my eyes on an unmarked spot on the wall.

Why am I drawn to the man with the cowboy hat, of all people?

He strikes me as the kind of guy who is used to getting what he wants. I can tell by the way the rest of the staff reacts that he's got pull and sway.

When he whispers something else, and a tray full of drinks and snacks is brought out, cheers rise from the group.

A few of the women exchange discreet looks.

The last thing I want is to get distracted by a man, especially someone like him. A man who is hungry for attention, obviously. Not my kind of man for sure.

It's not what exactly I'm here for. But I'm determined to see this trip through with as little drama as possible.

Chapter Four: Danielle

"So, cell reception is controlled except during the one hour a day when we're allowed to use our phones?"

Maureen, the blonde-haired receptionist who's spent the past forty minutes going over the rules with me, smiles and nods. "Yes, that's right. Mr. Steele feels like it's important to get the full effect of the place. And being on social media all the time isn't going to help with that."

I frown. "What if there's an emergency?"

"Then we can help you reach out to your loved ones, and there's a number that they can call you on. It's a landline."

I blow out a breath. "Wow, okay. You guys really aren't kidding when it comes to the technology detox."

Maureen stands up straighter and nods. "That's right. It's the same with the laptops. You can stream shows and movies. You can listen to music, and you can play games. But you cannot access the outside world directly."

"It's almost like a cult," I joke, pausing to skim over the agreement. "Are you sure we're not going to be howling at the moon and offering up a blood sacrifice?"

Maureen gives me a blank look.

"Sorry, it's a bad joke," I mumble, before averting my gaze. "So, are there any spa services around?"

"There's a schedule with all of the activities, and you can book an appointment with our in-house masseuse or the nail service."

I read over the last line again. "I'm sorry. What is this waiver for?"

Maureen leans forward and lowers her voice. "I understand that this is because you chose to add sessions with our in-house therapist. It's just a standard agreement. You're required to put down an emergency contact and basic information about yourself to help the therapist get started."

"Isn't that something we do in the session?"

"You can always give your therapist more information during the actual sessions," Maureen replies, after a brief pause. "But she does require that you sign the waiver. It indicates that you understand that if you appear to pose harm to yourself or others, she'll have to break doctor patient confidentiality."

I scrawl my name at the bottom. "What do you mean exactly?"

Maureen shrugs and retrieves the clipboard. "I'm afraid I can't comment on that. You'll have to discuss any concerns you have with Doctor Sheridan."

I link my fingers together. "Okay. Do you want me to sign over my firstborn too?"

Maureen gives me another blank look, and I offer her a weak smile.

I want to apologize for the jokes that I can't seem to stop myself from making.

Being forced to wait a whole hour just to get to my room is taking a toll on me.

I'm tired, hungry, and sweaty. And the only way I know how to cope with being uncomfortable is by making ill-timed and lame jokes.

It's a coping mechanism I've had since I was a kid, and I'm not proud of it.

But it's also gotten me out of some sticky situations.

More than I care to admit.

"Okay, there's just one more thing—"

The cowboy hat man I spotted earlier leans against the counter and flashes Maureen a row of perfect, pearly whites.

He still has his glasses on, so half of his face is covered. "Hey, Maureen. I was wondering if you could help me out with something."

I wave a hand in front of his face. "Um, hello? I'm standing right here. You don't even have the decency to say excuse me."

He twists to face me, and my stomach dips.

Up close, he's even more handsome. A chiseled jaw, beautifully tanned skin. Locks of brown hair peak from underneath the hat. And he has a body like a Greek Adonis.

I almost forget why I'm annoyed.

Until he raises an eyebrow and opens his mouth. "Excuse me?"

"I've been waiting for an hour, so you don't just get to come over here and bat your eyes and flash your million-dollar smile and think that's going to make things better."

His lips twitch. "You think I have a million-dollar smile?"

"Some people would describe it that way," I stutter, the color quickly creeping up my cheeks and neck. "But I don't, in case you thought I was one of those people or something."

He can't possibly think that I'm like all those women who go weak in the knees from his jokes.

Who the heck does he think he is? Just do your work, whatever your work is, and go away dude. I don't have time for you or your charm.

I don't want to care how attractive he is. Or what the ranch staff lets him get away with.

I don't even want to think about the surge of annoyance pumping through me every time another woman looks at him.

What the hell, Danielle? You can't be jealous. You don't even know the guy, shit, why do you feel so jealous?

He continues to stare at me, a furrow appearing between his brows. "I wasn't trying to delay the check-in process, Ms. Clark. I was just going to ask Maureen to give you something."

"Me?"

Why am I acting like a nervous high-schooler with a crush?

Get a fucking grip, Danielle.

He nods in Maureen's direction, and she reaches underneath the desk and pulls out a gift bag.

Wordlessly, she hands it to him, and he peers into it. After moving a few things around, he holds it out to me with a smile.

A smile that makes my knees feel weak.

And makes my stomach feel funny.

Goddamn it.

What is the matter with you, Danielle? You can't just act like some lovesick teenager when a man smiles at you. No matter how handsome he is.

I can't help the smile that spreads across my face. "What is this?"

"It's a gift bag," he replies, pausing to flash me another smile. "I know it can't make up for the delay, but consider it a start."

"Huh?" I am staring at him, completely lost now. The rest of the world has faded into the background

He takes a step towards me, and his answering smile sends the butterflies in my stomach into a frenzy. "The start of a really good apology."

Is he for real?

This man has no right to be this good-looking or this charming.

Because he's making my stomach do odd little flip-flops, making me reconsider my decision to remain celibate throughout the trip.

Wow! Maybe they are even right about couples finding each other here.

Stop it Danielle! You're doing it again. You see a guy smile at you, and you start fantasizing about him. By the time you're in your room, you'll be married to him and having his children.

I bring myself back to reality.

With his broad shoulders, long calloused hands, and easy smile, I know I'm in danger. Especially because he is still looking expectantly at me. I can see my own image in his glasses.

I wish he could remove his glasses so I could see his eyes. Meanwhile, I gape at him like a fish. Hastily, I snap my mouth shut and let my hand fall to my side.

Maureen, the receptionist, quietly slides a key card over to me. I'm not aware that I've picked it up until it's in the palm of my hand.

And I have no idea when I bridged the distance between myself and the handsome rancher, but now there are only a few inches of space between us.

This place is not half bad. I smile at the thought.

Why is my heart pounding wildly against my chest?

Fuck.

He is just a man.

Think about something else. Anything else. Before you do something stupid.

"Let me get your bags." He reaches for them before I can protest and makes a sweeping hand gesture. "Shall we?"

"Is this a habit of yours?"

"What?"

He holds the door open for me, and we step outside. "Swooping in to make yourself look better."

"Only if the guests are pretty."

I let out a nervous laugh and fall into step beside him. "Does that line actually work on women?"

"You tell me." He wheels the bags over the smooth and even terrain, and the sun is hot on the back of my neck. Beads of sweat have formed there, and on the sides of my face.

But I know I can't check myself with the phone camera. No matter how much I want to.

I don't need to be just another woman falling all over him.

"Are you going to tell me you've never used the line before?"

He touches two fingers to his chest. "Scout's honor."

I laugh and fan myself "So, you were a boy scout too? Why am I not surprised by that?"

Of course he was. He's like a perfect specimen of a man.

There are rows and rows of cabins on either side. All of them are painted the same shade of dark brown, and all have a small porch out front.

We stop outside of one of them, and he holds his hand out for the key card. After swiping the door it clicks unlocked, and he pushes it before stepping to the side.

I step in, and my eyes dart over the interior, taking in the double doors leading into a spacious bedroom with a window overlooking the greenery.

A small kitchen looks surprisingly sleek with modern appliances. And the living room set is brown leather and overlooks a fireplace with a mantle and a TV mounted to the wall.

In a daze, I venture further into the cabin and take in the tile-floored bathroom with a claw foot tub and a glass shower stall.

Although I have no idea what I was expecting, I know it wasn't this.

This is much nicer and bigger than I imagined.

"Everything is pretty straightforward." He leaves my bags by the door and lingers in the doorway. "If you've got any problems, just use the landline. We've got an in-house electrician and plumber."

I swivel around to face him. "This ranch really has thought of everything, hasn't it?"

His eyes glitter. "We aim to please, Ms. Clark."

I ignore the shiver that races up my spine. "Your boss has definitely thought of everything."

His lips lift into a half-smile. "He's worked hard to make this feel like a home away from home. I'm Adrian by the way."

"Danielle." I offer him a small smile. "You don't have to babysit me, you know. Don't worry. I won't leave a bad review or anything. I get that delays happen."

The luxury of the room and the surrounding beauty almost make up for the delay checking in.

And the less time I spend in the Greek Adonis' presence, the better.

His smile grows. "We welcome constructive criticism."

"Is that so?"

He nods. "Why don't I tell you about the ranch's activities? Every night, there's a campfire. It's considered a social event, but you've got a great view of the stars, and s'mores are involved."

I tilt my head to the side and study him. "That sounds nice. I saw some horses around too."

"We do offer horseback riding lessons. And our more proficient guests can go on solo excursions, provided they follow the safety protocols. There's also river rafting, and there's a waterfall nearby."

"I can see why your boss picked this place to build a retreat."

Adrian takes a step forward. "I'm glad you approve."

Heat climbs up my neck and stains my cheeks. "How could I not?"

"Mr. Steele, sorry to interrupt, but I need you to sign these slips." Maureen materializes in the doorway, looking harried, and with a clipboard in her hand. "I'm sorry, sir, but with Lorraine is out sick. We've all been trying to cover her workload. Or I would've gotten to this sooner."

He takes off the hat pulled low over his head, picks up the pen, and scribbles. "It's okay, Maureen. Just make sure you divvy her work up evenly amongst everyone, including myself. Lorraine will be back before you know it."

Maureen nods in my direction and gives him a grateful smile. "Thank you, sir."

Halfway to the main cabin, she sprints back and holds out an envelope. "Sorry, sir. This was dropped off for you." I can see the name on the envelope. Adrian Steele.

With that, she darts off. It isn't until after she disappears into the main cabin that Adrian looks back at me.

I'm filled with embarrassment; I glance between the main cabin and his face.

A small niggling sensation begins in the back of my head. And a sour taste in the center of my stomach. It spreads slowly till it takes root, and I gasp.

""You....you....you're Adrian Steele. You're the owner?"

He doesn't say anything.

"You're the owner of the ranch," I continue, my blood now pounding so loudly I can barely hear anything else. "Shit."

I am not off to a good start.

I don't want to be seen or remembered as the girl who was salivating all over the owner of this impressive place.

Ugh. Why do I even care so much?

A man this good looking is probably used to worse displays of affection.

"I….I had no idea," I add, weakly. "You really don't have to go through all of this trouble."

Adrian waves my comment away and gives me another one of his heart-stopping smiles "Oh, don't worry about it. I'm happy to help."

Another employee emerges. He and Adrian step away, their heads bent together in conversation.

A few short minutes later, Adrian comes back, one hand shoved into his pocket, and the other hanging limply at his side.

I'm still reeling from the shock.

And I want to slam the door shut, find the nearest hole, and crawl into it.

For the remainder of my trip.

Or at least until the strong visceral reaction I'm having abates.

I can't spend my vacation lusting after him.

Adrian steps into the cabin and motions to me. "Why don't I show you some of the amenities here?"

I follow him as he opens the cabinets to indicate some of the basics provided. "There's really no need for all of this."

Adrian doesn't respond as he shows me around the rest of the cabin. He stops in front of the fridge and gives me an encouraging smile.

I peer into it and look back at him. "This looks really impressive."

He swings the door shut and moves to the counter, where there are several gleaming appliances. "You've got a toaster, coffee maker, etc."

Adrian steps out of the kitchen and glances over his shoulders at me. "Let me show you how the faucet works."

In the bathroom, he holds his hands up to a sensor and water comes out. "Temperature is adjusted according to the weather outside, but you can also manually adjust it. The entire ranch is solar-powered."

"You know you don't have to keep trying to impress me."

Adrian makes his way to the other side and twists to face me. "Trying? You mean to tell me I'm not succeeding?"

My mouth is dry. "You're hot. I mean not. I mean you are. I just... Don't you have somewhere else to be?"

Adrian raises an eyebrow. "Are you trying to get rid of me already? Damn, I really need to work on my people skills, huh?"

I flush and make a vague hand gesture. "Your people skills are perfect. I mean, you're fine—they're fine. But I'm sure you have better things to do."

Because he is the owner of the ranch, and I'm rambling like some idiot.

I have never been more embarrassed in my entire life.

Nor have I ever before been so conflicted in the presence of a man.

You do not care what he thinks. He's just trying to leave a good impression. So that you won't leave a bad review. Plus, he's probably hoping you'll tell all of your friends, so more and more people can come here.

As far as he's concerned, Adrian is just being a good host and businessman.

I, on the other hand, need a serious reality check.

"A good host always makes time for his guests. It's not all about the business side of things," Adrian replies. With a smile. As if he read my thoughts. "Besides, I'm happy to help."

I take a few steps back and turn my back on him. "Do you want something to drink? I'm really thirsty all of a sudden."

I fill up a glass of water from the dispenser. When I turn around, Adrian has moved closer, his eyes moving critically over the cabin.

After he glances back at me, I eye him over the rim of the glass and forget what I'm supposed to be saying next. He offers me an easy smile, and someone knocks on the door.

As he walks away, I try not to gawk.

Holy hell.

I like having an unobstructed view of him.

Shamelessly, I drink in every inch of him. All the while trying to convince myself I shouldn't.

But his shorts are hanging low on his hips, and his shirt is skintight, highlighting every muscle, every last inch of him.

I picture pressing myself against his muscled back and breathing him in.

Then I see myself pulling the shirt up over his head. Running my tongue and lips all over what I'm sure is a gorgeous chiseled chest.

Goddamn it, Danielle. It doesn't matter how attracted you are. It's been too long since you've had a meaningful sex. And that doesn't mean you have to do the owner of the ranch, of all people. Find someone else, scratch that itch, and move on.

Only problem is that I have the sinking feeling that no one else will do.

Adrian says something to the person on the other side of the door and glances over at me. When he's done, he walks back over to me and offers an apologetic smile. "I've got to go. Duty calls."

"Can I get you a drink for the road?"

Adrian's smile is genuine. "Sure."

I hurry over to the fridge, pick the first bottle my eyes land on, and dart back over to him.

When our fingers brush, a jolt of electricity races up my arm, and I exhale, sharply. I lift my gaze up to his. He's got a peculiar look on his face.

We stand there staring at each other for longer than I'd like to admit.

All too soon, he withdraws his hand and leaves.

Through the thin slit in the curtain, I watch him and tell myself to get over it.

Adrian Steele is not going to satisfy your itch. He can't. Make your peace with it and move on.

Jeez.

I fan myself as I begin to pace the entire length of the cabin, wishing Savannah was here with me.

Chapter Five: Adrian

When I step out of my office, I make a beeline for Maureen, a headache already pounding in the back of my skull. I stop at the main desk and wait for her to finish typing.

Out of the corner of my eye, I see a flash of movement. Danielle steps into the main cabin, her entire face shiny with sweat.

Even with her dark hair piled into a bun on top of her head, and wearing a pair of faded old shorts, she is the most beautiful woman I've ever seen.

I haven't been able to stop sneaking glances at her since I spotted her a few hours earlier, when the fresh group of guests arrived.

Everything from her tall and lithe figure to the dimples on her cheek calls out to me.

In my line of work, I've come across thousands of guests, many of them attractive. But not a single one of them holds a candle to Danielle.

She's gorgeous without even trying.

And I can't tell if it's because of the way she carries herself, or if it's because of the fire in her hazel eyes.

All I know is that when I step away from the main desk, and she brushes past me, I have to resist the urge to pull her to me.

She smells so good. I wonder what perfume she's wearing. I want to bury my face in her hair. I want to hold her to me and inhale until the rest of the world melts away.

You are a professional. You know why you can't sleep with a guest.

Fuck.

I can't afford any mistakes here, nor can I afford to get distracted.

Still, I find myself struggling to move away from her.

With a great deal of difficulty, I sit down in one of the comfortable armchairs underneath the AC and pretend to scroll through my phone.

Danielle has one hand in her pocket. With the other she tugs on the shirt now plastered to her glistening, ivory skin.

Her tongue darts out to lick her lips, and my mind goes absolutely blank.

Shit.

No. You are not a teenager. Get it together, Adrian. Brian needs you, remember? This is about him, not you.

And it's definitely not about the dark-haired goddess who offers me a smile on her way out. I remain rooted to the spot for a while longer until I'm sure I'm not going to go after her.

Slowly, I rise to my feet and go back to Maureen. She takes out a covered tray and wordlessly hands it over to me, offering her a distracted smile.

I duck out the adjoining door, pause in a carpeted hallway, and take a deep breath.

Once I make it out through the other door, I have my back straight, and my rehearsed smile in place.

Brian is on the bed when I come in, his hands linked together over his head. The TV is on mute in the background. Carefully, I set the tray down and clear my throat.

"You good?"

Brian sits up and exhales. "I appreciate you doing this, man. I know you've got shit to do…"

I hold a hand up. "It's what brothers do. I am going to need you to put in the work, B."

Brian stands up and removes the cover from the tray. He sniffs the sandwich and frowns. "I don't like what you're implying."

"I'm not implying anything. I'm telling you. You're not just here to learn. You're also here so that I don't have to keep cleaning up your messes."

Especially because he always ends up right back where he started.

Every single goddamn time.

I don't want my brother to drown in a sea of his own mess, but I also can't save him from himself if he won't help.

The cover drops to the floor with a clatter, and he twists to face me. "I never asked you to clean up my messes."

"Not in so many words, but you're still my brother. And you know as well as I do that if you don't put in the work, you're just going to end up going back to that life."

Brian advances on me. "Oh, perfect little Adrian is pissed that I'm here ruining his precious ranch."

He takes a swing at me, and I move to the side. Before his fist can connect with the wall, I twist it behind his back and push him against it. "Calm the hell down. This isn't going to solve anything. I'm on your side. But I can only help you if you help yourself."

Brian is breathing erratically and squirming against my grip. "Get the fuck off of me. I don't need your help."

I maintain my grip. "Yes, you do. You're worth helping, Brian. I need you to know that."

Without waiting for a response, I release him and take a step back.

His eyes are blazing, and his entire body is coiled and ready to pounce.

"You're going to be meeting with the therapist in your room," I tell him, with a lift of my chin. "If you ever need something when I'm not around, contact Maureen. But only in case of emergency. Call me first every time. I can't afford people mistaking you for me. I know people do. All our lives people haven't been able to tell us apart. We even sound alike. So, please, please be very careful, don't leave your room for any reason."

Brian gives me an angry look and pushes his glasses up his nose "I don't need a fucking babysitter. I don't want anyone to see me or talk to me. I hate everyone."

"Start acting like an adult then," I snap. After giving him one last pointed look, I step out of the room and ball my hands into fists.

Anger and frustration are still bubbling inside of me when I step outside and inhale, the smell of earth and wildflowers wafting up my nostrils.

Without pausing to give myself a chance to process, I find myself in front of the riding arena, where Pablo is leading a white mare around.

"Looking good, Pablo." I give him a bright smile as he passes, and he grins in response. "How's she looking?"

"She's a sweet horse," Pablo calls out, after a brief pause. "I think she'll be ready to ride in a few days."

I offer Pablo another smile and watch as he leads the mare around using a loose piece of rope.

For a while, as I stand there taking everything in, including the whisper of the wind, and the sound of birds chirping, it almost feels like everything is going to be okay.

Like I'm not in way over my head.

But I know that isn't true, not by a long shot.

In spite of my tough love spiel, I know Brian is going to need more than that to snap out of it and get his life back together.

All I can do is hope that I'm able to give him what he needs and minimize the damage to the best of my ability.

You're doing the best you can. I'm sure Brian appreciates that even if he doesn't know how to convey it.

In my pocket, my phone buzzes, and I step away to answer it. "Adrian Steele."

"Mr. Steele, this is Matt Montgomery from the local newspaper. I was wondering if you have anything to say about your brother's situation or if you know his whereabouts."

I pull the phone away from my ear and stare at it in disbelief. "How the hell did you get this number? Who the hell are you? What newspaper?"

"Is that really what you want to ask, Mr. Steele? We just have a few questions about his last incident.

"Listen here you son of a bitch. There is nothing about my brother that you need to know. I don't know where he is. Leave him alone. My brother and I don't talk or see each other."

"But—"

"Don't you try to contact me again or print anything about my brother. If I find out about anything coming from your end, you're going to learn firsthand why they call my lawyer a shark."

"There's no need for threats—"

"There is every need. I will do whatever it takes to protect my family."

Without waiting for a response, I hang up and shove the phone into my pocket.

I inhale several lungful of air and wait for the thumping of my heart to decrease. When it doesn't, I step further away from the riding arena and duck underneath the shade of a tree.

I call my lawyer twice, but each time it goes to voicemail.

I mutter something unflattering under my breath and kick at a pile of leaves on the ground.

When I hear a low startled noise, I glance to my right. Danielle is leaning against the shade of the tree, covered in even more sweat than before.

She pushes her hair out of her eyes and gives me a sympathetic smile.

"You're the owner of the ranch. If you wanted cell phone reception, I'm pretty sure you can find a way around your rules."

"I've got cell reception," I stand up straighter and blow out a breath. "But sometimes, I regret the fact that I do."

"Let me guess. Real estate agent? Tele-marketer?"

"Reporter," I reply, pausing to tilt my head up to look at the clear blue skies.

After a few more deep breaths, I glance back at Danielle. She has pushed herself off the tree and is guzzling water like her life depends on it.

Then she unzips her fanny pack and takes out a pack of wipes. She uses one to wipe her face. "Hey, don't hate the whole profession just because of one asshole."

I raise an eyebrow. "Don't tell me you're a reporter."

Because I would hate to have to be careful around her.

I don't need one more complication to navigate.

"I'm a journalist, not a reporter." She crumples up a wipe and tucks it into her pocket. "There is a difference between the two, you know."

"Sure."

"I can see that you don't believe me." Danielle takes a step forward and sighs. "This is why I don't usually tell people what I do. You'd think I had some kind of rare disease or something."

I chuckle. "As long as you're not here to write a story about me."

Danielle snorts and puts away her pack of wipes. "Of course not. Considering that I didn't even know who you were when I met you or came here. Besides, I don't do gossip or whatever you'd call a story about you. I write hard-hitting, award-winning pieces."

"You actually write puff pieces, don't you?" I tease.

Danielle groans. "I don't know how you figured that out, but yes. For now, but I'm working on convincing my boss that I can do better. She's not the easiest person in the world to convince though."

"I'm sure you'll figure it out."

Danielle reaches into her fanny pack and unfolds a map. "I hope so. I would hate to be shoe-horned into something that was meant to be temporary. I only started writing puff pieces because I needed more time at home with my husband."

I ignore the pit of disappointment in my stomach. "How did that work out for you?"

"It didn't. It didn't do me any good. Now I'm divorced. And I'm not where I want to be in my career."

Hope surges through me as I step forward and take the map out of her hands.

When I hand it back to her, right side up, and smile, my hands linger near hers. "It'll be easier to figure it out if you read it like this. Also, you should probably take a guide with you, since it's your first day."

Danielle places a hand on her hips. "I know I'm a city girl, but I'm sure I can handle wandering the grounds."

"That's the spirit. I'm impressed. Want some company?"

I should head back to my office and start going through the mountain of paperwork and unanswered emails.

Yet, I can't bring myself to walk away from Danielle. Or leave her to fend for herself.

When she looks at me like that, she makes me forget who I am, or what I'm meant to be doing.

Fuck.

How can this woman have such a hold on me when I've only known her for a few hours?

Danielle tries to hide her smile. "As long as you don't spend the whole walk insulting my profession, we should be good to go."

"I make no promises." We start toward the trail.

Chapter Six: Danielle

Doctor Sheridan shifts from one side to the other and clears her throat. "You seem a little uncomfortable, Danielle. Why is that?"

"It feels strange to be sitting here expected to unburden myself to a stranger," I reply, with a quick glance around the office. "I don't know. Don't you ever think it's weird that people you don't know come in here, expecting you to have all of the answers?"

Doctor Sheridan writes something down. "It's only weird if other people think it's weird. In my experience, it's easier to talk to complete strangers. Something about them not knowing you helps."

I snort. "Yeah, but people can still be judgmental and mean."

Doctor Sheridan gives me a kind smile. "This is a safe space, Danielle. I'm not here to judge you. I'm here to help guide you."

I glance away and feign interest in the landscape painting of the beach hung up behind her small, rectangular shaped desk. "You've got your work cut out for you, doc."

"Why is that?"

I make a vague hand gesture. "Because I don't even know where to begin. I mean, do we start with the obvious—my failed marriage? Or do we start with the fact that I basically derailed my career for my ex?"

Doctor Sheridan writes down something else. "We can start wherever you want, Danielle. There is no right or wrong answer here."

I swing my gaze back to hers. "So, why all of the questions then?"

"I'm just getting to know you. This is our first session together, after all." Doctor Sheridan links her fingers together and gives me a reassuring smile. "Would it make you feel better if I shared a few things about myself?"

"I'm not sure. Can you?"

Doctor Sheridan's smile doesn't fade. "I've worked here for five years. I'm married, and I've got a son and daughter who hate that their mother is a therapist."

My lips lift into a half smile. "You can't blame them. It gives you an unfair advantage."

Doctor Sheridan and I talk for a while, sharing my feelings and my thoughts about what I want Four Elements ranch to do for me.

Doctor Sheridan gets up. "Unfortunately, that's all the time we have for today. But I'll see you soon. Your appointments are all scheduled for you. Please refer to your handout."

I stand up, and my hands hang awkwardly at my side. "That's it?"

"I'd like you to think about something, a defining moment from the past few years, and write it down. We can talk about it during our next session."

I glance from the door to her face. "Okay."

Doctor Sheridan stands up and holds the door open. "Have a good rest of the day, Danielle. Take care of yourself."

After the door clicks shut, I linger outside her office and frown. Then I spin on my heels and make my way back to my cabin.

While I'm changing into a different set of clothes, I turn the session over and over in my head, surprised that I don't feel dread and skepticism.

Instead, I feel a strange sense of hope and optimism.

And it stays with me until I come out of the cabin and head to the riding arena.

· ♥ · ♥ · ♥ · ♥ · ♥ ·

"She's going to throw me off."

Adrian secures my grip on the reigns and motions for me to breathe. "She is not going to throw you. But she is going to get agitated if you don't calm down."

I blow out a breath. "No one ever calms down after being told to calm down."

Adrian flashes me a smile. "Okay, don't think of it like that. Think of it as... the horse can sense your emotions. And you don't want to put negative vibes out into the universe."

I snort. "Does that actually help?"

Adrian slows to a trot, and I realize we've been moving this whole time, and that I am not as scared as I was.

When I grip the reins tighter, my horse, a beautiful white mare, makes a low whinnying sound and stomps her hooves.

He sidles up to me, a vision atop his own black steed, and rolls his shoulders.

"Loosen your grip," Adrian instructs, pausing to lean forward between us "Don't dig your heels in too hard."

I glance over at him and try to mimic his stance. "Okay, how's this?"

His hand brushes against mine, and my breath hitches in my throat. "You're doing great, Danielle. I'm sure you'll be riding like a pro in no time."

Considering I've only been here a few days, and I break out into a sweat at the mere thought of being thrown off, I doubt Adrian knows what he's talking about.

Still, I appreciate how patient and kind he's been about the whole thing.

Especially when I am, far and away, the worst rider here. I feel like the amateur I am.

"Did everybody else get private lessons or something?"

Adrian glances over his shoulders at the rest of the group, and a furrow appears between his brows. "Not everyone gets the hang of it so quickly. It really depends on the person. On their willingness to let go of their need to control. And on their willingness to bond with the horse."

I choke back a laugh and try to ignore the tingles racing up and down my body "Um, have you met me? Relinquishing control isn't exactly my forte."

Nor is putting my trust in a muscular and tanned ranch owner. But, hey, this trip is supposed to be about change.

And taking risks.

I open my mouth to say something else but pause when Adrian takes both of my hands in his and changes my grip on the reins.

My throat is dry, and I'm sure I've forgotten how to breathe as he gives me instructions in a slow, soothing voice.

But I can't make out anything he's saying. I'm not even listening anymore. I see his mouth moving and words coming out, but I can't make out what he says.

I like the timbre of his voice and how it unlocks a deep, primal response in me.

And I like how it feels to be so close to him, close enough to feel the heat emanating from his body.

All I have to do is lean forward and hug him.

Jeez.

He twists to look at me, and my stomach dips. "Did you get all of that?"

"Uh-huh."

He is still holding my hand, and I'm sure my brain is going to short-circuit any minute. As soon as the thought crosses my mind, he releases my hands and leans back.

I swear he can read my thoughts.

Then he pauses and reaches for the edges of his shirt. He pulls it over his head and drapes it over the saddle.

Then he leans forward to pat his horse and adjusts the hat on top of his head.

Sitting astride his horse in a pair of jeans with a large belt buckle at his waist, he looks like he walked off the set of a western.

And when beads of sweat start rolling down his stomach and back, my mouth is completely dry.

Again, I imagine what it would be like to run my tongue all over his taut stomach. And when I blink, I spot a few of the guests doing double takes and salivating over him.

Fuck. I get the sour feeling of jealousy again.

I need to get my shit together, and I need to ignore the jealousy burning through my veins.

I have no right to claim him or worry about the other women looking at him.

With a slight shake of my head, I gingerly steer the horse away and resist the urge to look over my shoulders.

The last thing I need is to see Adrian galloping towards me, like some fucking knight in shining armor.

For a while, I wander around the riding arena, muttering unintelligibly under my breath while Adrian tends to some of the other guests.

As I'm getting ready to dismount, Adrian materializes and helps me off the horse. His bare skin against mine sends shivers of desire racing up and down my spine.

It feels electric.

Like I'm being burned from the inside out.

Shamelessly, I lean into his touch for a while longer, longer than appropriate. Then, abruptly, I withdraw my hand and take a few steps back. "Thanks."

Adrian drops his hands to his sides. "You're welcome. Are you walking back to the main cabin?"

"Yes, I think I'll pass by the cabin for a quick shower and a nap."

Adrian nods. "Sounds like a good plan. See you at the campfire later?"

I offer him a dazed smile. "Sure."

He gives me one last look and saunters off. I eyeball him the entire time.

When he glances over his shoulders at me, I pretend to look away and fan my face, aware of the flush staining my neck and cheeks.

Lowering my head, I hurry past Adrian and in the general direction of the cabin. There, I slam the front door shut and lean against it while I wait for my heart to calm down.

It feels like it's going to jump right out of my chest.

And I know Adrian freaking Steele is to blame.

He's everywhere, and the harder I try to resist him, the stronger our pull becomes. I decide to skip the campfire.

In the morning, when he lingers over breakfast and makes conversation, I get lost staring into his eyes.

In the afternoons, he's there during our excursions. And I keep finding excuses just to touch him and be near him. Whenever I'm in the main cabin, I find myself looking for him.

I know I can't keep acting like this, but I can't seem to help myself. OMG! What did I get myself into? I can't get him out of my head.

And it doesn't help that with the sweltering heat, half the time he's half-naked.

I can't get the image of his taut and firm stomach out of my head as I push myself off the wall and head for the bathroom.

I wait for the tub to fill and trying to avoid thoughts of Adrian, then I strip out of my dirty clothes and get in.

The cool water soothes my aching muscles.

I squeeze my eyes shut and try to empty my mind.

But the image of Adrian is there too, holding his hand out and smiling at me.

With a groan, I submerge myself deeper into the tub and pull some of the bubbles towards me.

A short while later, still unable to relax, I scrub up and wash myself off. Then I wrap myself in a fluffy white bathrobe.

I throw myself, stomach first, onto the bed and hold my arms out on either side of me.

What the hell am I doing?

There is no spark between Adrian and me.

There *can't* be.

Whatever pull I'm feeling is the result of being trapped in a loveless marriage for too long.

Adrian just happens to be the first available attractive and interesting man I've crossed paths with since the divorce. So my psyche has latched itself onto him.

Deep down, I know it doesn't mean anything.

It can't.

Still, my skin tingles as I relive the feeling of his skin brushing against mine. I flip onto my back, stare up at the ceiling, and place a pillow over my head. I release a deep, frustration-filled groan into it and sigh.

Half of me wants to take out my laptop, just to give myself something to work on. But the other half of me knows it's not going do me any good.

Without social media to fill the silence and silence my demons, I have nothing else to do. Sighing, I stand up and wander into the living room.

After flipping through a few cable shows, I settle on an old black-and-white movie and sink against the couch.

I'm half-asleep when I hear the familiar buzz of my phone, bringing me back to the present with a jolt.

Half-asleep I pick the phone up off the nightstand. "Oh, thank God. I was beginning to go crazy not being able to talk to you."

"You're going crazy? I'm the one who got left in suspense here. What's happening with your cowboy hunk?"

I sit down on the edge of the bed and twirl a lock of hair around my fingers. "Okay, first of all, he's not my cowboy hunk. Second of all, he's not a cowboy....he's a rancher."

Savannah snorts. "Girl. He is so much more than just a rancher. He's Adrian Steele, stealing your heart." I hear her laughter.

"Sav, it's not funny. I told you to stop mentioning him. It's embarrassing enough that you know that I've got a thing for the owner. I don't want anyone else to know."

"Based on what you've told me, I'm sure the entire female population there is already in love with him. And at least half of them have thought about what it would be like to bang his brains out."

"You always did have a way with words."

"Babe, even I want to bang him from what you've told me. It sounds like you're living in a fantasy land with your hunk by your side. You think I don't know that you indulge in those fantasies."

"I don't," I insist, with a shake of my head. "Not to that extent at least."

Savannah says something to her cat in the background. I hear a door open and close then the sound of a hiss. "Sure, whatever makes you sleep at night. Anyways, what happened after breakfast yesterday?"

"What do you mean?"

"He got you a bowl of fruit instead of the one you spilled all over yourself, and…?"

I sigh and stop twirling my lock of hair. "And nothing. He gave me the bowl and wandered off to talk to some other guests. Let's face it, Sav. He's just doing his job, and I'm lusting over him like…. like some kind of animal in heat."

Savannah's TV blares in the background. "Sorry, babe. Hold on. Let me just find the remote. Bad kitty."

I let the bathrobe fall into a heap on the floor and stand in front of my closet, completely naked. "I don't know what to do. It's not like I can tell him to stay away from me."

"Why would you want to do that?" Savannah is munching on something. I have a vision of her in pajamas, glasses perched on top of her head, marinara sauce dribbling down her chin. "He's definitely into you too, D. It's pretty obvious from what you've been telling me."

"Or maybe I'm just mistaking basic human decency for interest." I select a flowery dress that falls just above my knees. "I don't know, Sav. I've been out of the game for a while and.... I don't trust myself."

"But you trust me, right?"

I set Savannah on speaker and pull the dress on. "Yes, but you know why I can't pursue anything with him. It would just complicate my stay here. And I've still got a little over three weeks left."

"I say, enjoy those three plus weeks and see where they take you," Savannah offers, suggestively. "Come on, D. Live a little. What's the worst that could happen?"

"I humiliate myself or I make a fool of myself in front of the rest of the guests."

"They'll get over it. And they'll move on to the next piece of gossip," Savannah replies, pausing to slurp on her drink. "Come on. I want to live vicariously through you. Don't deny me that."

"Read a romance like a normal person," I suggest, before settling on a pair of sandals. After putting them on, I examine myself in the full-length mirror and twist to and fro. "Or watch those period movies that you like."

"But I can just picture the two of you sneaking out to meet each other underneath the moon light and trying to hide your love affair from the rest of the guests—"

"I'm hanging up now."

Savannah laughs. "Okay, fine, fine. I'll stop. Just promise me you'll keep an open mind, okay?"

Without responding, I hang up and toss my phone onto the bed.

A few minutes later, I'm still giving myself a pep talk as I step out of my cabin and into the balmy night air.

The sky is lit up in bright lights, a kaleidoscope of purples and pinks that make me pause on the last step.

Smiling, my feet hit the ground, and I join the throngs of people heading towards the clearing further away from the cabins.

Conversation rises and falls around me as I concentrate on my steps.

The trees give way to a large clearing and the red and orange flames of the campfire.

A few instructors are standing around the fire, conversing amongst themselves including Maureen and Pablo, the horse trainer. When they see us, they smile and wave.

Awkwardly, I trail after the group, my eyes searching the semi-darkness, hoping against hope that Adrian is going to be there.

I know it's stupid. And I know I shouldn't be looking for him.

Especially because I know that as the freaking owner of the ranch, he's got better things to do.

He's definitely got better things to do than sit around a campfire, roast marshmallows, and tell stories. Come on, Danielle. What did you expect?

After I'm handed a cup of iced tea, I make small talk with some of the other guests. A few of them are doctors, one is a nurse, and the other is a lifestyle coach.

All of them are here based on recommendations, and they all seem to get along.

I feel like the odd one out, but they try and make me feel welcome.

It's not their fault that I'm only half listening.

As I stand underneath the pale light of the moon, feigning interest in their stories, I can't help but glance around the clearing, looking for that familiar face.

Amazingly, Adrian emerges from the woods. I stand up straighter and smile at him. I feel such relief seeing him walk toward the fire.

I realize I'm holding my breath waiting for him to come so I can breathe again.

Adrian offers everyone a smile and a wave, and his eyes linger on me.

Neither of us looks away until he walks up and draws the rest of the staff into a conversation.

My heart is hammering uneasily. I wish that I was part of the staff right now. And little pinpricks of desire race up and down my spine.

I try to focus on the group in front of me. On discussing the benefits of hiking versus horseback riding.

When I finish the last of my tea, I wander over to the cooler and pour myself some more from the jug.

The cup is halfway to my lips when Adrian sidles over to me. "Enjoying the night?"

I take a long sip of my drink and swallow. "I am. How about you?"

Adrian pours himself some iced tea and glances around the campfire. "Honestly? This is one of my favorite parts of the retreat. It's one of the reasons I started this business."

"Didn't you have enough campfires when you were a boy scout?"

Adrian chuckles. "Fair enough. But no, I didn't. But that's not really why. After college, I traveled the world for fun. And I ended up volunteering for a year at a retreat center in Peru. And it wasn't until I came back home that I realized what I wanted to do."

I twist, so I'm facing him directly. His entire body is bathed in moonlight.

It gives him a warm and intimate glow that does strange things to my insides.

Half of me wants to wrap a hand around his neck and pull him down for a kiss.

The other half of me wants to set my cup down and run in the opposite direction.

Instead, I sip on more of my suddenly lukewarm drink and shift from one foot to the other. "Oh, I get it. You wanted to be able to pester people all the time."

Adrian lets out another laugh. "Yes, that's exactly right. Am I that obvious?"

I hide my smile. "Only to me. You're not as subtle as you think."

Adrian gives me an amused look and sips on his drink. "And here I thought I was being really smooth."

I clear my throat. "So, what did you realize when you came back?"

"That I wanted to do something that hasn't been done before. I wanted to give people a completely transformative experience. On every single level. To help people to re-connect with the best versions of themselves."

I nod. "I think that's very noble of you."

Adrian shrugs. "I don't know about noble. But I know what it's like to watch the people you love suffer and struggle. This world isn't as kind as it should be. And I want to play a part in changing that."

I raise an eyebrow. "Oh, so that's your fatal flaw. You're one of those guys with a hero complex."

Adrian winces. "Guilty as charged. We all have our vices."

I pause. "As far as vices go, it's actually not bad. I mean, I'm not one to talk. I have a hard time letting people go. And an even harder time walking away from things. Even when I know I should."

"Yeah?"

I sigh and study the flames leaping and dancing and casting long shadows across the ground. "Yeah, and I keep trying. Because I can never quite bring myself to give up. Because I was taught to fight for the people that I love until I can't anymore."

Adrian brushes his hand against mine. "I'm sorry you've had to go through that. I can't imagine that turning your back on someone you love is ever easy."

"Yes, well I do have a good support system."

Out of the corner of my eye, I see a flash of movement. When I focus, I realize that Adrian is being called over by his employees.

He offers me an apologetic smile, sets his drink down, and wanders over. I wait until he leaves before my shoulders sag. Then I let out a deep, shaky breath.

I sit down on a fallen log and go over all of the reasons why this is a bad idea.

Starting with the fact that he's a handsome and successful billionaire who wants to do good in the world. While I'm a struggling journalist who just ended her marriage and has lost her sense of self.

There is no world where the two of us make sense.

Yet, I spend the rest of the night sneaking glances at him. And the butterflies in my stomach beat their wings mercilessly any time he looks at me.

Shit.

I'm totally and completely screwed.

Chapter Seven: Danielle

"Do I have to come down there and do everything myself?" I hear Skittles meowing loudly in the background and the sound of a door opening and closing. "What is the matter with you, D? He obviously likes you."

"He does not like me, Sav. He's just being nice."

And I can't imagine a world in which Adrian feels the same as I do. So I don't want to go down that path.

I don't need to waste my time or his on a silly infatuation. Not when I am a grown-ass woman who can pull myself up my bootstraps and get over him.

It's not like you were under him, to begin with. It shouldn't be hard to get over your little crush.

Savannah sighs. "D, you deserve to be happy, and you're on a vacation. It's practically a rite of passage to have a steamy and illicit affair. Trust me, it's all part of the healing process."

I bring one leg up over the other and lace up my sneakers. "I had no idea you were a lifestyle coach now."

"Fuck you. I know what I'm talking about. You need to make a move on Adrian before someone else does, and you spend the rest of the vacation moping and sulking."

I gather my hair up into a high ponytail and sigh. "Okay, look. I've got my second appointment today with the therapist. If I promise to talk to her about it, will you stop nagging me?"

"Yes, for now. So go. I'll check in later."

When she hangs up, I pull the phone away from my ear to stare at it. Then I shove it into the pocket of my jeans.

I run into Adrian on the way out. He is deep in a serious-looking conversation with Maureen. The two of them offer me tight smiles on their way past.

I straighten my back and march over to the main cabin where the therapist is waiting for me in a small but cozy air-conditioned room.

Like clockwork, when I open the door, she stands up and holds out her hand.

Doctor Sheridan is a petite woman with streaks of white in her blonde hair, kind brown eyes, and an easy smile.

She holds a clipboard to her chest and smooths out her skirt before taking her usual seat in the armchair.

I sit across from her on a comfortable brown leather couch and cross one ankle over the other.

Late morning sun is pouring in through the open window, causing tiny particles of light to dance on the floorboards.

She shifts from one side to the other and sets the clipboard down in her lap. Then she looks directly at me and waits.

"How are you today, Danielle?"

"I'm fine. How are you?"

Doctor Sheridan offers me a smile. "I'm fine, thank you. So, how do you feel after our last session? Have you given any more thought to our conversation about Trevor?"

I lean back against the couch and cough. "Yes, but I don't feel like blocking him is the answer. He's just going to find other ways to reach me."

Doctor Sheridan adjusts her glasses. "Do you feel like he'll be able to reach you through your friend Savannah?"

"No."

"So, what are you afraid of? Or are you trying to keep the lines of communication open in case of a reconciliation?"

I shake my head. "No, I don't want to get back together with him. I just don't see the point of blocking him because nothing he can say is going to make a difference."

Doctor Sheridan jots something down on her clipboard. "What do you feel is going to make a difference?"

"Me getting over him. And I don't mean just saying I'm over him. I want to feel it too. I'm so ready to move past that phase of my life and pick up the pieces."

"It's going to take some time," Doctor Sheridan tells me, with a calm smile. "You need to be patient with yourself. The two of you were married for three years, and you were together for a year before that, right?"

I nod and clasp my fingers together. "That's right."

Doctor Sheridan writes something else down. "Danielle, I want you to know that it's okay to grieve the loss of your relationship with Trevor. Even if he was awful to you. Even if it ended badly. It doesn't mean you can't grieve what was lost."

I glance away and stare at a spot over her head. "I know that."

"You can tell me whatever you want here."

I look back at her and uncross my ankles. "My ex isn't the issue here, doc. I mean, I hate what he's done to me, but I know it was wrong. And I know it's okay to miss who I was before all of this bullshit."

"So, what is the problem?"

"The problem is…. I'm attracted to someone, and I don't want to be."

Doctor Sheridan offers me a gentle smile. "Why don't you want to be? Is he like Trevor?"

I shake my head. "They couldn't be more different actually, but that scares me. Because I know this isn't the right time."

Doctor Sheridan sighs. "Sometimes, the timing of something doesn't seem great, but it doesn't mean you shouldn't pursue it. If you like this man, and he likes you, I see no harm in trying to make something with him."

"You sound like Savannah."

Doctor Sheridan jots something else down. "What does Savannah think?"

"To put it bluntly, Savannah thinks I need to get laid to get Trevor out of my system once and for all. And she also thinks it's okay if I pursue something with this guy if it'll make me happy."

Doctor Sheridan's eyes are bright and full of understanding. "I can see that you are seriously considering this. Is this man your friend?"

"No, actually he's.... a guest at the resort," I finish, lamely. "I've only known him a week or something. And I already can't stop thinking about him."

Doctor Sheridan motions for me to continue.

I shift from one side to the other and lick my dry lips. "I'm attracted to him. And he's easy to talk to. But I don't know, Doc. I don't know if it's enough."

Doctor Sheridan sets her clipboard aside and leans forward. She clasps her fingers together and clears her throat. "Danielle, I want to ask you a question. Why are you here?"

"Because I signed up for therapy as part of the treatment—"

"I mean why are you at the resort?" She interrupts me with a kind smile. "Can you tell me your reasons?"

"I want to find myself again. I want to get back on track after being waylaid by Trevor."

And I don't want to go home to an empty apartment. To feel the loneliness closing in on me while I lament the fact that my career has moved on without me.

Already the thought of moving out of Savannah's finding my own place and having to start over by myself doesn't sit well with me.

Trevor made sure I was reliant on him, too reliant if I'm being honest.

It's how he kept me in check for so long. But I don't want to be that person anymore.

Still, I'm not ready to tell the therapist any of this. So as I sit here, my mind racing to come up with a plausible explanation, and I think of Adrian.

About how kind, patient, and understanding he is.

Adrian doesn't deserve any of the baggage I come with.

Doctor Sheridan leans back against her chair and unlinks her fingers. "Okay, I want you to take several deep breaths. Hold them in for ten seconds and release."

I mimic her movements and feel some of the tension leave my body.

"I want you to work on your assignment for the week. Every day when you wake up, I want you to fill out a mood chart that I'm going to send you via email.

During our next session, you can bring your laptop along to show me."

"I thought we only had limited access to the outside world. So as not to interfere with the healing journey."

"That's true. So, I'll be sending the mood chart during the allotted hour. The mood chart is split into two-hour intervals. In each slot you can write down how you feel during that time period and why."

"Okay."

"I also want you to write down some of the fears and resentments you have when the intrusive thoughts come up. We're going to be unpacking and discussing them during our therapy sessions."

I press my lips together and say nothing.

"Most of my patients don't like homework, but it's part of the process," Doctor Sheridan adds, with an apologetic smile. "You'll start to really feel it work when you get into the habit of doing it."

"And in the meantime?"

"In the meantime, I'm going to send you some breathing exercises to help with anxiety and mindfulness. I also want you to remember something. You are here because you are looking for something different."

I tilt my head to the side and stare at her. "What do you mean?"

"It's okay to step out of your comfort zone to find your way back to who you were." Doctor Sheridan stands up and gives me a cryptic smile. "I'm afraid that's all the time we have for today. I'll see you soon, Danielle. Take care of yourself."

Hours later, I'm sitting by the campfire, jotting down a few things when loud laughter erupts.

The other guests are talking to each other and laughing. Suddenly I'm aware of Adrian's gaze on me.

With a sigh, I snap my notebook shut and wander away from the fire, the clearing, and the other guests.

Underneath the shade of a tree that's far enough away from everyone else, I lean against a trunk and squeeze my eyes shut.

"Summoning the spirits of your ancestors?"

My eyes fly open, and I see Adrian standing a few feet away, bathed in moonlight, carrying two cups.

He hands me one, and I give him a small smile. "Do you think it'll help me with my therapy assignment? Because I can use all the help I can get right now."

Adrian grimaces. "Oh, yeah. That's some heavy stuff. Therapy is never easy, and it's not meant to be comfortable. Even the spirit of your ancestors can't help you here."

I push myself off the trunk. "Thanks for that."

Adrian takes a sip of his own drink. "Do you want to know how I got through it when I was in therapy?"

"Tell me."

"You have to open yourself up to it. Therapy is hard work, and it's going to get harder before it gets easier. And it damn sure is going to dredge up some things you might think should stay buried. But when you make it to the other side, it is so worth it."

"You really think so?"

Adrian moves toward me and gives me a comforting smile. "I absolutely know so. I am living proof of this. It's going to be okay, Danielle. You've got this."

When he says my name like that, like a promise, and a prayer rolled up into one, I want to wrap myself in his embrace.

I want to kiss him until the world stops turning and changing, and we are the only two people left.

I tilt my head back to glance up at him, and whatever witty response I have dies on my lips.

Suddenly, Adrian throws his cup away, leaps toward me and takes me into his arms. I barely have a chance to register what's happening before he kisses me.

It feels like I'm falling but like I know I'm going to land in a bed of fluffy clouds.

It feels like coming home to a Christmas tree and the presents underneath.

I am aware of every inch of him through his clothes. Pressed against me and making me feel all sorts of things I shouldn't be feeling.

When he nips on my lower lip. I gasp and his tongue darts in. Then we stumble backward, so my back collides with the trunk, and a jolt of pain races up my back.

But I don't care.

All that matters is his mouth on mine. His hands all over me.

Burning and claiming every inch of my skin.

I want to drown in him and climb inside of his skin until the two of us are one.

With a sigh, I wind my fingers through his hair. He rubs himself against me, sending another jolt of desire racing through me.

I don't know how much time passes, or how long we stand there, kissing like our lives depend on it.

All I know is that when we come up for air, I'm consumed by my need for him.

He presses his forehead to mine and blows out a breath, and I feel it in my soul. "I didn't mean to do that. I've been wanting to do that since I first laid eyes on you."

I place my hands on either side of his shoulders to keep from sinking to the ground. "I've been wanting to do that too."

I've actually spent the past hour trying to convince myself not to try to kiss him.

And now that he has kissed me, I know we can't go back.

My lips are still tingling, and my body is humming due to his proximity.

"You know what, fuck it." Adrian takes a step back. He is looking at me intently. "I know you feel it too,

Danielle. I don't want to fight whatever this is between us."

I exhale, sharply. "I don't want to either."

Adrian clears his throat. "But the optics of me dating a guest don't look good…"

My stomach drops, and ice settles in my veins. "You want to keep it a secret?"

"Just for the time being. You'll be gone in a few weeks and then the optics won't matter," Adrian replies, the words pouring out of him in a rush. "I'm sorry. I wouldn't ask if it wasn't… necessary."

I can hear and see the sincerity on his face and in his voice.

It's a small price to pay for getting to be with him.

For experiencing more of those earth-shattering kisses.

Slowly, I nod. Adrian takes my hand, and we delve deeper into the woods.

When we're far enough away, he hoists me up. I wrap myself around his torso. He is kissing me with so much intention and ferocity that I feel like I'm going to combust at his feet.

Wave after wave of desire builds within me.

I claw at his back and fumble with his shirt.

Voices drift over to where we stand, and we freeze.

Reluctantly, Adrian sets me back down on my feet and turns away to hide the bulge in his pants.

I run a hand over my face and glance away, waiting for my heart to stop racing. He presses a quick kiss to my cheeks, and I hear the reluctance in his deep breath.

Adrian has disappeared. A group of guests walk past on the trail behind the trees a few feet away. One spots me and waves.

I wave back, but I can't muster up any words.

Or any kind of explanation for why I'm out here alone.

Reluctantly, I trudge back to the bonfire and glance over at Adrian when I sit down. He offers me an apologetic smile and turns his attention back to the conversation.

I spend the rest of the night staring at the flames, eye locking with Adrian's, trying to calm the racing of my heart.

Later at night, after I've staggered back to my own cabin, I'm jolted awake by the sound of a knock on my front door.

I rub my eyes, sit up, and stagger over to the door. Through the peephole, I make out Adrian, with a bouquet of flowers in his hand.

I throw the door open, pull him inside, and slam it shut.

Chapter Eight: Adrian

"I thought we were supposed to keep it discreet." She runs her fingers through her hair and resists the urge to yawn. "What's happening?"

"I had fun today." I cover the distance between us and takes her into my arms. "Also, I couldn't wait one minute longer to do this."

She kisses me back. My mind goes blank. My knees are weak.

Then she grabs a fistful of my shirt and holds on for dear life.

Danielle tastes like blueberries, and it's making the butterflies in my stomach go wild. In one move, I hoist her up and carry her over to the couch.

One hand moves to the back of her neck. The other glides down her back and pauses at her ass. I give it a firm squeeze, sending a jolt straight to her core.

She keeps one hand on my chest. The other winds itself through my hair. Little pinpricks of desire race up and down my spine.

When she nips at my lower lip, I growl into her mouth and hoist her up again.

Then I carry her over to the bedroom and set her down on the mattress.

I am buzzing with excitement as I pull my shirt up over my head and watch her do the same.

She is in just her bra and underwear when I start kissing her again. Her lean and tanned body presses against mine. There isn't an inch of space between us.

Then I rub my hands up and down her arms, and she shivers.

It feels like I'm going to explode already.

Every inch of my skin burns where she touches me. She arches her back and purrs when my hands move to her back and fumble with her bra.

Her mouth is searing and demanding as one of my hands darts between us to play with her nipples and the other traces a path down to her center.

I palm her over the thin fabric of her underwear. Her answering moan reverberates inside of my head.

"Oh, you like that, huh?" I press hot, open-mouthed kisses down her neck and over her jaw, leaving little goosebumps in my wake. "We're just getting started, baby."

With a growl, I push her underwear aside and stroke her.

Danielle is panting and chanting my name when I touch her core. The blood is roaring in my ears as I lower my head and take one nipple between my teeth.

She is clawing at my back when I move onto the other nipple. They are both as hard as pebbles.

When she mutters something unintelligible underneath her breath, I chuckle and use my tongue to trace a path back up to her mouth.

This time when I kiss her, I pour every ounce of emotion I can into the kiss. Hoping she can feel a fraction of what I feel. A glimpse of the yearning burning through me.

Her moans grow louder, and she begins to grind against me.

She's all I can think about or see or breathe.

When the force of her orgasm rips through her, she lifts her hips up off the mattress and cries out.

My fingers don't stop until she collapses back against the mattress, a thin sheen of perspiration erupting across her forehead.

Then with one move I rip her underwear, a smirk hovering on the edge of my lips. She glances up in time to see me throwing the tattered remains over my head.

"Oops," she says, breathlessly. "You definitely owe me a new pair."

"I'll get you as many as you want." I position myself at her entrance. In one quick move, I thrust into her.

She is soaking wet. It takes every ounce of control to think about her experience and not just mine.

I want this to be unforgettable.

I want Danielle to be panting and calling out my name well into the early hours of the morning.

But I also want to take my time with her and leave her desperately wanting more.

She runs her fingers over my shoulders and down the length of my back. Then she links her fingers over my neck and wriggles her body.

"Fuck. You're so wet." I ease out and slam back into her. "And you feel even better than I thought you would."

She lets her head fall to the side and squeezes her eyes shut. "Oh, God. *Oh, yeah.*"

Her voice is like butter, like music to my ears.

And I can't get enough.

I want more, I need more.

I thrust in and out of her in slow, practiced strokes. Then I lift her arms up over her head and hold them in a vice-like grip.

Her eyes fly open. When I take her in, draped under me with a look of raw, animal-like hunger on her face, it's almost enough to make me come undone.

I lower my head and give her another searing kiss.

She grinds against me. Her breathy moans reverberate through my head.

Then she sinks her teeth into my neck, sending dual waves of pain and pleasure ricocheting through me.

I throw my head back and growl. The bed dips and creaks with each movement.

My chest is tight, and my lungs burn as I run my hands up and down her arms. Each touch, each kiss, each movement brings me closer and closer to the edge of oblivion.

Nothing else matters.

Not even the fact that the entire ranch can probably hear us.

We move together with wild and animal-like abandon until another orgasm rips through her, prompting my own release.

When my body stops shaking, I roll off of her and collapse onto the mattress next to her.

I am barely breathing when I drape an arm over her shoulders and tuck her into my side.

She places her head on my chest, over the beating of my heart, and drifts off with a smile on her face. I press a kiss to the side of her head and squeeze my eyes shut.

The next few days are a blur of stolen kisses.

In the mornings, after making my rounds with the other guests and making small talk over breakfast, I wind up at her table, as if it's the most natural thing in the world.

I can see us having many more breakfasts together.

I hate having to get up and leave without her.

In the afternoons, during activities, I look for excuses to touch her and be near her. It's all I can do to control myself.

At night, we sit across from each other around the campfire, and I resist the urge to drag her off into the woods to have my way with her.

I feel like a teenager sneaking around behind everyone's back.

Somehow, this makes our relationship even more exciting.

Like I'm privy to something that no one else has or knows about.

During the rare occasions that we're able to be together, I hang on her every word. And I bring her flowers and chocolates. Spoil her as much as I can. For now.

But I'm scared it's not going to be enough.

By the end of the second week, I'm sure that I've started to develop feelings for Danielle. And now I have no idea what to do with myself.

How in the hell am I supposed to spend the next two weeks pretending like she isn't one of the best things to ever happen to me?

·♥·♥·♥·♥·♥·

I meet Danielle for a late night snack around the alpha cabin, which is in a restricted area.

I open the gate. As I hold her hand, we walk down a narrow trail to a small waterfall. The cabin is on the far right but we won't be going there tonight.

That's the VIP cabin reserved for super special guests. I treat myself and stay there once in a while.

I pull her to me, bury my face in the crook of her neck, and inhale.

She smells unbelievable.

It's the most intoxicating thing I've ever smelled. I want to be around her all the time.

All around us, nocturnal animals are coming to life. But I don't care.

All that matters is the two of us. On a blanket on the edge of this flat cliff. Overlooking the waterfall. Beneath the light of a pale, half-moon.

Over the past few days, I've spent every free moment that I can with Danielle. It still doesn't feel like enough.

Our late-night walks and stolen moments during the day leave me with a spring in my step and a smile on my face.

But I know that we can't keep it a secret forever. And I find myself looking forward to when we can openly announce our relationship.

Still, I'm terrified of what might happen when we're forced to leave our bubble and confront reality for what it is.

I haven't even told her about Brian yet.

Because I don't want to scare her off.

And I have no idea where to start

Danielle and I are on the precipice of something great. And I have a feeling that so far we're only scratching the surface because I've never felt this way about anyone before.

Danielle is the first woman, in a long time, to make me feel like who I am is enough.

Like all of the issues I have and all of the ways I try to compensate for them don't matter.

And it is the best feeling in the world.

When she draws back to look at me, a beautiful smile on her lips, I frame her face in my hands and kiss her.

I pour every ounce of emotion I can into the kiss, hoping she feels it too. She angles her head to the side, giving me better access, and I plunge my fingers through her silky hair.

It's not enough.

I inch closer to her, so we're pressed together, and I deepen the kiss. Her lips part, and my tongue darts into her mouth, beginning a sensual battle for dominance.

She tastes like wine and strawberries.

I want more.

I need more.

So, I move my hands from her hair, down the curve of her back. Then I stand and hoist her up.

My fingers move back to her ass, and I squeeze, hard. She makes a little mewling sound in the back of her throat that makes my blood turn molten.

Each thump of my heart, each staccato rhythm calls out her name.

I hold her to me and move her backwards. Slowly, I set her back down on the blanket. My fingers move to her dress.

Danielle is panting now and murmuring my name under her breath. With a smile, I lift the dress up so that it's pooled around her waist.

Her breath hitches in her throat as she leans up into my touch. She brings herself up and buries her face in the crook of my neck. Her skin is soft, like butter.

As I trace my fingers over it, goosebumps break out over her flesh.

Danielle shudders, and her hands move to my shirt. With a growl, she draws back and pulls my shirt up over my head. She flashes me a wicked smile as the shirt falls to the floor with a flutter.

Then her hands are all over me, running over the bare skin of my back and stomach, as if she has something to prove.

But I'm already hers.

With the sound of water rushing in the background, and our own heavy breathing, I lay her down on the picnic blanket again and drape myself over her.

Danielle wriggles and wraps her legs around my waist. I rub myself against her and place my arms on either side of her. She runs her fingers down the length of my back.

I lean back to look at her. When I see the stark, naked hunger written all over her face, it makes me want to rip off both of our clothes and bury myself inside her.

It takes every ounce of self-control I have to hold myself still and glance down at her, her tanned body bathed in the soft glow of the moon.

Danielle gives me a confused look. "Is everything okay?"

I blow out a breath. "Yes, everything is just perfect!"

Danielle's expression softens. "You feel it too?"

I search her face. "Yes, for sure. I just want to go slow. I don't want this moment to ever end."

Danielle sits up and gives me a smile. "Yeah, of course. Take all the time you want."

I give her another kiss. But before she can deepen it, I stand up. Offering her a wicked smile, I hold my hand out to her.

After a brief pause, she takes it. I pull her up to her feet. My eyes don't leave her face as I help her out of her dress, leaving her in her matching white cotton bra and underwear.

She's so beautiful it hurts.

I'm still smiling as I hurry out of my own clothes, leaving only my boxers on. "Let's go for a swim. The water is great."

Without waiting for a response, I pull my boxer down. Her eyes dart down and widen in surprise.

Her mouth parts. A flush moves up her neck and cheeks. I give her another wicked smile, take a few steps back, and pause.

Once I reach the edge of the small cliff, close enough that I can see the water glistening below, I take a deep breath.

And I jump in.

I'm suspended in the air for a few seconds before I crash and water is all around me. When I surface, I flick my hair out of my eyes and rub them.

My vision comes back into focus, but Danielle is nowhere to be found.

I squint in the darkness, struggling to make out her familiar figure, when I spot something out of the corner of my eye.

Suddenly, she is throwing herself through the air.

She is a flash of color in the night before she crashes into the water.

When she finally comes up for air, I'm waiting impatiently for her.

Immediately, I crush her to me. Our naked bodies are slippery and wet as we kiss. It feels like I'm trying to mold her to me, to mark her with something.

Meanwhile, she's pawing at my back and rubbing herself against me. I shift so that I'm at her entrance. Then I plunge two fingers into her.

Danielle throws her head back and moans. "Oh, fuck."

"You're so sexy," I murmur, into her skin. She wraps her legs around my waist, and my hands fall to her back. "Shit, you drive me crazy, Danielle."

I thrust myself inside her. Move in and out of her at a steady pace, pushing her closer and closer to the edge of oblivion.

She grinds against me then bucks and thrashes, eager for more. Abruptly, she arches her back and explodes, her entire body spasming and writhing with pleasure.

As she's climbing down from her high, my phone pings, the sound slicing through the air.

I ignore it and press my lips to hers.

She kisses me back with just as much fervor.

My phone rings again, and it takes a while for me to recognize the ringtone. When I do, I reluctantly, and with a great deal of difficulty, pull myself away.

With an apologetic smile, I swim away from Danielle and pull myself out of the water.

Droplets of water trail behind me all the way up to the cliff, and I'm exasperated. I pick up my phone and see Brian's message.

Danielle has one hand over her chest, and the other is held between her thighs. She shifts from one foot to the other and reaches for her dress. "Is everything okay?"

I sigh and pull my boxers on with a snap. "Yeah, I'm sorry. Work emergency. Do you mind if we head back?"

She looks disappointed as we roll up the blanket and carry the picnic basket back through the woods and to the ranch.

No one is around when we get to the ranch main area. I leave a few inches of space between us and send Brian a few messages.

When he doesn't respond, I leave Danielle in front of her cabin with a quick kiss and a sincere apology.

I find Brian on the floor in his room, staring up at the ceiling, a bottle of unopened scotch next to him.

His clothes litter every surface. His hands are clenched into fists at his sides. Wordlessly, I kick the door shut and slide onto the floor next to him.

When I link my fingers with his and wait, Brian makes a low noise in the back of his throat.

For a while, we sit there in silence. I wait for my brother to collect his thoughts.

Brian has never been good at sharing. And it's even harder for him to open up because of all the people who have taken advantage of him.

With a sigh, I rise to my feet and retrieve a large bottle of water. I'm halfway through it when Brian fixes his gaze on me and frowns.

"Why is your hair wet?"

"I took a dip in the stream." I set the bottle down on the dresser and fold my arms over my chest. "You want to tell me what happened?"

Brian sits up straighter and gives me a pointed look. "Not until you tell me what you were doing at the stream. You got a hot date or something?"

"You didn't call me here to talk about my love life."

Brian snorts. "What love life?"

"Exactly." I unfold my arms and pull the chair out with a screech. "What's on your mind?"

"I know you told me not to use social media during the my hour per day, but I couldn't help myself."

"Bri—"

Brian held his hand up then ran it over his face. "I know I screwed up. I just needed to see her, you know. After we left things, I wanted to know that she was okay. I know you understand, Ad."

I frown. "Even if I do, you can't keep pulling stunts like this. Didn't your therapist say you need to focus on yourself, and your journey to healing?"

"Yes, but we're also reliving certain events from the past, so it's got me thinking."

"About?"

"About Vanessa." Brian stands up and shoves his hands into the pockets of his shorts. "And how we left things. I'm sure that if she knew I was putting in the work, she'd want me back. You said yourself that this place works wonders, Adrian."

I exhale. "Brian, I think your enthusiasm and dedication are amazing. But you've still got a long and difficult journey ahead. And Vanessa has already made it clear that she can't wait around."

"It's because she thinks there's nothing to wait around for. But if I tell her the truth…"

"What are you hoping is going to happen?"

Brian shrugs and won't meet my gaze. "That she'll stop dating other pricks and find her way back to me."

I stand up and let my hands fall to my sides. "Maybe, but you have to put in the work first. You can't just say that you will. She needs to see a real change in you. Then maybe she will come back."

Brian's expression lights up. "Do you think I actually stand a chance with her?"

I pause. "I don't know. But it isn't the craziest idea you've ever had. And stranger things have definitely happened."

Brian stares at my face and doesn't say anything.

Slowly, he sinks to his feet and stares back up at the ceiling. I take my phone out and check the time.

Then I hurry out of the room and into the reception area where Maureen is about to clock out.

After giving her a series of instructions, I go back to Brian. He is standing in front of the window peering out.

Wordlessly, I pick up the jacket he hung up behind the door and toss it to him. He catches it mid-air and gives me a confused look.

"Everyone's asleep. So, come on. There's something I want to show you."

Brian pulls the jacket on and doesn't say anything. On our way out of the main cabin, I take the bag out of Maureen's hand and offer her a smile. "Remind me to give you a raise."

Maureen laughs. "You just gave me one."

Outside in the darkness, I switch the flashlight on and hold it up in front of me. Brian falls into step beside me, and we creep forward.

In the distance, a wolf howls, and the wind whistles. When we reach the clearing, the fire there has just died out. There are no guests in sight.

Relieved, I climb over the log and glance at Brian over my shoulders. "I know you don't feel up to group activities just yet, but I thought you might enjoy a preview."

Brian sits down on the overturned log and looks around. "You bring them out to the middle of nowhere? Half of them probably think you're a serial killer."

I choke back a laugh, sit down next to him, and take out a can of beer. After handing him one, I crack mine open and take a long sip. "As long as it doesn't taint the overall experience."

Brian sips on his drink and studies the night sky, where hundreds of stars are spread out and twinkling like a thousand diamonds. "Yeah, I don't know how the hell you came up with the idea for this retreat, but it's not half bad."

"It was actually partly inspired by you."

Brian rolls his eyes. "Yeah, right."

I take another sip of my beer. It trickles down my throat and settles into the pit of my stomach. "Do you remember the first trip you took after you got your first job? To Peru?"

Brian twists to face me and nods. "The silent retreat...Yeah, I remember that. I also remember mom being pissed. And Dad thought I was on drugs."

My lips lift into a half smile. "Honestly, I kind of thought you were on drugs too. So when mom and Dad told me I should go and check on you, I jumped at the chance. I was already traveling abroad. So I thought, why not?"

Brian snorts. "I knew you didn't to detour from your plan as a spur-of-the-moment thing. You're not that kind of person."

"I'm not. But you're my big brother. Even if it is only by a few minutes."

It's always a no-brainer for me to make sure he is okay.

Yet, rather than being knee-deep in drugs and unaware of anything around him, Brian had been surprisingly alert and calm.

I spent the entire time clinging to the shadows and watching him carefully, ready to swoop in at the first sign of trouble.

Looking out for Brian has always come as second nature to me and I've done it my whole life.

The retreat in Peru was no exception.

But the more I studied him back then, and the grace with which he held himself, the more relieved I was.

I ended up in another retreat. It was there that the plan for my own retreat took shape. And when I returned from my trip backpacking around the world, I couldn't get the idea out of my head.

Each country that I visited reminded me of my brother's face.

I've been trying to re-capture and recreate the feeling from that first retreat ever since. But I know it isn't the same, at least not for Brian.

He stands up and stretches his arms over his head. "Do you want to know what one of the last things Vanessa said to me was? She told me that I need to take a page out of your book and figure out how to get my shit together."

"You do realize she said that to hurt you, right?"

Brian shrugs. "She's not wrong. You're a fucking billionaire, Adrian. And I've seen how much your employees love you. I've also seen the way the guests talk about you…. That's not something I'm ever going to be able to do. And I'm okay with it. I know who I am, Adrian."

I stand up and take another sip of my beer. "I know. And believe me when I say it's her loss."

Brian exhales and looks back up at the sky. "I hate having this disease or whatever you call it. And I don't like being compared to you. But I appreciate your help."

"Of course."

In silence, we study each other. A short while later, we make our way back to the main cabin. Brian seems to be in a much better mood.

In his room, he doesn't even bother to look at his phone and instead throws himself onto the bed and switches on the TV.

I linger in the doorway for a while before making my way back out.

In my room, I toss and turn and think of Danielle.

And I can't help but worry about my brother. Am I even able to help him or is this going to backfire somehow and explode all over me?

I hope this retreat is the answer he's been looking for all along.

In the morning, I wake up when the first patches of light pour into the room, illuminating everything in a soft and buttery glow.

There is a headache in the back of my skull and my mouth feels dry. After brushing my teeth I set off for my morning run.

By the time I make it back to my room, I'm covered in sweat, and my heart is racing. I step into the shower and scrub myself. When I get out, I feel better.

I put on shorts and a T-shirt. I check in on Brian, who is buried in a heap underneath his covers and snoring loudly.

At breakfast, everyone is talking animatedly. Everyone except for Danielle, who is sitting by herself at a table near the back and sneaking glances out the window.

After greeting everyone else, I make my way over to her and lean against the chair. She brightens when she sees me. And the smile she gives me takes my breath away.

"Good morning. I wanted to come and tell you that I'm sorry about yesterday."

She tucks a lock of hair behind her ears. "It's okay. I hope everything is all right."

I pull the chair out and sit down opposite her. "It is now."

Chapter Nine: Danielle

"I still don't understand why I have to wear all of this." I zip up my sweater and glance down at the open-toed sandals I had planned on wearing today. "Also, wouldn't it be easier to wear sandals or something?"

Adrian shakes his head and holds the helmet out. "No, sneakers are a much better option for river rafting. It helps protect your feet from sharp objects."

I give him a dubious look. "Okay, that sounds dangerous."

"It can be." Adrian glances over at the life jacket I have propped up against the wall. "You're going to have to wear that too."

I sigh. "I know there's probably a good reason, but can I at least keep it under my feet or something? I promise to put it on quickly if there's a problem."

"You wouldn't have enough time. It's better safe than sorry."

I grimace. "Fine. But just so you know, I wanted to look nice today. And you're ruining it with the helmet and the life jacket."

Adrian smiles and secures the helmet around my head. "You'd look amazing in a paper bag."

I blush and reach for the life jacket. "At least let me put it on when we get to the river. There's no reason I have to walk around the camp like this."

After the other night in the woods, I don't need to give the other guests more reasons to give me strange looks.

Wandering around the main grounds in the night wasn't my best idea. Even though no one was around when we got back. But after Adrian dropped me off, I wasn't able to sleep.

I'd tried watching a show, reading a book, and writing in my journal.

But was so wound up and I knew that only fresh air would do me good.

I spent half the night spinning in circles just to work off the excess energy.

Adrian brushes his hand against mine as we climb down the steps and fall into step beside each other. "It's going to be a lot of fun, trust me."

"Is there anyone else coming?"

"You're the only one who signed up."

I grin. "So, I get you all to myself, huh? I like where this is going. On a completely unrelated note, how long has this river rafting activity been going on?"

Adrian throws his head back and laughs. "We've done it hundreds of times. I know what I'm doing, don't worry."

"I'm not saying you don't. I'm just wondering why there aren't any other guests."

Getting to spend an entire day out on the water with Adrian sounds too good to be true.

There has to be a catch.

"Today is spa day," Adrian says, with a quick look in my direction. "Have you even checked the schedule I gave you?"

"Sure, I have. And while we're on the topic of schedules, I suddenly realized that mine is full. Maybe we should try river rafting on another day when it isn't spa day."

Adrian laces his fingers through mine. "Come on. Tt's going to be a lot of fun. I promise."

"But is it going to be hot stone massage, facials, and pedicures kind of fun?"

"That's a tough standard to be held to." Adrian drew me closer and brought my hands up to his lips for a kiss. "But I think I can get creative."

My heart misses a beat. "Yeah? How?"

"You won't know until you come out on the water with me." He releases my hand, spins around to face me, and walks backward. "So, what do you say?"

"You're trying to seduce me into river rafting with you," I accuse, pausing to point a finger at him. "You should be ashamed of yourself."

Adrian shrugs. "I'm not ashamed."

With that, he darts off, and I scramble to keep up with him. As we wander through the woods, he finds excuses to stop and kiss me.

By the time we reach the river, I'm giddy and breathless and nothing can bring me down.

An inflatable boat is already waiting for us, along with two paddles. Adrian secures his helmet and life jacket before getting in and holding his hand out.

I take it and hoist myself up.

When we settle across from each other, our knees are touching. Adrian picks up his paddle. "Just do what I do, okay? We're going to paddle in the same direction."

I nod, the sound of birds chirping in my ear. "Like this?"

Adrian smiles. "You got it. You ready for this?"

I roll my shoulders and then square them. "I was born ready."

"Uh-oh. Have I discovered a competitive side to you?" Adrian begins to paddle, and we settle into a rhythm, moving further and further away from our path.

The water is rushing steadily underneath us as we drift past the rows and rows of trees on either side.

When I squint, I can spot a few mountains in the distance.

"You scared, Steele? Worried about a little competition?"

Adrian laughs. "I'm not worried. I like competition."

I give him a meaningful smile. "Good, so do I."

Eventually, Adrian stops paddling in slow, practiced strokes and sits up straighter. His eyes dart around before moving back to me.

My arms ache, and my muscles are screaming in protest. But I like seeing him like this.

Out in the wilderness, there's a softness to Adrian that I didn't expect.

Like he's connected to the earth and everything around him.

It makes me like him even more.

When he flashes me a smile, my stomach gives an odd little twinge.

I'm an idiot.

Adrian is going to lose interest in me once the novelty wears off, and there's nothing I can do to stop it.

With a sigh, I look away from him and let my eyes sweep over the terrain. "You know, I'm glad you tricked me into coming."

"I didn't trick you. You wanted to come."

I swing my gaze back to him. "Well, it's your fault. How do you expect me to say no to that smile and those abs?"

He gives me a slow and wicked grin. "There's more where that came from."

I point a finger at him. But I can't stop smiling. "Aha! See, I told you that you were being unfair."

Adrian holds his free hand up. "I regret nothing."

My smile fades. "I've been dreaming of going on a retreat like this for years. But there was always something stopping me from going."

"At least you're here now," Adrian offers, after a brief silence. "We can't change the past, Danielle. All we can do is learn from it and let it go."

I push my hair out of my eyes.

"You ever think about being a shrink?"

Adrian chokes back a laugh. "Oh, fuck no. I mean, I've got a lot of respect for the profession. But I couldn't do what they do. I'd probably get too attached and end up a wreck whenever my patients came in."

"Maybe it would be your superpower."

Adrian offers me a half smile. "I appreciate the vote of confidence, but I couldn't do it all the time."

"Well, for what it's worth, talking to you is easier than talking to my therapist. Doctor Sheridan is nice and all, but it feels weird to be put under the microscope."

"Doctor Sheridan reminds me of my old therapist."

I tilt my head to the side and study him. "Why is that?"

Adrian stops paddling and lets the water move past, at a steady and unhurried pace. He looks at me, and it feels as if he's seeing me.

Like he can see right into my soul.

It's exhilarating and terrifying, and I can't look away.

I want to get lost in his eyes and never come back down to reality.

"When my parents died in a plane crash, I was really angry. It felt like the world was out to get me. I just couldn't seem to make my peace with it. Jenny, the woman I was seeing at the time, suggested I see a therapist."

"Did it help?"

Adrian blew out a breath. "I hated it at first. I thought my therapist was a condescending prick who wouldn't know trauma if it bit him in the ass. Without my parents around, I was suddenly responsible for my family. I guess I just wanted someone to blame."

"I'm sure he understood that it wasn't about him. You were just trying to sort through some things."

Adrian gives me a grateful smile. "Yeah, but I still feel bad about how I treated him. I did apologize afterward. But I've always said that he had the patience of a saint to put up with people like me."

"People like you?"

"He told me that wanting to save the world is my problem. Because I can't save everybody."

Before I know what I'm doing, I reach between us and take his hands in mine.

I rub my thumb along the inside of his wrist and ignore the hammering of my heart. "I don't think there's anything wrong with trying."

Adrian gives my hands a firm squeeze. "There isn't, but I had to learn how to set boundaries and how to give myself a break too."

"See? You're a natural. How many people do you know who can actually accept therapy so easily?"

"It was far from easy." Adrian stands up and sits next to me. He is still holding my hands like they're the most fragile things in the world. "But it's so worth it."

"I guess we'll have to wait and see."

Adrian nods. "Yes, we will."

Slowly the inflatable boat comes to a sudden stop.

There are still butterflies in my stomach when we walk back to camp.

They stay there even though we are walking separately when we emerge onto the main part of the ranch.

Adrian doesn't look back at me as he walks away, and I sigh. In my cabin, I hum and whistle as I throw myself stomach-first onto the bed and squeeze my eyes shut.

Chapter Ten: Adrian

"Mr. Steele, I wasn't expecting to see you today." Doctor Masterson stands up behind her desk and pushes her chair back. "To what do I owe the pleasure?"

I let the door click shut behind me. "I thought we agreed you wouldn't call me Mr. Steele. It's Adrian, please."

Doctor Masterson gestures to the chair opposite her desk.

It's a modest-sized room with a matching leather set, a rectangular-shaped desk, and a large window that allows plenty of sunlight in. There's an excellent view of the ranch grounds.

In the background, I can make out the faint whirring of the AC.

"I know that you're bound by the laws of doctor and patient confidentiality." I sit down and fold my hands in my lap. "So, I can't ask you to tell me what you and my brother talk about during your sessions. But I do want to express some concerns."

Doctor Masterson's brows furrow together. "Have there been any complaints about my methods? I know I'm pushing Brian. But I'm trying a different method with him. In the hopes that it'll be more effective."

I shake my head. "I don't think it's you, doc. I think it's Brian. Do you feel like he's responding well to treatment?"

"It's been eighteen days since we started," Doctor Masterson replied, after a brief pause. "It's hard to say for sure because real progress takes time. But I think he's doing fine."

I exhale. "He had another one of his depressive episodes the other day. His messages made me rush back from swimming. I thought he was going to hurt himself."

Doctor Masterson's furrow deepens. "Did he say anything in his messages to indicate that?"

I frown. "No, but I keep an eye out anyway. As I've explained to you before, it's not the first time he's gotten in trouble or hurt himself."

Doctor Masterson reaches into her drawer and pulls out a file. She flips it open and makes a low noise in the back of her throat.

Then she looks up at me and snaps the folder shut again.

"If you'll remember, I did mention my concern regarding Brian's well-being. He took our parents' death pretty hard. And even though I tried to get him into therapy, he wouldn't listen."

Doctor Masterson links her fingers together. "Yes, I remember. Mr. Ste— I mean, Adrian. I assure you that I am keeping a close eye on your brother. So far he has not exhibited any suicidal tendencies."

I lean forward. "Has he spoken about his ex-girlfriend? He's still hung up on her."

Doctor Masterson gives me an apologetic look. "I'm sorry, but I can't tell you any of that information. Brian is my patient. I owe him my loyalty and discretion. I know you mean well, but you need to trust me to do my job."

I lean back against the chair and blow out a breath. "I know you're right, but I worry about him, you know. We've got a few distant relatives out there somewhere. But it is pretty much just the two of us left. I don't want to lose him."

Doctor Masterson takes off her glasses and polishes them. "I believe this is a conversation you need to have with your brother."

"Maybe you're right. I do try talking to him about things. It's almost impossible to have a serious conversation with him."

Doctor Masterson puts her glasses back on and twin pools of brown peer at me. "Mr. Steele, you know your brother better than I do. Which is why this isn't easy for me to say. Over the past couple of weeks, I've been observing your brother. I'm considering whether or not to prescribe him medication."

"He hates being on meds. He's taken anti-depressants before, but he says they make him feel fuzzy and wrong."

"Anti-depressants are perfectly safe," Doctor Masterson argues. "If the dosage is too strong, he can come back, so we can adjust it."

"Doc, I hear what you're saying, but I thought you said he was doing okay."

"I did. But based on your concerns, perhaps we need to consider a more serious form of treatment."

"I am not going to institutionalize my brother."

"That's an offensive term, Mr. Steele." Doctor Masterson doesn't look pleased when she holds my gaze. "Mental health institutions are a great way to give yourself a break from the hardships of the world. I do believe that Brian can benefit from such a break."

"He'll hate it." I stand up and wander over to the window. Through the glass, I see a group of guests in the riding arena, patting their horses and posing for pictures. "If he isn't open to it, it'll do more harm than good, I think."

"Your brother won't always make the best decisions for himself, as evidenced by his previous behavior." Doctor Masterson pushes her chair back with a screech. "I don't mean to upset you. But you might want to consider something a bit more drastic to enable you to help him."

"Like what?"

"Like a conservatorship."

I spin around to face her. "We haven't reached that point. And let's hope that we don't."

Brian can forgive me for meddling.

But I am not going to try to take his freedom away from him.

Not when I have no idea what kind of long-term ramifications it's going to have.

Brian means too much to me. I can't have him hate me for the rest of his life.

"He deserves a chance to fight and win against his own demons, Doc," I add after a brief pause. "And I want to give him the chance to do that. Without me hovering or controlling every aspect of his life."

Otherwise, he is never going to learn to survive on his own.

After a brief pause, I move away from the desk and move towards the door. I pause there with a hand on the knob and glance over my shoulders.

Doctor Masterson is sitting behind her desk with Brian's file open. She is skimming through it, a furrow between her brows.

When she glances up at me, I swallow back the rest of my retort.

Then I yank on the knob and pull on the door with a little more force than necessary.

I make it back to one of my offices, somewhere deep in the bowels of the main cabin. I mutter to myself and wonder if I made a mistake bringing Brian here.

Or hiring Doctor Masterson in the first place.

Of course, she wants to go for the drastic option.

As I sit down behind my desk and shuffle some papers around, I realize that there's no way for me to know if it'll work.

Not for certain at least.

Sighing, I press two fingers to my temples and rub in slow, circular motions. Then I pick up my phone and place a few phone calls, including one to Maureen.

I ask her to make sure she keep tabs on Brian the whole time.

Hours later, my entire body is aching, and I've got a crick in my neck.

Slowly, I push my chair back and stretch my arms over my head. Then I bend down to touch the tips of my toes and shake off some of the numbness.

When I draw myself back up to my full height, I realize the sun is dipping below the horizon, lighting up the world in hues of pink and purple.

With a slight shake of my head, I step out of the office and lock the door. On my way to my room, I can't stop thinking about Brian, or the best way to help him.

In my room, I shower, change into a clean pair of clothes. I order my meal and eat it while peering through the balcony doors.

A steady stream of guests are headed into the forest in the direction of the clearing where the nightly campfire is being held.

I spot a familiar head of dark hair, and I swallow, trying to ignore the nervous fluttering in the center of my chest. After brushing off the crumbs, I wash my hands and hurry out.

Several guests call out to me as I race past them and in the direction of the clearing.

It is half hidden in the shadows, with only the red and orange flames to light up the path.

Underneath the silver, crescent-shaped moon, I spot Danielle sitting on a log, twirling a lock of hair between her fingers, and sipping on her drink.

She is glancing around at the people gathered around, a thoughtful expression on her face.

When her gaze meets mine, I forget what I mean to say next.

Suddenly, I can't even remember why I'm so anxious.

My feet move toward her before I know what I'm doing.

As soon as I sit down next to her, she twists to face me. Her entire face lights up. "Hey."

Her smile turns my entire day around.

"Hey yourself." I nod towards her drink. "You enjoying that?"

She sets the cup down on the ground and looks back up at me. "It's okay. How was your day?"

I roll my shoulders. "Long. I've got this relative who needs help. But I'm not sure how to give him what he needs."

Danielle's expression softens. "I'm sure just the fact that you want to help counts. How bad is it?"

"He's got a lot of.... issues. Anger issues, some hallucination, other issues that I won't mention. I might be the only one who can get him the help he needs."

Danielle studies my face. "And you're worried that if you interfere too much, he'll eventually resent you?"

I release a deep breath and nod. "Yeah, exactly."

Danielle links her fingers together and folds them in her lap. "I think that if your heart is in the right place, he'll forgive you."

I look away from her and study the flames of the fire.

Conversations rise and fall around us.

"I don't think it'll be that easy. It's a lot of history," I reply after a lengthy pause. "And based on how he's reacted in the past... I doubt this'll go over well."

Danielle inches closer, and a gust of wind rips past, blowing the smell of her floral perfume in my direction. "I think you'll figure out a way to make things right, if things even get that far. But isn't it better than regretting it later?"

I swing my gaze back to hers. "What do you mean?"

"I don't know about you. But I'd personally would rather be sorry about how something turned out than have regrets about not doing what I should've done. Or about not having followed my instincts."

I pause. "I guess I get that."

"You do?"

"Yeah, of course," I tease, pausing to bump my shoulders against hers. "You're a lot more insightful and observant than you give yourself credit for."

Danielle makes a low noise in the back of her throat. "I don't think I could ever get used to hearing that."

I lean forward, so there's only a few inches of space between us.

Her pupils dilate, and her breath hitches in her throat.

"Trevor is a fucking idiot and an asshole, and every minute he spent tearing you down is because he was jealous."

Color crept up Danielle's neck and cheeks. "Thank you."

"I'm not just saying that, Danielle," I add, in a softer voice. "I mean it. You're an incredible woman."

The kind that any man would be lucky to have.

In two short weeks, she's made me feel like I'm not a screwup, and like there's hope for Brian and I to emerge from all of this relatively unscathed.

And she is the first woman in a long time to look at me and see the man behind the money and not the other way around.

It makes me feel invincible. Like I'm standing on top of the world.

"I've never met anyone like you," Danielle whispers, her flush deepening. "You want to hear something weird? I'm afraid this is all some kind of dream."

I stand up and tilt my head in the direction of the woods. "We'd better make every minute count then."

After another meaningful look, I wander over to some of the other guests.

For a while, I make small talk and listen to stories.

When I glance back at the log and realize Danielle is gone, I make my excuses.

Then I wander through the trees and the smell of earth. I find her leaning against a tree, scanning the darkness.

Wordlessly, I cross over to her and hoist her up so her legs are around my waist.

Once I kiss her, the rest of the world disappears.

She tastes like marshmallows and strawberry lip-gloss, and I can't get enough.

I'm addicted. And when I press her against the tree and my hand moves down the side of her body, the blood roars in my ears.

With a smirk, I lift her dress up, so it pools around her waist. She makes a low noise in the back of her throat that sends waves of desire through me.

Half of me is tempted to undress her and take her then and there.

The other-half of me wants to take my time, to continue to feel her hot breath on my cheek against my ears.

She is whispering my name now, a chant and a prayer falling from her lips. She tightens her legs and rubs herself against me, and the roar in my ears grows louder.

Molten-hot desire pumps through every inch of me.

I'm not afraid of how much I need her.

Or of how every inch of me yearns for her.

Her fingers dart underneath my shirt, and I shudder, goosebumps breaking out across my flesh.

She runs her fingers over skin, and it's all I can do not to bury myself in her.

Instead, I pin her arms up over her head and wrench my lips away.

I'm pressing hot open-mouthed kisses down the side of her neck and over her jaw when laughter from the campfire rises through the air.

Danielle deflates, and her eyes are wide and full of hunger when she leans back to look at me. "We should head back over to the campfire."

I kiss her again, with a passion and fervor that surprises me.

She's unsteady on her feet when I set her back down.

I give her another kiss and tuck her hair behind her ears. "I'll come and find you after the party. Leave your door unlocked."

The looks she gives me goes straight to my soul.

I spend the rest of the night trying to steer clear of her.

Later that night, I find my way to Danielle's cabin. I dress as discretely as possible and make sure no one sees me.

I just can't afford for a guest to see me entering another guest's cabin this late at night.

It was my custom to show up randomly at guests' cabins with complementary gifts during the day. I love doing that and seeing their reactions.

But creeping into a guest cabin late at night is a whole different story.

Chapter Eleven: Danielle

"I told you that you would enjoy getting to know Mr. Cowboy Hunk more often."

I pat my face dry. "You know that's not his name."

"Yes, but you swore me to secrecy. So we need a codename, and I was up most of the night coming up with it."

I open my eyes and peer at my reflection in the fluorescent light mirror. "You expect me to believe that you were up all night trying to come up with a nickname for Adrian and that's what you came up with?"

"I was also grading some assignments and going over lesson plans. I thought it was a good chance to multi-task."

I pick up the tube of sunscreen and squeeze out a generous amount. "Didn't you accept a date the other day? With the dentist?"

"Yeah, but I'm probably going to cancel. There's no spark. Nothing like you and Mr. Achy Breaky Heart."

I grimace and spread the cream all over my face. "Believe it or not, Cowboy Hunk is a better nickname."

Savannah laughs. "I thought you'd see things my way, so when are you seeing him again?"

"I don't know, probably tonight. But I was thinking I'd surprise him."

"I like where this is going. Wait, no more romantic excursions underneath the moon light?"

"Not tonight," I reply, before reaching for a brush and raking it through my hair. "He's been a little strange lately. I don't know. Maybe it's that relative of his who has issues?"

Or maybe he's trying to tell me something about himself.

Adrian is the first guy I've liked who doesn't make me feel like I need to change everything about myself.

With him, I don't have to jump through hoops or make myself smaller to feed his ego.

It is both refreshing and terrifying to realize how attached I'm getting.

I have no idea how or when he did it, but Adrian Steele has gotten under my skin.

And I don't mind.

I don't mind that I have feelings for him. Or that he's my first thought in the morning. And my last thought at night.

And I can't bring myself to regret anything that has happened between us.

Not when it feels this good.

Do not get too attached, D. The point is to have an affair, not fall in love, remember?

Except a part of me wonders if it's already too late.

We've spent the past few days together, and I still can't get enough of him.

"Whatever it is, I'm sure he'll get over it. The important thing is that he makes you happy. I'm so pleased for you, babe. I really am."

"Thanks, Sav. Anyway, my internet hour is almost up, and I need to download this new assignment my therapist sent me. I'll talk to you tomorrow, okay? Give Skittles a big kiss from me."

"Love you."

"Love you too."

Humming to myself, I step back into the room and pick up my laptop. After sinking against the couch, I wait for my email to load.

Moments after I download the assignment file, I lose my signal. With a sigh, I set the laptop down and wander into the room.

Later, I emerge from my cabin and head into the main restaurant for lunch.

Bright sunlight is pouring in from outside. Tiny particles of light are dancing on the hardwood floors.

Everything is bathed in a warm halo of light, and it takes a while for my eyes to adjust.

When they do, I see Adrian at his usual table in the back.

Adrian is using one hand to shovel food into his mouth and the other to scroll through his phone.

He doesn't react when I pull my chair out to sit down. When I pick up my fork to eat, he glances over at me, and my heart does an odd little somersault.

His lips spread into a slow smile, and I stop with the fork halfway to my lips.

"Why are you looking at me like that?" I shove the fork into my mouth and chew on the lettuce and tomatoes slowly and thoughtfully. "Do I have something on my face?"

"You look beautiful," Adrian tells me, his eyes moving steadily over me. "Being on the ranch suits you."

I blush and look down at my plate. "It's not too much color?"

"I don't think so. Tan and healthy is a good look for you."

I peek up at him, and he's still looking at me and smiling.

Something warm and unfamiliar unfurls in the center of my chest. "You look good too."

He puts the phone on the table and gives me his full attention. "I've got some work tonight, but I might be able to stop by later if you're still awake."

"Ok, I'll be waiting for you in my room. I have special lingerie to try on for you," I offer, once I unglue my tongue from the roof of my mouth.

Adrian gives me a wicked smirk. "I like a woman who knows what she wants and how to make everything so special."

"What a coincidence, so do I. You know what else I like?"

"Hmm?"

I lean forward and hold his gaze. "I like a man who can go all night. Imagine all of that sweat, and all of those different positions…"

Adrian chokes on a piece of his salad. His face turns a bright shade of red. I give him an innocent smile as I lean back in my seat.

He thumps his chest and gives me a look that I feel in the pit of my stomach.

If it weren't for the guests around us, I'd climb over the table and pull him to me.

If it wasn't for our agreement, I think he'd rip my clothes apart, drape me over one of these tables, and lose himself in me.

I blink. Adrian guzzles his water. "Cat got your tongue?"

He sets his glass down and clears his throat. "Tonight, you and I are going to put that tongue to good use."

"Is that so?"

"I'd suggest you take a nap before I come over." Adrian sits up straighter and gives me a suggestive look.

I give him a slow and sensual smile. "You've got yourself a deal."

Underneath the table, his hand darts out and grazes my knee. I kick off my ballet flat and lift my foot up. Then I use it graze his thighs.

When it's between his legs, Adrian stiffens, and a single bead of sweat forms on his forehead.

With a smile, he pushes his chair closer, and his fingers move from my knees to the inside of my thighs.

Fuck.

Are we really doing this?

One of the guests, a tall and pale man with wisps of blonde hair comes over, and Adrian stops. Reluctantly, I let my foot fall back onto the floor and turn my attention to my food.

During the rest of lunch, guests keep coming up to the table. When I get up to leave, I feel Adrian's eyes follow me out of the dining room and into the hot afternoon air.

In my room, I strip down to my underwear and try to cool down.

I'm halfway through the first episode of a show when I realize I have no idea what's happening on the screen. Frowning, I turn the TV off and pick up a book.

After reading the same page several times, I throw the book onto the couch and bury my face in my hands.

What's the matter with you? You can do this.

I don't realize I've fallen asleep on the couch till I flip over and land on the floor with a thud.

My eyes fly open, and my entire body aches, so I stand up and stretch. I look at the time. I haven't been out long.

Time to change into something more comfortable. I slip on a black thong and a matching lacy bra. After pulling a cotton dress over the outfit, I study myself in the mirror.

Adrian is going to have no idea what hit him.

On my way out, I get a few strange looks. Or am I just imagining things because I'm just so nervous?

In the main cabin, I wait in one of the comfortable leather chairs and unfold a newspaper.

Over the top, I study the people coming and going until I spot Adrian in a pair of cargo shirts and a bright green shirt.

Hastily, I fold the newspaper back up and dart off in his general direction. He stops and goes into his room, leaving the door ajar.

I lean against the wall and wait.

He comes back out, shakes his head, and disappears down the hall, leaving his door propped open.

My heart is racing as I hurry into the dark room and out of the dress. I kick it away, climb onto the king-sized bed and prop myself up on my elbow.

There is a small beam of moonlight coming into the room, providing just enough illumination to discern the outlines of the objects within.

Then I shift, push the cover away and place a hand on my hips.

When I hear Adrian coming, I peel off my bra and thong and pull the cover over the lower half of my body.

I'm half-sitting up, a smile painted on my face, when he comes in. He has a tray of food and a bottle of beer.

He sets it down on the table by the door but doesn't look at the bed. With a smirk, I lift my arm up over my head and wave.

He lets out a muffled protest and I let the cover fall all the way off and give him my most seductive grin. I point a finger at him and beckon him forward.

Adrian makes a strange noise in the back of his throat.

Then he opens his mouth the rest of the way and lets out a scream. "What the fuck?"

Wincing, I jump out of bed and scramble for my lingerie and shoes. Adrian is still yelling and screaming unintelligibly when I fumble in the dark for my dress and pull it on. I manage to grab my shoes too.

My heart is pounding in my ears as I race past him and nearly run straight into a wall. Without pausing, I keep my feet moving as quickly as possible. I can't get out fast enough.

Halfway to the main cabin, I pause to straighten my dress, keeping my head ducked. My feet are bare, and my face is no doubt flush with color.

On the steps of the main cabin, I hop into my shoes and resist the urge to glance over my shoulder. I don't stop walking until I'm back in my own cabin.

There, I throw myself onto the couch and groan.

Then I bury my face against the nearest pillow and let out a muffled scream. When I stop, I stand up, go into the bathroom, and fill up the tub.

While I wait, I turn the whole thing over and over in my head, growing more and more confused with each passing second.

A part of me wants to stomp back over to Adrian's room and demand an explanation.

The other part of me is too horrified to set foot outside my room.

Now I'm worried that the ranch staff is going to be talking about the half-naked girl in Adrian's room. Do they know it was me?

I can already hear the rumors swirling.

This is not good!

Or maybe I'm blowing it out of proportion. As far as everyone else is concerned, women throwing themselves at Adrian is normal.

Hell, I'm sure a few of them have even gotten creative over the years. But I'm sure none of them have ever run out of his room while he screams bloody murder.

I let my dress fall to the floor with a flutter and pause to throw my lingerie into the laundry basket. The water is lukewarm and soothing against my flushed skin.

So, I sit there and soak and try to unravel the enigma that is Adrian Steele.

By the time I come out, my skin is shriveled and I'm no closer to understanding him. With a sigh, I wander into my bedroom in my fluffy robe and climb onto the bed.

I alternate between watching a show on my laptop and staring at my phone. Even though I know Adrian can't reach me because of the rules, a part of me is hoping he'll break them.

Even if only to explain his bizarre, over the top reaction to my being in his room.

In the morning when I wake up, I am covered in sweat, and I've got popcorn crumbs all over me. After I clean up the bed, I step into the shower and wonder what I'm going to say to Adrian.

As I rummage through my closet, I'm struck with the urge to call Savannah and get her take on things.

The urge is so strong I imagine myself walking away from the ranch and stopping only after I get a signal.

In the end, it's my growling stomach that propels me out of my cabin and onto the main path that leads to the dining room.

I run into a few guests on the way there, but other than one quick nod in my direction, no one acknowledges me.

I'm starting to think nobody's even heard about what happened until I step into the dining room and everyone is whispering.

However, when I join the line at the buffet table, I realize that nobody has a clue.

This fills me with a small amount of relief.

I add some tomatoes and cucumbers to my plate.

When I reach the omelet station, I still don't hear anything alarming. Weakly, I give the chef my order and shift from one foot to the other.

I retrieve a bowl of yogurt and skip the line near the toaster, color creeping up my cheeks the entire time. I'm nervous as hell to face Adrian, what do I say to him?

I find a table in the back, pull my chair out, and sink lower into my seat.

I'm moving my yogurt around the bowl and counting the minutes till I can leave when in he walks.

He's dressed in a pair of jeans and a button-down shirt. His hair is tousled to the side, giving him an artful yet brooding look.

His bright blue eyes are scanning the room while he greets the other guests.

Those eyes land on me, and I hastily look away.

Shit.

In spite of my better judgment, I look back up and find Adrian weaving through the crowd, pausing now and again to greet more of the guests.

He gives them all smiles and waves. By the time he reaches me, I'm a nervous wreck. Sweat has formed on my forehead and on the sides of my face. My shirt clings uncomfortably to my back.

I want a hole to open up and swallow me.

I also want to reach across the table and give Adrian a firm shake.

Neither of those things happen as Adrian pulls the chair out and sits down. He links his fingers together and smiles. "You look beautiful today. I'm sorry about last night. A few things came up."

My throat is dry. "Thank you." A few things came up? Is he being real now?

"I got a lot of work finished last night," he continues in the same pleasant voice. "Sometimes, I really hate the managerial side of things. It's a lot of paperwork, you know."

I give him a weak smile. "Sure."

Is he trying to give me an out, a chance to redeem myself for last night?

I can't tell for sure.

All I know is that not talking about what happened isn't making me feel better. Why isn't he saying anything about last night?

It's actually making me feel worse.

And the longer we sit there, making small talk about anything and nothing in particular, the more uncomfortable I feel.

But I can't bring myself to say the words and watch his face fall.

I've been humiliated enough as it is.

"Are you okay?" I lean forward and lower my voice. "Because, you know, you seemed a little…. off yesterday."

Adrian takes a grape off of my plate and shoves it into his mouth. "Yeah, I'm fine. I think it's just the stress of the job."

I blow out a breath. "You can talk to me about things, you know. If anything is bothering you, I mean anything…"

Or if there's anything he wants to get off his chest. I don't know how to bring that up. His behavior was so bizarre I don't even know how to start.

I'm starting to wonder if he even knew it was me in his room.

I don't want a heavy cloud over us, but Adrian offers me another smile and shrugs. Then someone comes in looking for him, and he has to get up.

As he walks away, I begin to wonder if he was trying to tell me something the other day.

Is the relative who has issues really Adrian? Is he the one with anger issues? Is he the one he's been describing to me? Maybe he's too embarrassed to admit that it's him. OMG! How can I even bring that up?

I don't get the chance to ask him because he's not available for the rest of the day.

And when I get back to my cabin after a day of yoga and horse-back riding, I'm sore and sweaty and my mood hasn't improved.

Not even the series of cute pictures of Savannah and Skittles that comes in during my internet hour makes me feel better.

Why did I get involved with him in the first place? Why can't I control my urges? Why do I get myself in the weirdest situation always?

I close my eyes and I still have no answer. But the memory of last night flashes full color in my mind.

Chapter Twelve: Adrian

"Okay, I'm confused. Can you repeat what happened again?" I let the curtain fall back into place and spin around to face Brian.

He is pacing his room, one hand shoved into his pocket, the other moving through his hair.

"Which part is confusing to you?"

"The whole thing," I reply, pausing to move away from the window. I perch on the edge of the bed and twist to face Brian. "So, you left the door to your room open, and when you came back, and it was dark, and you heard a woman?"

"A naked woman," Brian emphasizes, with a shake of his head. "And she wasn't even apologetic. She just kept trying to get me in bed with her."

I frown. "Are you sure you didn't come back to the wrong room? And how do you know she was naked if it was dark?"

Brian stops pacing and gives me an incredulous look. "No, I'm sure it was my room. Plus, I'm the one who left the door open. I just went out to get my food. It was late last night. No worries I went undercover. I didn't want to cause you trouble. I covered up and I came back very fast. I didn't talk to anyone. Sneaked in and out without being seen. I made out her vague silhouette as she ran past me."

I hold both hands up. "Maybe a guest got confused and went into the wrong room? It happens sometimes. And Brian, you were not supposed to go out like that, remember. No one knows you're here or that I have a twin brother. Do you see the confusion it could cause?"

Brian grimaces. "So, why would she come into my room and think it's a good idea to undress and try to get me into bed?"

I shrug and stand up. "I don't know. She probably...most likely.... Maybe she was drunk.... I don't know, I really don't know, Brian."

Brian made a face. "She seemed sober to me. I don't know, Adrian. It seems like you've got some weird people staying at the ranch. What if she comes back and tries to seduce me again, just when I've lowered my guard?"

I pause. "That's extremely unlikely, but I'll look into it. You might want to be sure before you startle my whole staff next time. Don't leave your room and don't leave your door open."

Now I'm worried. Is he hallucinating? He does have a past history of it.

Brian folds his arms over his chest. "And in the meantime, we should change my room just to be on the safe side. I don't need any more of this. It's fucking with my life."

I sigh. "Okay, if it'll make you feel better."

With a frown, I pick up the phone and dial the main desk. "Yes, I'd like someone to pack my brother's things and have him moved to another room. I'm not sure what is happening or why it happened. We have no clue or evidence of this incident, but we don't want it to happen again."

Maureen is already typing on the keyboard. "Of course, sir. I'll have it taken care of immediately."

I exhale. "I'll be with Doctor Masterson if you need me."

"Of course. Have a good day, Mr. Steele."

"You too."

I shove a hand into my pocket and step out of Brian's room and down a series of hallways.

Doctor Masterson's door is slightly ajar. She's sitting at her desk, hair piled into a bun on top of her head, a pencil between her lips.

She glances up when I walk in. A flicker of confusion moves over her face.

"Is this a bad time?"

She shakes her head and gestures to the chair. "Not at all, Mr. Steele. How can I help you? Have you given any more thought to the conservatorship?"

I sit down and fold my hands in my lap. "I'm not here to discuss that. I'm here to talk about the side effects of the psych medications you prescribed."

Because I already regret agreeing to them on a trial basis.

I should've known Brian wasn't ready for them.

Doctor Masterson sat up straighter. "Is there a problem?"

"My brother appears to be experiencing delusions or paranoia. Maybe he even hallucinated the whole thing. I'm not sure to be honest."

Doctor Masterson reached into her drawer and flipped a folder open. "What kind of delusions?"

"A naked woman in his bed trying to seduce him. Yesterday, he was in his room screaming. But when the staff got there, nothing seemed to be wrong. And they didn't find anyone or anything to indicate that there was something amiss."

Doctor Masterson wrote something down. "So, you believe the woman wasn't actually there?"

"Is it possible that his new medications are having an adverse effect on him?"

Doctor Masterson doesn't respond for a long time.

"It can cause hallucinations. But that's only in rare cases," Doctor Masterson replies with a frown. "I've prescribed it hundreds of times before, and I've never seen this kind of reaction."

"Can you prescribe something else?"

The last thing I need is to have Brian running around the ranch seeing things that aren't there and hurting himself.

The pills are supposed to make him feel better not worse.

Doctor Masterson sets an empty bottle down on her desk and lifts her gaze up to mine. "Mr. Steele, I hate to be the one to point it out. But it's much more likely that the pills would have a negative impact if they were being mixed with something else."

I stand up so quickly the chair falls backward. "My brother is not on drugs."

Doctor Masterson pushes her chair back. "I'm sorry, Mr. Steele. I understand that this is a difficult thing to reconcile yourself to, but—"

I hold a hand up. "No, he's not on drugs. We are not entertaining that idea. I want you to prescribe something else."

"Mr. Steele—"

"Or I'll find someone else who will," I interrupt, giving her a steely look. "I need someone who can get my brother the help he needs, Doctor Masterson. Not someone who is going to entertain conspiracy theories."

Doctor Masterson stiffens. "Of course, Mr. Steele. I apologize."

I nod and press my lips together.

When she sits back down, I turn around and leave the room.

Then I make a beeline to Brian's new room.

He must be in the bathroom.

His room has been recently cleaned. It sparkles and gleams in the late morning sun. Lemon and citrus and a whiff of something I don't recognize.

Dread settles in the center of my stomach.

I burst into the bathroom. Brian is in the tub. His head is thrown back, his arms at his sides. "Can you come back later? I'm busy."

I step into the tile-floored bathroom and fix my gaze on an empty spot on the green-colored wall. "We need to talk."

"Can't it wait?"

"It can't. I need to know what you've been mixing your pills with. I know you heard me, Brian. I don't have time for this bullshit. I am trying to help you, but I can't do that if you're not honest with me."

He scowls. "I'm not on drugs. What kind of dumbass do you think I am that I would do drugs while taking those medications?"

"Are you a dumbass? Because if you are, and you're not serious about getting your shit together, then don't waste my time."

Brian stands up. Water sloshes over both sides of the tub.

He reaches for the towel draped over the back of a dresser chair. "So instead of having some compassion for your brother, who had his room broken into, you want to make this about drugs? Are you fucking serious?"

"I am fucking serious," I respond, with a lift of my chin. "I told you what my conditions were for bringing you here. And I am doing my best to keep you safe—"

"I am taking this seriously," Brian interrupts, after securing the towel around his waist. "So maybe you should look into whatever shitty security system you have in place that allowed her to break into my room in the first place."

I dig my nails into my palms.

I don't want to keep having this fight with Brian, not if he's lying to me.

Because I can deal with a lot in order to protect my brother.

But the one thing I can't save him from is himself.

I stare at Brian. "I am looking into it, but if you're lying, I swear to God—"

Brian crosses over to me and holds my gaze. "I am not. Do whatever test you want. I am clean."

I study him for a while longer. "Fine. I already have people looking into what happened. I'll let you know if we come up with anything."

Anger is pumping through me as I walk out of his room and find myself back in the main cabin in the cool AC air.

As I peel the wet shirt away from my chest, I spot a flicker of movement.

Danielle comes in through one of the side doors, hair plastered to her forehead, and a yoga mat rolled up underneath her arm.

I like her in the tight black yoga pants and a teal tank top.

It makes me want to pull her into an empty storage room and lose myself in her.

Some of the tension leaves my body as I walk over to her and smile. "How are classes going?"

She shifts from one foot to the other. "It's fine." She has a serious look on her face.

"Yeah? I'm glad to hear that. I saw you riding earlier. It looks like you're getting the hang of it."

Danielle blinks. "Yeah, sure. I guess."

"I've had the most insane day," I continue, my smile never faltering. "Do you want to go for a walk or something tonight?"

She tilts her head to the side and studies me. "Don't you have a lot of work to finish?"

"I can make time," I reply, my smile fading. "Are you okay?"

Danielle clears her throat. "Yeah, I'm fine. Why?"

I make a vague hand gesture. "oh nothing, I was just wondering." She keeps avoiding making eye contact.

Danielle takes a step back and averts her gaze. "Probably just tired. I've had a long day too. Raincheck on that walk?"

"Why don't I walk you back to the cabin?"

Danielle hesitates then shrugs.

On our way out, I hold the door open for Danielle as she steps through. Then I hurry after her, slowing to a brusque yet even pace.

She is clutching the straps of her gym bag like her life depends on it.

I keep trying to brush my hands against hers, but I can't.

She's as stiff as a statue, and each time I move closer, she shifts away.

Like she can't stand to be around me.

All too quickly her cabin materializes. She quickens her pace. "Well, this is me. You didn't have to walk me to the cabin, you know."

I stop at the foot of the stairs. "I wanted to."

Danielle twists to face me, a myriad of emotions dancing across her face. "I'm sure you have better things to do."

"I can't think of anything else I want to do."

Danielle raises an eyebrow. "Really?"

I nod and give her a small smile. "Really."

She takes a step back and climbs up the stairs. At the top, she pauses to toss her hair over her shoulders and look at me. "I guess I'll see you around."

I offer her a bigger smile. "Definitely."

After throwing another look in my direction, she uses her card to open the door. Then she ducks inside, without a backward glance.

I stare after her until the door clicks shut, and I'm left alone again.

Through the slit in the curtain, I spot her peering at me. With a shake of my head, I make my way back to my office... hmmmm... that was strange!

I am shuffling papers and scowling at my screen when Brian messages me to come to his room. I leave my office and walk to his room.

Brian takes a long sip of his drink. "What's happening in your love life. You have a woman?"

I ignore the flutter in my chest. "What woman?"

"I know what you're like when you like someone," Brian continues as if he hasn't heard me. "You get all moony-eyed, and you become hyper-focused on everything like you're trying to make sure everything goes according to plan."

I lean back against my chair and eye Brian over the rim of my glass. "What's your point?"

"You two get in a fight or something?"

I don't want Brian to know about Danielle.

Not yet.

I'm not ready to share her with the world.

Still, as I sit across from Brian, the two of us lost to our own thoughts, I wonder what it would be like to confide in him.

Especially when I don't remember the last time the two of us had a normal conversation that didn't revolve around Brian and his life.

So I have nothing to say where Danielle is concerned.

And I have no idea where she and I stand.

Her attitude makes me wonder if she really was tired today, or if she has some kind of issue with me.

I stare at the wall for a moment. Still going over it all in my head. Still trying to understand what I did wrong.

Unfortunately, as Brian and I sit in the room and stare at each other and make small talk, I'm no closer to finding answers than I am to controlling my brother's fate.

And it frustrates me to no end. Why is everything so complicated all of a sudden?

Chapter Thirteen: Danielle

I flip onto my back, bring my arms behind my head, and sigh.

Then I continue to count backwards from a hundred. Then I twist onto my side and tuck my hands underneath the pillow. Still, sleep evades me. My entire body is wired.

Sighing, I throw the covers up and stuff my feet into a pair of slippers. Slowly, I wander over to the windows and pull the curtain aside.

It is pitch black. And I don't see a single person outside.

I check the clock on the wall above the fridge and frown.

It's still only eleven at night. And despite the long day I had, I don't know what to do with myself.

After hours of mindless TV and another half an hour of a book that put me to sleep, I don't know what to do with myself.

I can't get Adrian out of my head. His scream the other night is still ringing in my ears.

With another sigh, I shuffle back into my room and rummage through the closet for something to wear.

I leave the nightgown draped over the edge of the bed and shimmy into a pair of shorts and a t-shirt.

After lacing up my sneakers, I go back for a sweater. The Montana air gets chilly at night.

I pull it on and listen to the sound of water rushing in the distance, punctuated by the occasional howl. Nocturnal animals are coming to life around me.

Listening with a half-smile, I make my way to the main cabin.

I'm already sweating by the time I reach the steps. Inside, I sit in on of the chairs and link my fingers together.

A man with slicked-back hair and dark brown eyes is sitting behind the desk. He nods in my general direction, and I offer him a tight smile.

I am drumming my fingers against my thighs and wondering what to do when I hear Adrian's voice spill out from the hallway at the end of the main cabin.

Abruptly, I sit up straighter and wait. His voice drifts off and disappointment settles in the pit of my stomach.

I rise to my feet and wait till the employee's back is turned before I duck down the hallway that leads to his room.

Where did his voice come from? I can't seem to find him anywhere.

My feet are light and soundless against the carpet. But my heart is pounding so loudly in my ears that I'm sure everyone can hear it.

When I reach Adrian's room, I see myself in my cotton dress with the lingerie underneath, and I flush.

I lift my hand up and linger. Before I can talk myself out of it, I rap against the wood and take a step back.

You're doing the right thing, D. You deserve to know what happened the other day. And if he can't bring it up, you're going to have to.

A long moment passes before the door creaks open.

An older looking woman in a short dress with silver hair piled on top of her head answers the door.

"I'm sorry," I begin, color creeping up my neck. "I didn't mean to disturb—"

"Who's at the door?" A man with laugh lines and salt-and-pepper hair appears. "Can I help you?"

"I must have the wrong room." I glance between the two of them and offer an apologetic smile. "I'm sorry to disturb you."

Before they shut the door, I spot two children sitting on a couch overlooking the TV. Then the door slams shut, and I wince.

I lean against the nearest wall and bite back a groan. While I have no idea why Adrian has changed rooms, I know it can't be a good thing.

Not with things being what they are.

Between us.

I try not to dwell on it as I walk back to my cabin and climb into bed.

In the morning, I'm still trying to think of an explanation when Adrian comes into the dining hall. He has a spring in his step, and he looks as handsome as ever in his shorts and t-shirt.

Suddenly, a mixed, sweet and sour feeling grips the core of my body. I begin to ponder the extent of Adrian's mental health challenges.

He mentioned a relative with anger and alcohol issues, and now I can't help but wonder if he was subtly referring to himself... Oh poor Adrian!

Reflecting on our conversations, all the pieces start falling into place. He spoke about the benefits of therapy and how it was initially challenging for him.

I shake my head, releasing a heavy sigh.

Concern fills me as I wonder whether he is still seeking help. I feel a tightness in my chest and a squeeze in my heart, imagining the struggles he faces in keeping this side of himself hidden.

Managing a successful business while grappling with such unpredictable challenges must be incredibly difficult.

Realizing how challenging it must be for him, my heart goes out to Adrian.

Now I start to understand the importance of allowing him the space to share, rather than pushing him to discuss it.

It's clear he's dealing with something deeply personal, and I want to support him in his own time

The main question is, do I want to continue my intimate relationship with him?

In an instant, a wave of emotions crashes over me—sadness, anger, empathy, sympathy, annoyance, frustration, all converging at once.

The intensity builds, and I find myself yearning to release it all, to scream out loud, but I don't.

His eyes sweep over the room, and they linger on me. Then he straightens his back and links his fingers together.

"Good morning, everyone. I've got some good news. Since the weather is getting better, it's now safe for us to go on a hike."

A cheer rises through the room.

"Anyone who wants to join should sign up. We have only a limited amount of space to ensure everyone is being tended to. So please write your names down as quickly as possible. The sign-up sheet will be posted on the bulletin board next to the main desk."

Another murmur rises through the crowd.

Adrian looks away from me and smiles. "There will be more hikes throughout the week if you miss this one. Looking forward to seeing you all. Thank you."

With that, he spins on his heels and leaves. Why am I disappointed that he didn't come to my table? God, I want him. And at the same time, I don't think I should want him.

How can I settle this fight inside me? Do I want him or do I not?

I linger over breakfast, hunched low in my seat. Then I carry my tray over to the nearest bin and leave it there. On my way out of the dining room, I'm still searching for Adrian.

In the hallway outside the dining room, I bend down to tie my shoe laces and spot something out of the corner of my eye.

When I turn towards it, Adrian pokes his head out of a nearby room and motions to me.

He disappears inside, and I stand up.

Adrian pulls me into the room, kicks the door shut and presses me up against the wall. I barely have time to react when his lips descend on mine.

He tastes so delicious. I missed this so much. I whimper when he places one hand on my waist. The other frames my face.

His touch is electric, and the effect is instant.

I know I'm supposed to be mad at him, but I can't help myself. When he kisses me, I kiss him back with just as much fervor and passion.

Like I need him to be able to breathe.

His hands move down to my waist, and he hoists me up. I wrap my legs around his torso. He rubs himself against me, his days' old stubble prickly against my skin.

My breath hitches in my throat when he wrenches his lips away from me and presses hot, open-mouthed kisses down the side of my neck and over my jaw.

My head is spinning, and I have to hold on tight to Adrian to keep from falling.

Every last part of me burns as he touches me.

Without warning, he sets me back down on my feet and presses his forehead to mine. "I've missed you."

I release a deep, shaky breath. "I missed you too."

Adrian rubs his nose against mine, and I hear the smile in his voice. "I can tell."

I squeeze my eyes shut. "That was…intense."

Adrian laces his fingers through mine. "That was nothing, trust me."

He draws back and reaches into his pocket. Wordlessly, he hands me a note with a pressed flower in it. "You don't have to read that right now. I just wrote you something."

I smile, and my heart swells to twice its size. "You wrote me a love letter?"

Adrian clears his throat. "Something like that."

I tuck it into my pocket and link my fingers over his neck. "I'll read it later."

Adrian's hands circle my waist, and the smell of him and a spicy cologne wash over me, unfurling some of the knots in my stomach. "I'm sorry about the past few days. I've had a lot on my mind."

I blow out a breath. "It's okay. You're coming to the hike, right?"

Adrian pulls back to smile at me. "I'm going to try my best to make it."

I pull him down for another kiss, and he growls into my mouth, sending shivers racing up and down my spine. All too soon, his phone buzzes, and I have to remove my arms.

He gives me one last smile over his shoulders and pats down his hair. Then he steps out into the hallway and glances down both sides.

On my way past, he gives my ass a firm squeeze, and I swat him away.

The rest of the day, I find myself smiling and humming, feeling ever so joyful.

When Savannah calls, I am still distracted. I barely hear a word she says.

That night, after I go for a quick jog around the ranch, I stop at the main cabin. I am stretching my arms over my head and peering at the sign-up sheet for the hike when Adrian walks past.

He waves and flashes me a million-dollar smile. My knees go weak. I lean against the closest wall and fan myself.

The memory of a few nights ago is vanishing from my mind. I'm sure whatever it is Adrian is dealing with will be okay since he is probably getting treatment for it.

I put my name down on the list, the butterflies in my stomach erupt into a frenzy. I have a spring in my step as I walk back to my cabin, the smile never leaving my face.

I'm in a good mood for the rest of the day, and Adrian is never far from my thoughts. I even end up socializing with a few guests, letting some of my fears and anxiety melt away in the process.

At the end of the day, after a quick shower, I crawl in between the sheets and pick up the book on my beside table.

But I'm thinking of Adrian as I try to read.

It's his image I see when the hero is described. And instead of the windswept hair, the large coat ,and with a white see-through shirt, I picture a shirtless Adrian astride his horse.

His jeans hanging low on his hips, and his hat tipped in my direction. Sighing, I snap the book shut. The image of Adrian holding his hand out to me, giving me his mega-watt smile appears before me.

Why can't I stop thinking about him? And why can't I stay mad at him?

He still owes me answers about why he freaked out. And that's when I remember the note he gave me. I jump up and reach for my shorts.

With trembling fingers, I unfold the letter and climb back into bed to read it. Slowly, I set the pressed flower down on the nightstand and hold the letter up to my face.

I can't stop thinking about you. You're my first thought in the morning, and my last thought every night.

I read and re-read the note, growing giddier and giddier with each passing minute.

Finally, when my eyelids grow too heavy, I press the flower back inside the note and tuck it into my nightstand drawer.

Then I bring my arms up over my head and sigh.

Sleep comes quickly, and all of my dreams are of Adrian.

In the morning I'm still giddy and breathless. After a quick shower and a quick bite, I reach for my fanny pack.

I am one of the last guests to join the hiking group, but when I glance around, I can't spot Adrian anywhere.

I ignore the tight knot in my stomach and set off at a brusque pace, catching up to the instructor easily.

Why isn't Adrian here?

Maybe he has work, or maybe he slept in. You're not his keeper, Danielle. And you need to ease up a little.

I am sipping on my drink underneath the shade of a tree when I spot Adrian.

Rather than leading the group, he is trailing behind.

He has a backpack strapped on, a rather large pair of sunglasses that cover half his face, and a large baseball cap down to his ears.

He has both hands shoved into his pockets, and his head is lowered as if he's staring at something on his shoe.

The guests standing a few feet from him are talking. They don't recognize him.

I don't blame them. Look at him. He looks rather different than his usual self with the long sleeved shirt and the loose jeans hanging on his waist.

I pretend to stretch my muscles and wait for him.

But he's walking far to the right, as if he's ready to leave the trail. What is he doing? Is he having a mental break down?

Frowning, I try to follow him with my eyes as the guests walk together in an orderly fashion. Adrian shifts to the left, just behind the last group.

I keep stopping and trying to figure out where he is and what he's doing.

I wait for him to reach me at one point. But I get close enough to say hi, he looks the other directions and walks right off the path as if he didn't even recognize me!

Okay fine then.

Except I can't let it go. Even when I'm far ahead of him and annoyance is pumping through me. I decide to just lower my head and walk the path. To not look around for him anymore.

But I can't help it. I look around for him but don't see him. What the hell is this? Why was he undercover like that? Is he spying on his guests? What is wrong with him?

Did I do something to upset him? Or for the love of God, how ill is he?

Why is history repeating itself?

Because you attract a certain type of man, that's why. When are you going to learn, Danielle? You like chasing after guys and obsessing over them. It's who you are.

Only I told myself that Adrian was different.

Over the past few weeks, I've seen nothing to indicate that he likes playing games.

On the contrary, I've marveled at how different Adrian is from anyone else I've been with. And how safe he makes me feel.

Unfortunately, between the incident in his room and him steering clear of me right now, I'm not sure what to think.

But I do know that I'm not walking away without a fight.

At the very least, I deserve answers.

As we climb up the wide path with thick foliage on either side of us, I fall back. Using the back of my hand, I wipe the sweat off my face. Then I place my hands on my hips and inhale several mouthfuls of air.

When my heart is no longer pounding, I start walking again, until I reach the rest of the group.

I take my phone out and pause to snap a few pictures. Some of the other guests do the same, so I offer to take a few pictures of them. When I'm done, they do the same for me.

I'm swiping through the pictures when I realize that I'm looking away and towards the horizon in all of them. Like I'm searching for something.

We reach a steep incline, and I lose my footing.

One of the guests is there to help me find my balance, and she gives me a bright smile before continuing the hike.

A sense of shame and embarrassment starts burning through me.

Is this why he wanted to keep us a secret?

Because he's ashamed to be seen with me?

He's a billionaire and one of the most eligible bachelors in the city. I don't know what you were expecting, Danielle. This isn't one of the romance books you like to enjoy. And no matter what Savannah says, this kind of thing doesn't happen in real life.

I frown as I hoist myself up over the incline and spin around.

More and more of the guests are finding their footing and reaching the top.

When I wheel around, the beauty of the scenery takes my breath away. The mountains in the distance. The clear blue skies. The thick foliage down below.

It's one of the most beautiful things I've ever seen.

I move closer to the edge and inhale, the crisp air filling my lungs and making me feel better.

Adrian is nowhere to be seen. The more I think about his behavior, the angrier I get.

What the fuck happened to you, Adrian? What happened to being different, huh?

Chapter Fourteen: Danielle

It must be signal hour. My phone buzzes in my pocket as I try to find good footing for my next step.

I take the phone out and see the text from Savannah. I'll have to answer her later. I shove the phone back into my fanny pack and take another sip of my water.

Out of the corner of my eye, I see Adrian again. He's far back, behind a row of trees. I can't make out what he's doing.

It looks like he's intentionally staying away from the crowd. Then he walks away again toward the ranch's main cabin.

I have no idea why I'm this nervous.

Adrian and I have spent hours talking to each other, about anything and everything we can think of. While it scares me to know how attached I've grown to him in such a short amount of time. However, it's also not surprising.

He's an easy man to talk to, and even easier man to fall in love with.

And I know beyond a shadow of a doubt that my feelings for him are real.

But I have no fucking clue what I'm supposed to do if he's going to alternate between hot and cold all the time.

On the one hand, I understand why he feels the need to keep me at arm's length in front of the other guests for now.

On the other hand, he always manages to find a way to reassure me and let me know that he's still thinking about me.

Today that's not happening, and I have to wonder why.

Am I coming on too strong?

Have I scared him off already?

I'm so out of my depth that I'm tempted to step away, just to call Savannah. It isn't until I realize that my signal hour is over that dismay settles over me.

Not only am I on my own, but Adrian is nowhere to be found. Once again.

What is the matter with me? Why am I falling back into old habits and trying to build the courage to speak up?

It's not like I'm asking Adrian for much, just the bare minimum. And the thought makes me sad.

As we begin to descend the hill, I start to think about the warm and loving Adrian I have gotten to know.

Where is the warmth and the fire I've gotten used to? Where is that smile that makes me go weak in the knees?

I have no idea what's happening, but I have a sinking feeling that the man I encountered today is nothing like the Adrian I have come to know.

Not by a long shot.

Then, abruptly, I skid to a halt and glance over my shoulders. But I'm still on my own, deep in the bowels of the woods. With no one around.

Am I lost? Are there wild animals around here? I shiver with fear.

I place a hand over my chest and lean against the nearest tree. I don't realize I'm crying till I touch a hand to my face.

I've got scrapes and bruises, and I can't tell if I'm crying because they sting or because of Adrian's brutal rejection.

All I know is that I'm all alone in the woods, with no idea where I am, and no one who will notice I'm gone.

At least no one who cares enough to come after me.

Fucking Adrian.

I tried to warn you. I tried to tell you it wouldn't be a good idea to get involved with someone like that. Of course he tricked you. Men like that don't go for women like you, remember?

I brush away the tears and take several deep breaths.

A deep ache settles in the center of my chest as I push myself off the tree and glance around. Nothing but trees for miles on end. I take out my phone and squint, but there's no signal.

With a frown, I pat my pockets in search of the compass Savannah got me as a joke. I'd grabbed it at the last minute when I headed out the door.

After I pull it out, I hold it up to the light and squint at the sky.

In the distance, thunder booms, and a flash of yellow lighting streaks across the sky.

I place one foot in front of the other, the squelching sound the only thing I can hear other than the thumping of my own heart.

In spite of the ache settling in my bones, and the tender bruise I can feel from my earlier fall, I keep moving. I duck under branches and climb over fallen logs until I can't anymore.

Still, my muscles ache, and there's no sign of civilization anywhere.

By the time it begins to rain, panic is clawing its way through me. And I have no idea what I'm going to do. I'm soaked through when I duck underneath a tree.

I rifle through my pockets and fanny pack for something that could be of use.

A fresh wave of tears starts as I sink to the wet ground and draw my knees up to my chest. Then I shove a stick of gum into my mouth to give myself something to do.

"Why are you punishing me?" I throw my hands up in the air and look up at the dark skies. "I don't deserve any of this."

Exhausted, I push myself back up to my feet and stumble through the woods. In the distance, I hear something familiar, like tires screeching on the asphalt.

My heart misses a beat as I stagger forward and fall face-first onto the ground. I shove my wet and matted hair out of my face and keep moving until the trees give way to a street.

Squinting, I make out the vague silhouette of a truck in the distance.

Then, trembling, I jump into the middle of the street and wave my arms up and down. Finally, the tire slows to a halt, and a man sticks his head out the window. "Are you okay? Are you from the Four Elements Ranch?"

"I got separated from the group," I reply, pausing to rub my hands up and down my arms. "Do you know how I can get back?"

"Hop in. I was headed in that direction anyway."

I'm too tired, cold, and miserable to argue with the stranger who pushes the passenger door open. I'm too tired to even think that this could be dangerous.

Carefully, I sit down on the old newspaper he places on top of the seat. Then I rub my hands together and peer through the windshield, struggling to make out anything in the torrential downpours.

The Four Elements Ranch looms in the distance, and I sag in relief.

He rolls to a stop outside the edge of the property. "Thank you."

"You're welcome. You be careful out there, okay?"

I thank him and push the door open, making a beeline for the main cabin.

When I stumble in, several of the guests are standing around talking amongst themselves.

Maureen looks relieved to see me and immediately hands me a towel. "We were putting together a search and rescue team. Are you alright?"

I swallow. "I'm fine."

"Thank God you're okay." Adrian materializes, his hair in tufts on top of his head, and a stiffness to his movements. "Are you hurt? Do you need a doctor?"

"Nothing I can't handle," I tell him, coldly. Is he for real. Now he sees me and wants to talk to me? I don't want to talk to him or explain anything to him.

His problem is way bigger than I thought. I don't want to be involved with him anymore.

Confusion splays out across his face, but I don't wait for a response. Instead, I give Maureen a grateful smile and spin on my heels.

By the time I make it back to the cabin, I'm shaking again. And a deep ache has settled into my bones.

I'm fumbling with the card when Adrian appears next to me and uses his own card to swipe the door open.

"I don't need your help." I step in and try to slam the door in his face. "I can take care of myself."

"Danielle. What happened out there? Where did you go?"

I wheel around to face him, and I'm bristling now, some of the sadness replaced with red-hot fury. But I have to hold it back.

I don't even know what to say to him. Do I tell him that I know he has mental issues? I stare at him, "Are you pretending that you like me and you care?"

He runs a hand over his face, his wet shirt clinging to his form. "Danielle, of course I like you. I just had a few issues on my mind lately that have shifted my mind a bit. But I'm working on them."

I hold a hand up. "I'm sure you're working on them. But I just don't have the patience for it. I don't want to play games, Adrian. I thought you and I were on the same page, but we're not."

Adrian shakes his head, sending droplets of water flying in every direction. "That's not true. I don't know what this is about."

I take a step back. "Of course you don't."

From the day I laid eyes on him, he's had me wrapped around his finger.

Adrian opens his mouth to protest, his face etched in sadness, but I push him back. He looks startled as he staggers back, allowing me to slam the door shut in his face.

I turn my back to the door and sink to my feet. I rest my head against my knees and listen to Adrian walking away. Eventually, I push myself up to my feet and head toward the bathroom.

In a daze, I strip out of my dirty clothes and get into the shower stall. The hot water mixes with my tears and swirls beneath my feet.

I have never been more tired or more confused and humiliated in my entire life.

As soon as the adrenaline wears off, I climb into bed and wrap my hair in a towel. For a while, I sit there, staring at an unmarked spot on the wall and turning everything over and over in my head.

Unfortunately, the more I think about it, the less it makes sense. So, I throw the covers off and in pace my room in my bathrobe.

Outside, it's still raining, punctuated by the occasional clap of thunder.

There are heavy footsteps outside my door, so I freeze.

Then I hurry over to the curtain, and I see the back of Adrian's head as he walks away. His clothes are clinging to his skin, and he looks defeated as he walks away with his head lowered.

Frowning, I open the door and find a tray of food and a bottle of wine. Angrily, I bring the tray inside and leave it on the counter.

I take out the corkscrew and open the bottle angrily. Then I pour myself a glass.

I take a long sip, and the liquid burns a path down my throat before settling in the pit of my stomach.

I take a few more sips and wait for the wine to work its way through my veins, but it isn't enough.

Because I want it to erase Adrian altogether.

So much so that I'm tempted to pack up my things and book the first available flight out of here. I might be cut off from the outside world, but I'll be damned if I let Adrian control what I do next.

When I sit down on the couch and tuck my legs underneath me, I feel a pleasant buzz. I alternate between taking sips of red wine and studying the screen in front of me.

Then I reach for the wallet tucked in between the couch cushions and stare at my credit card.

It's for the best, Danielle. You knew it was a bad idea to get involved with Adrian, but you went ahead and did it anyway. You've had your fun, so it's time for you to go home now.

Except I can't bring myself to do it. Not with how much this place has helped me already.

In spite of toying with me, Adrian didn't lie about a single thing.

This place is transformative, and I've felt the change growing inside of me. I'm not ready to turn my back on this place and everything it still has to offer.

So, if that means having to figure out a way to deal with Adrian, so be it.

I am not going to let him take this trip away from me, not if I can help it. And I'm not going to be his therapist to try to help him and make him better.

It's not my job or my responsibility to tell him anything.

Chapter Fifteen: Adrian

I push myself off the wall and step into her field of vision. "Good morning."

"Morning," Danielle replies, stiffly. She pulls the door shut behind her and draws herself up to her full height. "What are you doing here?"

I shove both hands into my pockets and give her a small smile. "I thought this was a good chance for us to talk. Now that you've had the night to sleep on it."

Or if she's like me, she hasn't slept at all.

Throughout the night, I found myself caught in a whirlwind of restlessness, grappling for answers. Puzzled about Danielle's cold reaction.

I'm very aware of the emotional roller coaster she's been going through. That's what brought her here.

I understand the toll her past marriage has taken on her emotionally. It's obvious that she's lost trust in men, indicating the need for a delicate approach in addressing her feelings.

With as much patience as possible.

Otherwise, I risk alienating her even further.

And considering I don't know why she's upset to begin with, I need to tread very, very carefully.

She folds her arms over her chest. "Do you honestly think that sleeping has made me feel better?"

"It should." I take another step toward her, and I give her a gentle smile. "Talk to me. I can't fix this if I don't know what happened."

And I desperately need her to not be upset with me.

Not being able to talk to her and confide in her is killing me.

More than it should. I didn't intend to fall in love with her. It was just a little fling in the beginning. And now all I think about is her.

Danielle gives a slight shake of her head. "If you honestly don't know why I'm upset then there is nothing I can say to make you understand."

"I would if I knew what it was."

Danielle studies me. "I thought that you were different, Adrian. I kept telling myself that I finally met a man who knows how to be open. A man who knows how to acknowledge his mistakes and learn from them. But I guess I was wrong."

I frown. "Don't you think that's a little harsh?"

Danielle's expression shifts and falls. "See that's the problem. You don't see the problem. So how can you fix it if you can't even see it? I can't tell you how to behave. You have to see it yourself and tell me."

I take another step and reach for her hand, but she snatches it away. "Danielle, I—"

She takes a step back and averts her gaze. "I'd better go before another one of your guests sees us together. Wouldn't want to cause you any further embarrassment."

"Embarrassment? Danielle, I'm not embarrassed by you. I...I care about you, but—"

She holds a hand up as she brushes past me. "Save it for the next woman, okay? I've got to go before I miss breakfast."

Without waiting for a response, she shoves both hands into the pockets of her jean shorts. I stand on her front porch, gaping at her back and wondering where it all went wrong.

All I can think is that Danielle has a lot of emotional baggage that she needs to unload. It's not fair that she's making assumptions about me. I hope her therapy sessions take care of it for her.

She can't be like this, especially now that I'm falling in love with her.

Then I snap my mouth shut and run a hand over my face. Heat shimmers and rises up from the ground. I use the back of my hand to wipe beads of sweat off of my face.

Why does everyone seem to be against me these days? Nothing is working and everything is falling apart. It started with my brother and now it's happening with Danielle.

Exhaling, I climb down the stairs and take the back route to my office.

As soon as I get there, I get a message from Brian to go to his room.

When I reach his room, Brian is sitting there with one leg crossed over the other, and a phone in his hand. My earlier frustration grows. "What is it? How're you feeling?"

Brian lowers the phone and sits up straighter. "We need to talk."

I let the door click shut behind me and I'm thinking... Oh boy. "Look. No offense, but now really isn't a good time. I've got a lot of shit to deal with."

Including trying to decipher Danielle's actions. Because I'm getting the feeling that a verbal apology just isn't going to cut it.

Not this time.

Brian takes off his glasses and polishes them. "This is important shit, okay? I can't do this anymore. I wanna leave."

I sit down behind my desk and pull my chair closer. "What do you mean? You know you can't do that."

Brian shakes his head and leans forward. "I don't know if this is working. I'm frustrated, I feel like I'm cut off the world. I just can't take it anymore. You don't even let me go out. I went out for a bit. Don't worry. I was all covered up. But I got too scared and came back. I don't even enjoy being outside. I feel like I'm in prison, Adrian."

I press two fingers to my temples and rub in slow, circular motions. "Not now Brian, please. Can you give me some time to figure out how I can fix that for you?"

"I don't know. I'm clean now. You know that. Why can't I just go? What do you need to figure out?"

My hand falls in front of me. "I'm sorry, but I have to talk to your psychiatrist, Doctor Masterson."

Brian looks unsatisfied with my answer. "What can she do for me? The medication she has me on is making me feel sick. I don't need her nor want to see her again. I'm fine. Can't you see that already?" Brian is starting to raise his voice at this point.

Throwing his arms in the air as he looks around. Trying to convince me that he's fine and needs to leave.

I make a low noise in the back of my throat. "Not now, please, Brian," I almost beg.

He stands up and brushes the lint off of his collar. "Anyway, I need an answer soon. Have them change my room again at least. This is like the smallest room so far. I'm far from everything and everyone, like if I have a disease. Give me a bigger, better room, Adrian. You're fucking rich and you have plenty of big rooms."

I exhale. "Is that going to make you feel better? I have given you a big room. This is one of our bigger rooms. Why do you need a whole suite? We have guests who request those suites and they pay for them too. We have limited quantities and I can't give you one."

"I can't stand this room anymore. All I want right now is to go back home to Vanessa and beg her to take me back."

I scrub a hand over my face. "Alright, fine. If it'll make you feel better, I'll make sure Maureen takes care of all of the details right away and gives you another room. But I can't promise that it will be bigger."

Brian flashes me a forced smile, and I open the door and leave his room.

I close it behind me and stand in the hallway, close my eyes and take a few deep breath to calm my pounding heart.

Back in my office, I pick up the landline and dial the front desk. A short while later, Maureen materializes in her pressed suit, her hair pulled into a high ponytail, her bright smile in place.

She lingers in the doorway while I finish another phone call. Then I motion to her, and she pushes the door open with a creak.

Maureen stands opposite my desk, hands clasped behind her back, and an expectant look on her face. "You wanted to see me, sir?"

I hang up and sit up straighter. "Yes, we're going to need to move my brother again. He's sick of his room."

Maureen furrows her brows. "Okay, sir."

I shake my head. "Thanks Maureen, you are a life saver."

She pauses and shifts from one foot to the other. "Anything else I can do to help, sir?"

I link my fingers together. "Just have Brian's things moved to another room, discreetly of course. And please ask Doctor Masterson to come and see me as soon as possible."

After a clipped discussion with Brian's psychiatrist, during which the headache in the back of my skull continues to expand, I find myself exhausted.

Since his doctor and I can't come to an agreement about the medication, she agreed to lower the dosage and monitor him.

I wonder if it's going to be enough.

What happens if this doesn't work for him, and he end up going back to his old habits?

I stand up, stretch my arms over my head, and roll my shoulders. Then I answer a few more emails before powering down my laptop.

When I'm sure there's nothing else that needs my attention for the day, I duck out of the same back door I came in through.

The balmy evening air hits me directly in the face.

I inhale, the crisp mountain air filling my lungs, and some of my angst dissipates. I'm rolling up the sleeves of my shirt and idly glancing around when I spot Danielle astride her horse.

She is wearing shorts and a low-cut shirt, gripping the reins securely in her hands, a look of fierce concentration etched onto her face.

She's easily the most beautiful thing about this place.

I slow down, let my hands fall limply to my side, and watch her.

Over the past few days, she's gained more and more confidence in herself, giving her the grace and self-possession to take charge with her mare.

Her hair is billowing behind her. And in spite of the tightness around her eyes, she looks happy. Whatever she was going through the other day must have passed already.

She seems to be at peace now.

Like she belongs.

I want to take her into my arms and kiss away the furrow between her brows. I want to rush to her, carry her off of the horse, and take her back to my room.

Then I want to spend the rest of the night showing her just how much she means to me. Unfortunately, I know I can't do any of that.

Not yet at least.

When I step forward and stand on the other side of the fence surrounding the riding arena, she still hasn't seen me.

She tilts her head to the side, squeezes her eyes shut, and a myriad of emotions dances across her face.

The sun is dipping below the horizon, bathing her in hues of pink and purple. Her face is silhouetted in a warm, ethereal glow, making her look even more vulnerable and enticing.

My heart is hammering unsteadily the entire time.

I wipe my palms on the sides of my shorts and lean forward to keep watching her. Eventually, she slows to a trot, and her eyes fly open.

Her head whips in my direction, and when she recognizes me, the easy smile on her face falls. I stand up straighter, offer her a small smile, and wait.

She frowns as she rides past me and heads in the direction of the stables.

Before I know what I'm doing, I'm running after her.

When I burst through the stable doors, she is leading her mare to the empty stall. There, she pauses to take off the saddle and give her a firm pat.

Then she reaches for a brush and runs it over the mare's back, a contented sigh passing between her lips. I try not to breathe too loudly as I walk towards her.

"I told you that I didn't want to talk," Danielle says, without looking at me. "Which part of that was hard for you to understand?"

"All of it." I stop outside the stall and fold my arms over my chest. "It's hardly fair that you get to cut me out without talking to me."

Danielle shakes her head and throws her hands up. "No, I'm not doing this. I can't keep going round and around in circles with you. I came here to get away from all of this bullshit not find myself getting sucked back in."

"Danielle." I stare after her as she walks away. "Wait."

She keeps walking, and I don't do anything to stop her.

And I have no idea why.

Is it because, deep down, I know she deserves better?

Or is it because I haven't been completely honest with her about everything?

Either way, I know I can't make things right when she's still this angry. With a sigh, I reach for the nearest horse, a sweet-tempered chestnut mare.

After leading her outside, I secure the saddle, and the stirrups and climb onto her back. I ride until sweat is pouring down my back and the sides of my face.

I ride until my legs ache, and my lungs burn.

And when I can't run anymore, I slow to a trot. As if I can outrun all of the feelings bubbling up within me.

Eventually, when it's too dark for me to ride, I lead the horse back to the stables, and offer her an apple.

Then I walk back to my room. Darkness surrounding me. A strange churning in the center of my stomach. What is happening to me? Why does my life feel so out of control in every direction?

Chapter Sixteen: Danielle

I peek through the curtain, see the back of Adrian's head, and frown. Reluctantly, I unlatch the lock, and the door creaks open.

Immediately, Adrian stops walking and glances at me over his shoulders.

When I glance down and see the bouquet of flowers, the bottle of red wine, and the handwritten note attached to it, some of the ice around my heart melts.

Am I being too hard on him?

Over the past two days, he's done nothing but seek me out at every opportunity. Even in front of the other guests. Just to grovel and plead.

He's left me flowers, wine, and every type of chocolate imaginable.

And he's even taken it upon himself to write me letters, short but sweet letters that leave me even more confused than before. I can't deny my feelings for him.

Especially not when he's lavishing me with attention.

But I'm afraid of opening myself up to him. He needs help and I can't help him. I'm not in a position to be able to help him with his mental health. I need help myself.

I've seen how easily he can flip his own emotions on and off. It's been so painful to see him ignoring and avoiding me like that and it's not even his fault. It's the fault of his illness.

Slowly, Adrian twists to face me. So when he walks towards me, my breath hitches in my throat.

I know I should slam the door in his face and scream about how unfair it all is.

But when he finally bridges the distance between us, the last of my defenses fall, and I find myself leaning into him.

He wraps his arms around me and shudders. "I thought you were never going to forgive me."

"I'm trying to," I say, in a muffled voice. The familiar and warm smell of him washes over me, chasing away some of my doubts. "I'm not sure if I've forgiven you completely yet."

But in spite of my better judgement, I want to try.

Because I miss Adrian with a fierceness that surprises me.

The past couple of days without him have been hard, harder than I ever imagined.

All I want is to drag him inside and curl up against him on the bed. To wrap his arms around me, whisper in my ear, and make me forget the past few days ever happened.

Unfortunately, I know that even Adrian isn't that good.

He reaches for my hand and grips it tightly. "I am truly and sincerely sorry about whatever I did that upset you. I would never intentionally hurt you, Danielle. You mean too much to me."

So, he doesn't even realize he's doing it. Oh Adrian...my hearts aches for you.

I stir and draw back to look at him, releasing his hand. "Aren't you worried the other guests are going to see?"

Adrian frames my face with his hands and looks into my eyes. "I don't give a shit."

I hold his gaze, and the butterflies in my stomach erupt anew. "Good answer."

His lips lift into a half smile. Wordlessly, he takes my hand again and kicks my front door open the rest of the way.

I stumble after him, pausing only to kick the door shut with the back of my leg.

He carries me over to the couch, places me on his lap, and buries his face in my hair.

Several long moments pass while I sit there, struggling to remember how to breathe.

I turn everything over and over in my head, but I keep coming back to the same conclusion. Adrian has issues he doesn't want to tell me about it.

Or issues he doesn't even know about.

How can someone who is doing so well for himself in life hide it so easily?

Not all mental disorders are the same, D. You can't bring it up and embarrass him like that. What if he doesn't want to talk about it?

Or worse.

What if he doesn't know and I'm the one who ends up shattering his illusion and forcing him to acknowledge reality?

I can't be the one to do that to him.

Besides, none of it matters when Adrian and I are alone. When he holds me like nothing else in the world exists.

Not the hike, not the incident in his room, and not the other guests.

When Adrian holds me like this, I can't think of a single place I'd rather be. Or anyone else I'd rather be with.

We are so deeply intertwined that I can't imagine a world where we aren't.

Nor do I want to.

He's under my skin and in my veins, and I wouldn't have it any other way.

Idiot. You've gone and done it now, D. How the hell do you think this is going to end, huh?

I ignore the vicious voice in the back of my head and draw back to look at him. "No more games, okay? Whatever is going on, we'll face it together."

Adrian's arms circle my waist, and his expression is solemn when he looks at me. "Yes."

I cover the distance between us and kiss him.

It's feels like I'm freefalling.

But instead of the ground rising up to collide with me, it's Adrian.

He meets each kiss with one of his own. Each stroke of his touch sears through me. When he makes a low guttural sound in the back of his throat, my heart misses a beat.

Then he flips me over so that my back is pressed against the couch. Without breaking our kiss, I stretch out.

Adrian looms over me.

I see nothing but him, he's everything and everywhere.

But I still can't get enough of him.

He makes a low humming sound when I pull his shirt up over his head. He breaks our kiss and tosses the shirt over his back, where it falls to the floor with a flutter.

With a smirk, he reaches for the edges of my nightgown, and I lift my arms up over my head. I shiver when I'm left in only my bra and underwear.

Adrian's eyes move over me, drinking in every inch. "You're so beautiful."

I link my feet over his torso and draw him closer. "I'm glad you like what you see."

"Very much," he smiles, and his kiss is feather-light and delicate. I make a low impatient sound and kiss him harder, earning a low and throaty chuckle.

He laces his fingers through mine and presses himself against me. Wave after wave of desire builds within me. I'm desperate and eager for his touch.

It makes me feel half-mad.

In one quick move, Adrian unhooks my bra and rips off my panties. He throws them onto the floor as I fumble with his boxers.

After I manage to slide them down over his backside, I pause.

Adrian growls, stands up, and kicks them away. Then he's draped over me. Now there isn't an inch of space between us.

It still isn't enough.

Each stroke, each touch, each breath pushes me closer and closer to the edge of ecstasy. Adrian drops a hand between us and strokes me.

I arch my back and moan, the sound reverberating inside of my head.

He pushes one finger in then another, and I go absolutely still. When I throw my head back, the blood pounding in my ears, he begins to move his fingers inside of me.

Shivers are racing up and down my spine. And a familiar warm feeling settles in the center of my stomach. I rake my fingers across Adrian's back and call out his name.

He wrenches his lips away from mine and presses hot, open-mouthed kisses down my jaw and over my neck. Then he kisses a path down the slope of my chest.

He takes one nipple between his teeth and tugs, and my vision goes white.

I hiss. "Oh, Adrian. Fuck, that feels amazing."

He moves to the other nipple and does the same. "You taste like butter."

I whimper. "I want you, Adrian. Please."

Without responding, he sinks his teeth into my neck. Dual waves of pain and pleasure ricochet through me. I squeeze my eyes shut as I hurtle closer and closer to the edge.

His fingers are moving quickly and deftly now, and my breath quickens. Rivulets of sweat are sliding down my back and the sides of my face. I lift my hips up off the mattress and cry out.

My entire body is shaking and writhing as I ride out my orgasm.

The spots are still dancing in my field of vision when Adrian removes his fingers and thrusts into me. I suck in my breath hard, and my eyes fly open.

He is looking at me. A look of pure hunger etched onto his face. A strange glint in his eyes. I still my body and adjust to having him inside me.

Then he eases out and slams back into me with smooth, practiced strokes. I sink my fingers into his waist and exhale.

He continues to ease in and out of me, his eyes never once leaving my face.

Then we begin to move together with wild abandon, like two frenzied animals.

Like we are trying to outrun something.

I twist my head to the side and squeeze my eyes shut. He laces his fingers through mine. My heart is pounding so loudly that I'm sure he can hear it.

The couch dips and creaks underneath us as we move together, taking and giving in equal measures. Eventually, I sit up. Our bodies, sleek with sweat, press together.

He stretches out his legs on either side of me, and I link my feet behind his back. To my surprise, Adrian draws back to look at me and holds my gaze.

Neither of us look away.

I begin to shake, and another orgasm rips through me. Adrian holds me to him. His own release follows quickly after and he thrusts and shudders inside me.

I wrap my arms around him, close my eyes, and blow out a breath. I'm still unsteady when Adrian eases out of me and lets me fall backward onto the couch.

Completely naked, he wanders into my kitchen and bends down to rummage through the fridge. I prop myself up on the pillows to watch him, a smile hovering on the edge of my lips.

"What are you doing?"

Adrian takes his phone out. "I'm going to get you some breakfast. I'm messaging room service."

My smile grows bigger. "You don't have to do that."

Adrian smiles that irresistible smile. "I want to. What kind of eggs do you like?"

"Scrambled." I sit up and pull Adrian's shirt on. It falls just above my knees. "I've got therapy in an hour."

"Don't worry. That's plenty of time." He moves toward me. "Why don't you relax while I take care of this?"

I pad over to him and pull out one of the high chairs. "Don't you have work or something?"

"I have nowhere else to be right now."

After he finishes texting the order, I watch him set the table. He moves with his usual strength and grace. I can't help but wonder how long he will be mine.

Adrian is joking and telling me stories, but I spend the whole time terrified that he's going to slip away from me.

· ❤ · ❤ · ❤ · ❤ · ❤ ·

"So, you're worried that your boyfriend—"

"He's not my boyfriend."

"You're worried that Mr. X is going to break your heart," Doctor Sheridan corrects, pausing to jot something down on her clipboard. "Why do you feel like that's inevitable?"

I run a hand through my hair. "I don't want it to be inevitable, but I feel like it is."

Doctor Sheridan leans back into her chair and motions for me to continue.

"Doc, he's hot. He's cold. He's up and down. He's into me then he doesn't even recognize me," I say, the words tumbling out of me in a rush. "I don't know how to explain any of it."

Doctor Sheridan frowns. "It sounds to me like he has serious commitment issues."

"If he does, he's not telling me about them. In fact, I don't think he's telling me a lot of things."

Doctor Sheridan nods. "And why do you think that?"

I place my hands in my lap and straighten my back. "Honestly? I'm afraid that he's hiding something from me."

Doctor Sheridan's brows furrow together. "Like a girlfriend or a wife?"

I shake my head. "No, like a mental illness."

Doctor Sheridan raises an eyebrow. "That's a very big leap, Danielle. What makes you think that?"

I make a vague hand gesture. "Think about it. One minute he's all over me, and the next he can't get away from me fast enough. When we're alone, he's sweet and caring. But sometimes when we're in public, it's like I'm invisible to him."

The warning signs are all there.

But saying them out loud changes things.

A part of me is reluctant to connect the dots, especially when I can see where they're taking me.

But the other part of me knows that denying it isn't going to help anyone, least of all Adrian.

As far as I can tell, he doesn't need my judgment or my pity. What he needs is help, but I'm not sure I can be the one to provide him with it.

I'm not a therapist.

Hell, I'm not even qualified to diagnose him. Yet, here I am, sitting across from an actual therapist. It feels like I'm telling her a story.

Despite the fact that I know how outlandish it sounds, I can't stop the words from leaving my mouth.

Admitting my suspicions to Doctor Sheridan doesn't make me feel any better. On the contrary, it makes me feel worse.

I half-expect her to shake her head at me and smile, letting me know that I've been jumping to the worst-case scenario conclusions.

Instead, she nods along while I tell her about all of my evidence, being careful not to give too much information. She only stops to jot a few things down on her clipboard.

I'm tempted to snatch that clipboard out of her hand and see what on it.

What good is that going to do you? It's just going to make you feel worse, Danielle. You know that as well as I do. You don't actually want to know what the doc thinks about you.

"....and then I came here to the session," I finish, noting the strained sound of my voice. "I know it sounds crazy, and I know it's a big leap to make, but what else could it be?"

Doctor Sheridan presses her lips together, her expression turning thoughtful. "It's not crazy, Danielle. I don't like to use terms like that here."

I blow out a breath. "What else should I call it then? At least if he does have a mental illness and doesn't know it, maybe I can figure out a way to help him."

Doctor Sheridan presses her lips together.

"I know that's an awful thing to say," I continue, in a smaller voice. "It's not that I want him to have issues. I just...it's just that...."

"It would be better than realizing you're getting played?"

I sink against the couch and bury my face in my hands. "I'm an awful person, aren't I, doc? What is the matter with me that I can't attract a nice and normal guy?"

It's like I'm stuck in a loop where I jump from one asshole to the next.

Damaged, unavailable, and self-involved men seem to be my specialty.

Through the slit in my fingers, I see Doctor Sheridan set the clipboard down on the table next to her and link her fingers together.

I continue to peek at her. She leans forward and clears her throat.

"Okay, first of all, there's nothing wrong with you. Second of all, it's okay to feel like you're attracting the wrong kind of people. It's because you don't think you deserve better."

I don't realize I'm crying until I wipe my face. "I do deserve better, doc. And I want to do better. I didn't come here to get caught up in whatever this is. I want to get my life back on track, and I definitely don't want to repeat old habits."

Doctor Sheridan stands up and kneels down in front of me. She takes both of my hands in hers and holds my gaze. "Danielle, just the fact that you're admitting what you want and realizing what you don't want is a huge step. A good step."

I sniff. "It is?"

"You're not going to make the same mistakes you did before because you're self-aware now and because you know better," Doctor Sheridan continues, softly. "Do you understand what I'm trying to tell you?"

I swallow. "What if my luck with men hasn't changed?"

Doctor Sheridan shakes her head. "I don't believe that. I think you should give yourself a lot more credit than that. Regardless of whether or not your Mr. X has mental health issues, the fact that you're paying attention makes all of the difference in the world."

I search her face. "So, what do I do now?"

Doctor Sheridan releases my hands and stands up. "You take it easy. One step at a time. And you listen to your gut. Don't be afraid to have an open and honest conversation with him, Danielle. Mr. X isn't Trevor, remember?"

I nod and release a deep, shaky breath. "Yeah, you're right."

Doctor Sheridan retrieves a box of tissues and hands it to me. "Whatever you decide, you're going to be okay. You are a resilient and smart woman. Just give yourself time to figure things out."

When I leave my session, I feel much better than when I went in.

And for the first time in days, my relationship with Adrian doesn't feel so hopeless after all.

He and I might actually have a chance. And I might not be losing myself all over again.

Chapter Seventeen: Danielle

I flip onto my side and curl up against Adrian. He drapes an arm over my shoulders and presses a kiss to the side of my head. "I wish we could stay in bed forever."

Adrian chuckles and stretches his legs out. "Maybe not forever. We'd have to get up for food, water, and showers."

I lift my head up and press a kiss to the base of his neck. "Fine, so we can just stay in my cabin for the rest of my trip."

Adrian gives me another kiss. "I wish we could."

I snuggle up against him, the smell of his soap and spicy aftershave filling my stomach with butterflies. "You know you can tell me anything, right? I don't scare easily, Adrian."

Adrian yawns and lifts his arms up over his head. "I know."

It's been a few days since my breakthrough with Doctor Sheridan, and I'm no closer to getting Adrian to admit he has a problem.

Not that he's exhibited any symptoms lately.

Still, I can't forget his strange actions from the past. And it's become more and more apparent to me that he has no idea that he has a problem to begin with.

And short of dragging him into Doctor Sheridan's office myself, I can't think of how to broach the subject with him.

Unless I confront him directly, of course.

And I'm not ready to do that just yet. What if it bursts our cozy little bubble?

I want more mornings cuddled up in bed and more afternoons spent swapping inside jokes and enjoying the fresh Montana air.

And I want more nights of him sneaking into my cabin. More of the two of us spending hours getting lost in each other. More time with him where nothing and no one matters but us.

I want all of it and more with Adrian.

A part of me is terrified about how all of this is going to unfold, but another part of me is determined to enjoy the present.

Regardless of how everything unfolds between us, I want to remember how it feels to be held by Adrian. Like nothing bad can happen when I'm in his arms.

When I flip onto my side, I study his profile, bathed in the warm glow of the early morning light. It makes my chest ache.

If only I could reach out and capture it all and tuck it away.

Adrian must feel me looking at him, because he twists onto his side, so he's facing me directly. "Penny for your thoughts?"

I hesitate. "How did you end up handling the problem your relative?"

Adrian's eyebrows furrow together. "My relative?"

"The one who you have a tricky history with? The one with the issues, anger, stuff…?"

Comprehension dawns on Adrian's face, and he averts his gaze. "Right, right.. yes…yes. It's going a lot better, yeah a lot better. I think he's finally getting the help he needs to get his life back on track."

I touch his arm and linger. "I'm sure he really appreciates it. He's lucky to have you around."

Adrian shrugs and brings one arm up over his head. "I'm not sure about that, but I am doing my best."

"I'm sure it's more than enough. It's all you can do. Just remember to go easy on yourself, you know."

Adrian tilts his head and gives me a look. "You're very introspective this morning."

I make a low humming sound but don't look away. "It's something Doctor Sheridan said about taking things one day at a time and not being so hard on myself."

Adrian kisses the bridge of my nose and throws the covers off. "She's right. That is really good advice."

I sit up and pull the cover up to my chin. "That advice can apply to everyone. Not just me."

Adrian nods and walks to the bathroom. "I know."

When he ducks inside, I deflate and run a hand over my face. Adrian re-materializes and holds a hand out to me. "You coming?"

I let the cover fall and stand up. "Sure."

In the shower, he runs the soap bar all over my body, taking care to scrub every inch of my skin thoroughly. He peppers me with wet, open-mouthed kisses until I feel like I'm burning from the inside out.

As soon as he's finished, he spins me around so that my stomach is pressed against the cool tile wall. He is right behind me. His hot breath makes the hairs on the back of my neck rise.

My skin is still tingling when he wraps me up in a towel and carries me out of the shower and over to the bed.

Slowly, he sets me down and gives me a slow and sensual kiss. I melt and wind my fingers through his hair. He smiles into the kiss and climbs onto the bed, moving the towel away as he does.

I'm naked and panting when his cell phone rings, slicing through the air.

Adrian continues to kiss me, and I link my feet over his torso.

He is tracing a path with his tongue down the slope of my chest when his phone rings again. He groans and buries his face in my neck. "I'm sorry. I should probably get that."

I sigh. "Do you have to?"

He leans back to look at me. "I'll be quick."

Without waiting for a response, he stands up and picks his phone off the nightstand. He presses it to his ear and turns his back on me. Grinning breathlessly, I stand up and wrap my wet body around his.

I kiss and leave a path of wetness from the back of his neck down to the curve of his back. With a smile, I touch his ass, and Adrian's voice turns husky.

He says something in a low voice, hangs up and tosses the phone away. "Where were we?"

"You tell me," I mumble, in a throaty voice. "I'm having a hard time remembering."

Adrian smirks and hoists me up. "I can definitely help with that."

We fall into a heap on the bed, and my smile stretches from ear to ear.

·♥·♥·♥·♥·♥·

Next morning,

"This breakfast spread looks amazing."

Ahead of me, Adrian reaches for the tongs and fills his plate with a few slices of cheese and some sausages. "It does."

"Eating light today?"

Adrian shrugs. "I'm not that hungry."

I drift closer to him and glance around to make sure that no one else is paying attention to us.

With everyone else lingering over their coffee cups and their plates, the two of us aren't drawing any attention. Smiling, I casually brush my hand against Adrian's waist.

He brushes against the back of my hand, then he moves further down the buffet.

"You're going to need a lot of energy for later," I whisper, focusing my gaze on the array of cereals in front of me. "I know I will," I giggle.

Adrian chuckles and stops at the omelet bar and says something to the chef.

I stand next to him and place my plate next to his. "Make sure his eggs are nice and runny. He likes that."

Adrian gives me a warm look. "You remember."

"Of course I do." I give him a sweet smile. "I'll see you later?"

Adrian picks up his plate, waits for his eggs, turns to me "I have a quick staff meeting down the dining hall. So, I'll see you soon."

I wave at him as he goes, watching as he walks over to Maureen and a few more staff members. I carry my own plate back to an empty table in the back.

All through breakfast, I can't take my eyes off of him. Neither can any of the other woman in the room.

It annoys me to no end, especially when he smiles and wave at them at one point.

Get a grip, D. He's just doing his job, remember? Besides, it's not like you and Adrian are officially together or anything.

Hell, I'm not even sure we can be until he admits he has a problem.

Still, as I slouch against my chair, alternating between pushing my food around and sneaking glances at Adrian, I can't help but imagine what it would be like if we were really together.

I imagine days where we lounge by the pool, watch shows together, and have conversations that last well into the early hours of the morning.

Adrian tilts his head to the side, and he has that signature half-smirk on his face. I sit up straighter and down an entire glass of water.

Then I push my chair back with a screech and pick up my tray of half-finished food.

I stop to leave the tray on top of a stack of others. After brushing crumbs off of my outfit and flipping my hair over my shoulders, I glance up.

But Adrian is not where he was a second ago. He's gone now, probably off to his office for that staff meeting. I can't help but feel disappointed.

Stepping outside, I feel the sun's warmth on my skin, a perfect day unfolding.

My heart is light and filled with joy from the beautiful moments Adrian and I have shared the past few days.

I retrieve my swim suit from my cabin and walk back to the pool with a beaming smile.

Then I grab a towel from a stack of towels by the pool. My plan is to embrace the day, a day woven together with love and sunshine.

Suddenly, I spot Adrian on the other side of the pool wearing a large hat and glasses, same as the ones he had on during the hike.

My heart drops. Is his problem flaring up again? He sure changed clothes fast. What happened to his staff meeting?

Never mind.

I position myself deliberately, eager for his attention, hoping he is as excited to see me as I am to see him.

However, he remains oblivious. He turns and ambles toward the distant edge of the pool, near the beginning of the trail that's snaking its way back to the southeast cabins.

A wave of discomfort settles in the core of my stomach.

Adrian!

I want to call out his name. But something stops me.

Instead, I put my robe on and walk to the main cabin. I sit in a chair in the corner and cross one leg over the other.

Again I pretend to read the newspaper. But all I'm thinking is: What am I going to do now?

Eventually, I walk out of the main cabin and step into the balmy afternoon air. On my way back to my own room, there's a heaviness in my step. My blood is humming.

I'm concerned about Adrian. I don't feel like hanging out by the pool anymore.

When I step out of my cabin a bit later after changing out of my clothes, I spot Adrian in the distance, leaning over the fence in the riding arena.

I start walking toward him but he's not even looking in my direction.

Am I invisible to you?

He is looking down at his phone, not paying attention to his surroundings.

As I try to take a short cut to him, I circle back around the pool, making my way toward the arena. I notice Adrian suddenly lifting his gaze.

A surge of anxiety races through me. My heart starts to race. I don't know why I'm so nervous.

He looks briefly in my direction, so I wave, trying to get his attention. I'm too far to call out his name without attracting the notice of the other guests.

He looks ahead and then swiftly looks away. With a sudden burst of speed, he turns on his heels, vanishing behind the rows of cabins to the left of the riding arena.

He's too far away for me to run after him. But still, I am so tempted to follow him.

Tension hangs in the air around me, as I ponder him, puzzled and intrigued by his enigmatic behavior.

The tension stays with me until I finish riding my mare and sweat pours down my back and the sides of my face.

I search for Adrian the whole time, but he's nowhere to be found. I slink back to my cabin and spend the whole shower turning the matter over and over in my head.

Chapter Eighteen: Danielle

I gesture to the bartender, and he pours me another shot. Slowly, I lift the glass and study it in the light.

Then I toss it back, and the liquid burns a path down my throat. When I signal for another shot, I realize the bartender is frowning.

And I know why.

Because I'm sitting here by myself muttering and shooting the other guests annoyed looks.

I'm jealous over how happy and simple their lives look.

Meanwhile, I can't even get Adrian to admit he's with me, much less that he has real problems that need to be dealt with before we can be together.

After the incidents at the riding arena and the pool, I try to steer clear of Adrian for the rest of the day, even opting to eat my dinner in my cabin.

There was a note outside my door this morning, but I didn't read it. I just left it inside and went to breakfast, where Adrian was socializing with the other guests.

By the time he circled back to me, I had pushed my chair back and was carrying my empty tray back to where it needed to be.

And he didn't even try to stop me.

The worst part about all of this?

Not knowing where I stand with him.

At least if I knew that, I wouldn't be sitting here, searching for answers at the bottom of an empty glass.

In the background, jazz music continues to play, punctuated by the occasional sound of laughter.

Now and again a few other guests wander over to the makeshift dance floor in the middle of the bar and sway to the music.

Seeing their happiness is like rubbing salt into my gaping wounds.

Why can't Adrian be the one chasing me?

Why can't I pluck up the courage to be honest with him?

You already know the answer to that, D. Do you really want to go down that path?

The longer I sit there, indulging in my drinks and turning the matter over and over in my head, the worse I feel about the whole thing.

I'm chewing on my bowl of peanuts when Adrian comes in, looking handsome in his shorts and tight shirt. With a frown, I push my drink away and stand up.

He doesn't notice me as I brush past him and head to the middle of the dance floor, where a small group of people are swaying to the music. I sidle up to them and smile.

My blood is pumping in my ears as I sway.

I lift my arms up on either side of me and slide them down my body, slowly, sensually, imagining Adrian's hands on me the entire time.

He sits at the bar and leans over to gesture to the dark-haired bartender. After pouring him a drink, the bartender glances over at me with a worried look.

I'm tired of playing by the rules. Of coloring inside the lines. Of not getting anywhere.

Why am I always the one waiting on the sidelines for scraps?

Why can't be I more like those women who go after what they want unapologetically?

All of these thoughts are running through my head as I move to the music. It's a low pulsing beat that I don't recognize. I keep sneaking glances at Adrian.

He is sitting with his back to the bar and looking directly at us. Unfortunately, he keeps looking around the bar as if he's waiting for something.

Or someone.

Maybe he's waiting for someone better than you to come along. Come on, D. You're smarter than this. Read the signs already.

Little bursts of anger pump through my veins, but I don't want to act on them.

Because I still have no idea how much of this is Adrian, and how much of it is his illness.

And I still don't want to be the one to point out the obvious. That Adrian has a serious problem, and it is not going to go away anytime soon.

Or ever.

But with the right medication and specialist, I'm hoping he can get it under control.

You sure do know how to pick them, don't you, D? Always going for the damaged ones. Always trying to be the heroine who swoops in and saves the day, fixing up everything that comes her way.

With a slight shake of my head, I turn away from Adrian and fix my gaze on the group of men and women dancing in front of me.

We all exchange smiles.

Then I pick up a shot from a passing tray and down it.

When I realize that my head is swimming and my heart is pounding steadily, each staccato rhythm calling out Adrian's name, I suddenly decide to leave, making sure Adrian doesn't see me when I do.

I have no idea how I'll make it back to the cabin, and I don't even realize I'm crying until I fall face-first onto the mattress and sniff, pulling the shovers over me.

I toss and turn and try to escape my thoughts of Adrian, but they won't leave me alone.

To escape them, I bury my head further against the pillow. But I catch a whiff of Adrian's cologne, which sends another wave of sadness washing over me.

With a huff, I throw the covers off and stumble into the bathroom. There, I grip the sink and wait for the room to stop spinning.

As soon as it does, I flick the lights on and wince. Spots dance in and out of my field of vision.

Then my eyes clear, and I find myself staring into the mirror at my bloodshot eyes and matted hair.

I look awful.

With a frown, I splash cold water on my face and gather my hair up into a bun. Swatting at the errant locks of hair escaping, I point a finger at the mirror. "You are not going to let him ruin this for you. Remember why you came here."

I splash more water on my face and shiver.

When I glance back at the mirror, some of the puffiness is gone from my face. I sigh, peel my dress off, and slip into the shower.

While I wait for the water to heat up, I listen for Adrian's familiar voice, hoping against hope he'll show up on my doorstep.

Again.

No. I shake my head slowly at first then faster. You do not want him to show up at your door. You are better than this. You are better than whatever scraps Adrian gives you.

Steam fills the room, and I get into the shower.

My back slides down the tile walls, and I find myself on the floor. Dazed and confused, I stare at the sliding door and then up at the shower head.

I draw my knees up to my chest, and it isn't long before my tears mix in with the water.

When I finally get out, my chest is no longer tight, but I am totally exhausted. I wrap the towel around myself and squeeze out some toothpaste.

After brushing my teeth thoroughly, I exit the bathroom and step into the kitchen. I grab a cheese and bologna sandwich from the fridge. I know I just brushed, but I'm suddenly so hungry.

I end up on the bed, filling the sheets with crumbs and scrolling through movie channels on the TV. Adrian welcome video is playing on the retreat's own channel.

His handsome face is turned sideways. He has an easy smile on his face while he talks, walking and showing off the ranch. Talking about the benefits and amenities.

Nothing on his face gives away the fact that he is dealing with devastating personal issues.

When I'm done with my sandwich, I set the plate down on the nightstand and sit up straighter.

I watch movies until my eyes are burning, and the ache in my stomach has settled.

Then I retrieve my laptop from the nightstand and go through some of my homework assignments from Dr. Sheridan.

After a while I close it and get out of bed to move it to the coffee table. I can't look at the screen anymore. I'm done for now.

With a scowl, I trudge back into bed and draw the covers back. I fluff up my pillows, settle against them, and scowl at the living room table, where the laptop now lies dormant.

Reluctantly, I pick up the book on my nightstand. As I try to focus on the words, someone raps on my door.

My heart misses a beat when I hear Adrian's voice calling my name.

Oh God! My prayers were answered. But I'm suddenly too nervous.

I snap the book shut and tilt my head to the side.

The thought of facing him is just too much for me.

He calls out my name, but I don't answer.

Instead, I sit there till I hear the now familiar sound of his feet moving away. Once he's gone, I breathe a sigh of relief and sink back against the mattress.

Given how vulnerable and shaken I feel, the last thing I need is Adrian in my room.

Because I know we'll just end up naked in my bed.

And as much as I enjoy having sex with Adrian, I know it's not enough.

It's never going to be.

So, what's your plan here, Danielle? Pray he sees the light? Play his little game until he sees the truth?

I press two fingers to my temples. "Urgh, shut the fuck up, okay? I just want to sleep."

With that, I throw myself backwards onto the bed and squeeze my eyes shut. Then I curl onto my side and wait for sleep to come.

Chapter Nineteen: Adrian

Danielle has been giving me weird looks all morning. Ever since I walked into the airy and spacious yoga studio and unrolled my mat next to hers.

It's only two of us. It's not the usual class time, and the studio is empty except for us.

Lately, any time I try to brush my hand against hers or lure her into an empty storage room for a romp, she pulls away.

While she's not as cold as she was before we made up, something about her behavior is off. I'm worried that something is wrong.

It feels like I'm about to lose her at any moment.

Why can't life just cut me some slack, huh? Why does it always have to be one problem after another?

"You're looking fine in those yoga pants," I whisper, with a quick look around the room. "Do you know what would look even better?"

Danielle lifts her up and stretches her legs back. As she leans forward, she tilts her head sideways to look at me. "I'm trying to focus."

My eyes dart over to her ass and then flick back to her face. "So am I. Any chance you can do the downward dog in reverse?"

Danielle blushes, and her lips twitch. "No. Now, shush."

Calming music is playing in the background and bright sunlight is filtering in through the large bay windows.

When Danielle lowers herself onto the yoga mat, she's bathed in a soft halo of golden light.

I sit down on my own mat, but I keep glancing over at her and finding excuses to stare at her.

I can't get enough of her.

And I'm beginning to care less and less what the other guests will think and say if they see us together.

Danielle keeps swatting my playful hands and giving me annoyed looks. "Stop."

"I can't help myself," I murmur, before inching closer to her. With a smile, I brush my hand against hers. "Let's get out of here."

"Shhhh," she whispers.

Danielle's eyes fly open as she gets down on all fours and arches her back. "Adrian, seriously. I don't know what game you're playing, but I'm actually trying to take this seriously."

"It's very sexy," I murmur, my mouth inches away from her. She shivers, and the blood in my ears is roaring louder. "Come on, you know you want to."

"Not now. We can talk later."

She gives me another dirty look, and I chuckle. When I lean in closer to her, Danielle swats me away and pauses to tuck her hair behind her ears.

Then she throws her head back and lets out a slow and deep breath. I should just grab her and melt her heart with a kiss.

Not super appropriate during a yoga session.

But I can't seem to stop trying to move my body closer to hers.

And to touch her.

I want Danielle to know how much she means to me. And that my secrecy has nothing to do with hiding our relationship from the other ranch guests. And everything to do with me and my issues.

Specifically one very demanding and damaged twin brother.

Yet, every time I think of bringing Brian up and coming clean, I break out into a cold sweat. A part of me knows I can't keep him hidden away in his room forever.

He has a habit of going backwards every time I loosen my grip on him. It's like he has to be constantly under pressure or restricted in order to behave.

I'm not ready to deal with him roaming free around the retreat. He's not ready yet either.

I'm afraid of what will happen once Brian is no longer in the shadows. When he's out in the light and a part of our lives, it'll no longer be just the two of us.

Still, whether I like it or not, Brian has to come first. At least until he finds his footing.

And as kind and understanding as Danielle is, I doubt this is something we can see eye to eye on.

Unfortunately, the more I think about it, the more I realize how unfair I'm being to her.

To us.

Am I even giving us an actual fighting chance, by keeping her a secret?

I have a feeling that's one of the reasons she's mad at me. She probably wants to openly announce that we are dating, but I can't right now. Not with Brian here and in the condition he's in.

Or am I just biding my time until she leaves. Hoping it will be easier when she's no longer a paying customer?

We both know that you're going to let her go back to the city. And that you'll let the connection fizzle out till she's nothing but a memory. Because that's what you always do. It's what you'll always do when it comes to the women in your life.

Except I don't want that to be me and Danielle's fate.

I don't want her to end up as a mere memory I revisit whenever I'm sad or lonely.

I'm at a point in my life where I yearn for a deep connection, a shared journey with a special woman.

A desire to settle down is pulsing inside me, a slow, steady drumbeat. And she makes my heart dance with excitement whenever our eyes meet.

The prospect of building a life together with her feels like the most natural and fulfilling choice.

"Are you at least going to pretend you're trying?" Danielle flashes me an annoyed look as she raises her arms and adopts the warrior pose. "You're supposed to be setting a good example for the others."

After flashing her a winning smile, I spring easily into the warrior pose.

"I can multi-task."

I give her a suggestive look,

Danielle rolls her eyes and shakes her head.

My eyes rake over her, from the top of her head to the soles of her feet. "I can think of something else we can do with our time."

Danielle blushes and pauses to tie her hair up into a high ponytail, showing off her long and slender neck. "You are the worst distraction ever."

"Or am I the best distraction?"

I lift one arm up and link my fingers together.

"Think about it. I'm forcing you to focus that much harder."

Danielle shoots me another exasperated look and mimics my position. "That's not a good thing. I'm supposed to clear my mind and relax."

I shrug. "It's not my fault you can't focus."

Danielle tilts her head in my direction and lowers her voice. "What do you expect when you show up here and start flirting with me like nothing is wrong?"

I frown and don't respond.

Danielle scowls. Her face is even redder when she gives me another dirty look. My lips are twitching as we lay down on our mattress and stretch our bodies out. I follow her every move.

I brush my hand against hers, and with a sigh, but Danielle inches away.

In spite of her obvious exasperation, I know it feels right to be like this.

As if we don't have a care in the world.

Why can't I just tell her the truth?

I can feel Danielle's eyes on me, so I twist to face her. Her bright eyes are full of so much heat and fire….

Something low and warm unfurls in the center of my chest.

The things grows when she inches closer and reaches between us to touch my face. Her touch is soft and gentle, making me feel all sorts of things I've never felt before.

Wide, searching eyes. Unflinching when she looks at me.

Mesmerized by her eyes and her beauty, I lose myself in her.

I have little hope of finding my way back to reality.

She stares into my eyes, into my soul, as if trying to uncover a secret. My insides are all twisted by the time she withdraws her hand and smiles. "This is a good look on you."

I clear my throat. "Right back at you."

"Yes, I'm sure the sweat and wheezing is very attractive."

"It is very attractive."

Danielle sighs and flips onto her back. She lets her hands fall to her sides, and I watch her inhale and exhale. After a few more moments pass, I blow out a breath and stare up at the ceiling.

Then I stand up and roll up my mat. Danielle lifts her head up and watches as I cross over to the door and duck outside.

Through the glass, she is still watching me, a myriad of emotions dancing across her face.

I don't look away from her until I collide with a harried-looking Doctor Masterson. Papers fly in every direction as I bend down to help pick them up.

I hand her everything back, and Doctor Masterson pushes her glasses up her nose. She brightens up when she realizes it's me and clutches the folder to her chest.

"I was on my way to see you, Mr. Steele. I've got your daily report on Brian's progress."

"Let's walk to my office and talk." She falls into step beside me as we make our way past the studio. "How are his sessions going?"

"Good."

"Doc, I know you can't talk about what goes in during the sessions, but can you at least tell me if the therapy is working?"

I don't want to feel like all the strain this situation is putting on my relationship with Brain is for nothing. That would be counterproductive.

And I definitely don't want to feel like I'm dooming my relationship with Danielle by keeping secrets for her for no good reason.

If Brian is making progress, then everything is worth it.

It has to be.

"I feel like he's making good progress," Doctor Masterson replies, after a lengthy pause. "He's probably going to need more sessions though. But he's been complaining about wanting to leave."

I nod. "I had a feeling you were going to say that. I guess I'll try to enjoy this while it lasts."

We stop outside my office, and I twist the knob. "It's been nice not having to shoulder all my responsibility for Brian while I'm alone. Being in a real relationship with a woman, something I can't even remember the last time I had, has made dealing with it easier. But dealing with Brian is also straining the relationship."

Doctor Masterson steps in behind me and lets the door click shut. "Do you feel like you have to choose between caring for your brother or getting to have healthy relationships?"

I step behind my desk and sit down. "I don't feel that way. I know it for a fact."

Doctor Masterson frowns. "Mr. Steele, I hope I'm not overstepping when I say this. But you're the one who has been adamant about Brian needing to stand on his own two feet and learn to survive on his own. But you are keeping him in his room and hiding him from the ranch guests, which isn't healthy for him or you. While still making unhealthy sacrifices for him."

I open my laptop and wait for it to start. "Yes, I know but I can't just abandon him."

Doctor Masterson's frown deepens. "You don't have to give up your life for his. He has to bear some responsibility. You need to set limits and give him a bit more credit."

I raise an eyebrow. "I thought I was following your advice."

Doctor Masterson shakes her head. "I was wrong about him in some ways. You should talk to your brother. He's a lot more perceptive than you think."

Without waiting for a response, she leaves the room. I answer a few emails, her words lingering in my mind the entire time.

I duck out to check on Brian, finding him in his room, scrolling through his phone. I step in, let the door click shut.

"You got a minute?"

Brian doesn't respond.

"I wanted to talk to you about something. I've been spending my time with this woman," I blurt out.

"I knew it," Brian interrupts, his head whipping in my direction. Then he holds the phone up to my face and points. "See? I knew Kevin was going to make a move on Vanessa when I was out of the picture. I never liked him."

I peer at the picture on the screen and then look back up at his face. "You should be trying to avoid social media. Keeping tabs on Vanessa isn't going to make you feel better."

Brian waves my comment away. "Everyone has their own coping mechanisms. I don't judge you, do I?"

I cross my arms over my chest. "This isn't healthy, Brian. You need to be looking forward, not back."

He gives me an incredulous look. "How can you say that when you know how much she means to me?"

I open my mouth and slam it shut again.

Brian goes back to his phone, and I exhale.

When I leave the room, there's a pit in the center of my stomach, and I'm angry at Doctor Masterson for getting my hopes up.

Brian is nowhere close to being ready. He's still the selfish and distracted, obsessed with the past.

And until he gets himself together, my days with Danielle are numbered and fleeting.

Chapter Twenty: Danielle

I pick up my phone and toss it back onto the couch. Then I practice some deep breathing while trying to empty my mind, I wander over to my laptop.

When I sit down at the desk, my fingers pause over the keyboard. I've avoided my therapy homework all day, but I know I can't show up empty-handed.

Not unless I want deal with Doctor Sheridan's disapproving looks.

I hate not staying on top of things, but it feels like there isn't enough space in my brain with everything else happening.

Every time I think I'm closer to understanding Adrian and getting a handle on his triggers and mood swings, he proves me wrong and takes me right back to where I started.

A part of me hates that I hang on to his every word, waiting for scraps of his affection whenever he has the time to toss them my way.

The other part of me knows I'm too invested to walk away.

It's too late for me to turn my back on him, but I can't help but wonder what would happen if I did. With a frown, I minimize the empty Word document and glance at the airline's web page.

I use the cursor to hover over the closest date, two days from now, and frown.

In spite of my better judgment, I spend my entire internet hour with my hand hovering over the cursor, and a headache beginning in the back of my skull.

Why can't I figure out what I'm supposed to do next?

Because you know it involves going home and leaving Adrian behind. And you're not ready to do that yet. You just want everything to change to your liking and to be exactly the way you want it to be.

Cursing, I push my chair back with a screech. I'm stretching my arms over my head when someone raps on my door.

With a sigh, I press my face to the peephole, and my heart gives an odd little twist.

Adrian is on the other side of the door, holding a bouquet of flowers.

I open up. Wordlessly, I take them from him and set them down on the table next to the door. I have a feeling we'll end up naked in bed again.

"It's a nice night out. Want to go for a walk? Before you say no, I'd like the chance to apologize for the other day."

Some of my anger has dissipated at the sight of Adrian, the familiar pull between us drawing us closer together.

At least hear him out. It can't hurt, right?

I nod and dart inside for my sweater.

When I return, Adrian is standing with his back half-turned to me, and he is studying the sun as it dips below the horizon.

I let my gaze sweep over him, taking in the lock of hair falling over one eye and the tightness in his jaw.

My stomach dips as we fall into step beside each other, with Adrian charting a path in no particular direction.

"How was your day?"

"It was fine. Yours?"

"It was...interesting," Adrian replies, with a quick smile. "I think I'm really making some headway with that relative I told you about."

I press my lips together and don't say anything.

Adrian brushes his hand against mine. "I know it's not exactly the kind of thing we should be talking about, but I really appreciate you listening to me. And I'm sorry all of this is messy and complicated."

I wonder if this is as close to a confession as I'm going to get.

Is Adrian trying to tell me he's getting help?

That he's putting in the work to get better?

I pause. "I feel like I can tell you things I've never told anyone, but I need to know that I'm not wasting my time here, Adrian."

Adrian helps me over another log, and we step through the trees, pausing on the edge of the cliff. "You're not."

I place my head against his shoulders, and some of the knots in my stomach unfurl. "I love this place. I can't believe it's almost time for me to leave."

Adrian drapes his arm over my shoulders. "You could extend your stay."

"I have to get back to work and to my life back home at some point," I whisper, squeezing my eyes shut. A cool breeze tickles the back of my neck. "But if it helps, I wish I didn't have to."

In silence, I open my eyes and study the crescent-shaped moon.

Bathed in the half glow of the moon, Adrian turns to me and takes me into his arms.

He kisses me until I'm breathless.

Until my toes curl inward.

Until I forget my name.

Then he takes my hand in his and leads me back to the main path. He doesn't release me as we weave in and out of the cabins.

Adrian smiles as we duck in through a backdoor and down a series of hallways.

He stops in front of the door to a room and takes a key out.

The room is sparsely furnished, with a dresser underneath a TV mounted to the wall, a shower cabin in the tile bathroom, and a king-sized bed overlooking the TV.

Adrian motions to the patio, and we step outside. Underneath a blanket of stars, I curl up to Adrian on the blanket he spreads out.

He has one arm around me, and the other is tracing idle patterns on my arm. "You're not wasting any time, Danielle."

My breath hitches in my throat.

"I've been holding back because I didn't want to scare you off," Adrian continues, without looking at me. "I'm falling in love with you, Danielle. I've never felt this way about anyone before."

I lean back to look at him, my heart racing away inside of my chest. "Adrian, please don't tell me that if you don't mean it." Can we even be? With so much unknown between us?

He turns so that he's facing me completely. Then he takes both of my hands in his and looks into my eyes. "I mean it. I've meant every word, every look, and every moment between us. I know things are complicated. And there are things I have to deal with that have nothing to do with you. Someday, I want to tell you about them, but I— I don't want you to leave, Danielle."

Tears prick the back of my eyes and emotion swells in my chest. "I'm falling in love with you too."

Adrian brushes his thumb across my jaw. "Stay with me tonight."

I glance between the bed and his face, and I nod, slowly. "Okay."

When I start to fall asleep, Adrian stands up and dusts off his pants. Then he bends down to sweep me into his arms, carrying me into his room.

My head is resting against his chest, over the steady thrum of his heart, and it's the best thing I've ever heard.

I want to stay in his arms forever. I forget about everything he's done wrong and all the pain he has caused me so far.

I'm sure there are explanations for all of it and I will find out everything when the time is right.

All too soon, Adrian pauses to draw the covers back. Slowly, he sets me down on the mattress, pausing to slip my shoes off. They fall to the floor with a clatter, and he pulls the cover up to my chin.

My hand darts out and closes around his wrist. Adrian glances at my hand, then at my face, a smile hovering on the edge of his lips.

With a sigh, he kicks his shoes off and pulls his shirt up over his head.

My mouth is moist when he climbs into bed next to me, and I curl into his side.

He drapes an arm over my shoulders and presses a kiss to the side of my head. "I wish I could stay here forever with you."

I squeeze my eyes shut and throw my leg over him. "Me too."

His hand moves from my hair, down the length of my back. His touch is sure and smooth against my flushed skin.

Goosebumps break out across my flesh as I bring my head to rest against the crook of his neck.

When I press a kiss to the base of his neck, Adrian makes a low noise in the back of his throat. His grip tightens, and his breath hitches.

With a sigh, I flip onto my side, so my back is pressed against his stomach.

He buries his face in my hair, and I listen for his even breathing.

In the morning, the sound of a phone drags me back to reality. With a groan, I pry one eye open and then the other, trying to think of how to escape the blinding white sunlight in the room.

I squeeze my eyes shut and take a few deep breaths.

When I open my eyes again, the room is dark, and the noise has stopped.

The front door clicks shut, and I sit up straighter.

Adrian is nowhere to be found, but there is a note propped up on the table. Smiling, I read over his words and sigh. I will do as he asks.

Humming to myself, I pull on last night's clothes and slip on my shoes.

After glancing down both sides of the hallway, I sneak creep over the carpet and out of the room. Outside, I pause to tilt my head up to the sun and enjoy its warmth on my face.

On my way to the cabin, I keep my head lowered, and I don't meet anyone's gaze.

Inside, I race through shower and skid into the dining hall minutes before breakfast is over. I shovel down a bowl of cereal and some yogurt.

Using Adrian's note, I follow the instructions until I reach a secluded part of the ranch, off the beaten path.

Then I burst through a small cluster of trees until wrought iron gates come into view.

Since the ranch itself is private and fenced, seeing a gate in the middle of the property doesn't surprise me.

What does surprise me is that when I punch in the code that Adrian wrote down in the note, the gate shudders open to reveal a pool with a small waterfall and a few chaise lounges scattered overlooking it.

There is also a cabin on the far left right overlooking the small water fall.

Adrian is already waiting for me, his tanned and taut chest glistening underneath the morning sun. He hoists himself out of the water and sits on the edge, letting his feet dangle.

With a smile, he pats the tile floor next to him.

In a daze, I leave my bag on a chair and hurry over, only pausing to kick off my flip-flops and take my clothes off so that I'm in my bikini.

As soon as I sit down, Adrian pulls me onto his lap and kisses me.

I'm falling and flying and everything in between. I forget all the misery I felt about him and his strange behavior.

I'm all his again. My body craves him and wants him. And I'm going to give it what it needs.

His hands are on my waist and my arms, on every inch of skin not covered by the bikini. He stops at my chest and gives my breasts a light squeeze.

Moaning, I rake my fingers over his back, pausing at his behind. I give it a firm squeeze, the blood roaring in my ears. Molten hot desire pours in my stomach as we sit there fondling each other.

Suddenly, I'm having a hard time remembering why we can't do this all the time.

My fingers are trembling when they move down to the waistband of his swimming trunks. One hand ducks inside, and the other splays over his stomach. Adrian jerks against me and growls into my mouth.

Abruptly, he removes my hand and pulls away to look at me.

The heated look in his eyes is enough to make me melt into a puddle at his feet.

"I didn't ask you to come here just for this," Adrian says, in a thick voice. "I just thought we could spend some time together. This pool is pretty secluded. None of the guests know about this place. This is another VIP cabin that I use for very special guests."

I sigh and bring my head to rest against his shoulders, my heart still pounding unsteadily. "It is beautiful."

Adrian wraps an arm around my shoulders. "Not as beautiful as you."

With a smile, I lean back to look at him. "When did you get so corny?"

Adrian chuckles. "It's called being romantic."

Without waiting for a response, he stands up, links his arms together and dives into the water. When he emerges, he shakes his hair out, sending droplets of water in every direction.

I shriek and am about to move away when Adrian wraps his arms around my waist. In one quick move, he hoists me up over his shoulders.

"Put me down," I say, in between peals of laughter. "Come on. I've got makeup on, and I can't get my hair wet."

"You didn't say the magic word," Adrian teases.

"Come on, you know that isn't how things work in life," I counter.

Adrian's expression turns mischievous. "No, that's the wrong answer."

With that, he lifts me up and tosses me into the pool. I sink into the water.

Sputtering and gasping, I kick my way to the surface and scowl. Then I shove my hair out of my face and give Adrian an angry look. He is clutching his sides and laughing.

"You're going to pay for that," I warn, pausing to splash some water in his direction. "When you least expect it, that's when I'll strike."

Adrian is still laughing. "Yeah, sure. I'm so scared."

"You should be." I stand up straighter and puff my chest out. "You won't see me coming."

In the background, Adrian's phone rings. He exhales and lifts himself out of the pool.

I am admiring the smooth muscles of his back, and the generous view of his behind. He bends over to retrieve his phone from the lounger.

He spins around, presses it to his ear, and my breath hitches in my throat.

Drenched in water, his swimming trunks hanging dangerously low off of his hips, he is easily the most attractive man I've ever seen.

And I still can't believe he's with me of all people.

You've been too hard on him, D. He's just a hard-working man with a lot of stress and pressure.

I lick my lips and stretch my arms up. I'm floating on my back and staring up at the blue skies when I hear a low whistle.

Slowly, I lift my head up and see Adrian kneeling by the edge of the pool, an apologetic expression on his face. Sighing, I wade closer to him and lean against the edge.

"Duty calls?"

Adrian lowers his head to give me a sweet kiss. "Unfortunately. Lunch in my room later? I'll send you a note with the time."

My heart misses yet another beat. "I'd love to."

Adrian's eyes travel down and linger on my lips. "You have no idea how much I want to stay right now."

My hands move behind my back, and I untie the straps of my bikini top, allowing my breasts to spill forward. "It is a shame."

Adrian makes a low noise in the back of his throat. Abruptly, he leans forward and pulls me out of the water, crushing me to him.

He gives me another searing kiss that makes my head spin. But before I can deepen it, he wrenches his lips away and takes a few steps back. Then he gives my ass a firm slap and walks off.

I am still smiling when I snatch up my bikini top, exit the pool, and pad over to the chaise lounge.

Later, smiling and humming to myself, I head back toward the main pool. Inches away from the clearing, I hear laughter and happy voices coming from all directions. Everybody here sure is happy.

When I step out onto the path, I'm startled to see Adrian in the jacuzzi, again with the baseball sunglasses, ducking behind a row of chairs.

What is he doing?

My heart drops. Not again.

I'm even more confused now. I thought he had an urgent matter to take care of. How did he change his clothes so fast? And why?

His episodes are increasing in frequently.

Perhaps it's worse than I imagined.

It's like he has two completely separate personalities. Personalities who are not even aware of each other. This is so messed up.

I stopped suddenly and just watch to see what he's up to. I'm standing right in his path of vision. So he should have no problem seeing me.

There are lots of people walking around us and no one seems to notice him. He looks in my direction at one point but then he looks away.

Did he see me?

Is he avoiding me again?

My heart is pounding in my chest so fast that I can't even breath.

His head is tilted back, and he is talking into his headpiece. I have no doubt that he saw me.

My pulse quickens as I set my towel down and peel off my clothes. I'm not taking my eyes off of him. But this time I'm not going to walk up to him or attempt to remind him that he knows me.

Quietly, I creep forward on the tips of my toes, pausing to put my stuff down on a chair. I dive into the water and surface on the other side of the pool at the closest point to Adrian.

By that time, he's already gone. I watch him disappear behind a row of cabins.

Why is this happening now? Why does he have to be this way?

I have so many unanswered questions.

I didn't come here to fix a broken man. It's not my job or my desire.

Why can't a normal man love me?

The smile on my face and the joy in my heart has vanished.

With trembling hands, I exit water, wrap my towel around me, and stare at a point on the chair. All kinds of thoughts are floating around in my head.

The more I think, the worse I feel about everything. Finally, I pull on the rest of my clothes and make my way back to my cabin.

I'm fumbling with my keycard and trying not to cry when Maureen finds me.

I'm thankful she can't see the rest of my face, half-obscured by the glasses.

Wordlessly, she hands me a note and walks off.

When I walk into my cabin, I kick the door shut and look at the paper she gave me.

It's my billing statement.

I crumple up the paper, and throw it away. I spend the rest of the afternoon holed up in my cabin, torn between wanting to cry my heart out and wanting to break something.

In the end, I settle for curling up on the couch and channel surfing until my eyes burn.

I feel numb.

Even Adrian's voice outside my door doesn't pull me from my stupor.

Chapter Twenty-One: Danielle

"I don't even know what to say anymore."

"Just come home," Savannah pleads. "You've been wanting to anyway."

I slam the refrigerator door shut and spin around. "But you're the one who's been telling me to toughen up and not let Adrian ruin my vacation."

"Honey that was before I realized what a fucked-up asshole he is," Savannah replies, her voice rising. "You're supposed to be at the ranch to heal and take some time for yourself. At the rate you're going, you're going to be worse off than when you arrived."

I run my hands through my hair. "Maybe if I just talk to him about it… But I can't even bring it up, you know…We just met. What do I even say? 'Adrian, you seem to be fucked up bad and I don't want to have anything to do with you.' Does that sound good?"

In reality, I know that I don't want to say that to him.

I want these issues to go away.

I want to end up with Adrian, happily ever after.

But how?

"Just a sec hon," says Savannah. Then I hear her talking to her cat.

I set my phone down on the kitchen counter and bury my face in my hands.

Why am I still fighting for Adrian?

Why can't I just let him go before this whole thing consumes me whole?

For the life of me, I can't understand it. I hear Savannah call out to me and I pick the phone back up

"Babe, I'm not trying to be harsh, but what is talking going to accomplish, huh? Didn't you try that already. And wasn't he sweet and reassuring? He has lots of issues to overcome and you have to be right by his side while he does so. Do you have the energy and the will to do that? Do you love him enough to sacrifice your own sanity for a while? Until he gets better?"

"Well, I don't know...."

"He has issues, serious issues by the sound of things, and it doesn't matter what either of you feel if he doesn't get help."

I swallow. "I know."

"Until he does, you can't save him from himself," Savannah continues, in a softer voice. "No matter how much you want to."

Otherwise, he's going to end up dragging me down with him.

Did I work so hard to free myself of my old life and its shackles, only to end up right back in another man's clutches.

It doesn't matter how different I think Adrian is.

Or how great I feel when I'm around him.

"Your therapist would probably agree with me," Savannah adds, after a brief pause. "You need to keep your distance, at least until he sorts himself out."

I sigh. "Okay. Listen, Sav, my hours is almost up. I'll talk to you tomorrow, okay?"

Savannah exhales. "Okay, I love you. Please don't do anything stupid."

I wince. "I'll try not to. Love you too. Give Skittles a hug from me."

With that, the line goes dead, and I'm left to the mercy of my thoughts again. Frowning, I change out of my pajamas and into a pair of shorts and a t-shirt.

When I step outside and see the wilting flowers and boxes of chocolate outside my room, I feel even worse.

I put them inside, my sandals sinking into the wet ground with a squelching sound.

As soon as I set foot in the main cabin, I breathe a sigh of relief.

Adrian is nowhere to be found, and the bar is largely empty.

I hoist myself onto a barstool, push my hair out of my eyes, and signal to the brown-haired bartender who is wiping down the counter. He comes over to me with a smile, and I sit up straighter.

"Hi, I'd like a dirty martini, please."

"Coming right up." He spins around and reaches for a bottle from the shelves behind him and then mixes the cocktail.

He places a green olive on top of my drink and sets it down in front of me. I down it in one gulp and exhale.

"I'll have another, please."

He raises an eyebrow and says nothing.

I'm on my third drink when more guests start pouring in. A few lean over the counter to gesture to the bartender. Others take up seats at the green vinyl booths and peruse the menu.

A blonde-haired waitress sets a bowl of peanuts down in front of me. I nod and then shove a handful of nuts into my mouth and chew.

A pleasant hum runs through my veins.

The headache in the back of my skull has receded, and the knots in my stomach are no longer as tight.

Unfortunately, the longer I sit here with my mind clamoring for a solution, the less certain I am about what I'm meant to do.

A part of me wants to pack up my bags and take the first plane ride out of Montana.

Another part of me isn't ready to leave the ranch behind yet.

Being here, getting to experience the outdoors, and attending my therapy sessions has had a positive impact on me, more than I thought it would.

Regardless of whatever else Adrian has done, he got that part right.

I came to the ranch looking for a fresh start and a way to get my life back on track. Slinking back home with my tail between my legs doesn't feel right.

Come on, D. What else are you going to do? You're obviously not going to stay away from Adrian if you stay here. So, what other choice do you have?

I signal for another drink and mull over my options a little more.

Out of the corner of my eye, I spot a flash of my familiar light brown hair and turn to it. Adrian is in a pair of cargo shorts and a shirt that shows off his toned and fit physique.

He earns a few looks from the women on his way past, but he pays them no mind. Once he reaches the bar, he leans over the counter and motions to the bartender.

He's got an easy smile on his face, and he looks unperturbed. He hasn't seen me yet.

I stumble to the dance floor and half-heartedly sway to the music.

Then I give a quick glance over my shoulders to see if he has noticed me, but his back is to the dance floor. I straighten up. Then I run my hands over the dress to smooth out.

Pausing, I step out of my uncomfortable heels and hold them by the straps. Determined, I weave in and out of the little groups of people till I reach Adrian.

I wait until he's seated at the bar again before I stumble over to him and lean against the counter. "You owe me an explanation."

Adrian looks at me. "What are you talking about? Are we still on for lunch?"

"You know what I'm talking about." I push myself off the counter and sway a little. "I can't keep doing this with you. I don't want to keep doing this with you."

He must feel something for me.

He has to.

What if he's just in it for the sex, huh? How are you going to feel then?

Adrian twists to face me and raise an eyebrow. "Sorry, I just have a lot on my mind right now. Another time? I promise."

His words are like a knife through my heart. He knows that he has a problem. I say bye to him and walk out, crossing back by the pool.

Shame and humiliation builds up within me, but I push those emotions away.

None of what I think matters anymore. I'm tired of this. I'm nothing but a fling to him.

That's all I am and all I'll ever be.

And I can't tell if the realization makes me feel angry or relieved.

On the one hand, it feels good to recognize that truth of what I am to Adrian. On the other hand, it feels awful. I want to cry and scream and yell about the unfairness of it all.

And I want to shake Adrian until he snaps out of it.

I take an uneasy step back, and my back collides with a passing waiter. The tray flies out of his hand, sending shards of glass everywhere. I slip on the liquid and land on my ass, staring up at the sky.

Pain shoots through me and a cacophony of voices surrounds me. I struggle up, reaching for the shoes that fell a few feet away.

Then I stutter an apology, suddenly grateful that my sunglasses are covering half of my face.

A niggling sensation starts in the back of my skull, so I press two fingers to my temples and rub in slow, circular motions.

It does nothing to keep the headache at bay.

Or ward off the ache in my chest and around my heart.

I struggle to get up, conversation rising and falling around me still.

Then a hand darts out to help me to my feet, and I find myself looking up into Adrian's startling eyes. "Are you okay?"

I search his face, bile rising in the back of my throat.

Why can't you admit that you have a problem?

Why can't I attract a nice and normal guy?

And why can't I just accept that he is refusing to acknowledge his problems?

What I want isn't going to change the facts of the situation.

No matter how badly I want it to.

Wordlessly, Adrian drapes my arm over his shoulders. He leads me away, out of the pool area.

I try not to dwell on how good it feels to have him next to me, or how intoxicating he smells.

Outside, the evening air is crisp, and it smells like marshmallows. I shuffle forward, hating that my entire body is reacting to being in close proximity to Adrian.

I hate how easily he makes me forget my anger.

Or how much I crave his touch, yearning for it with an ache that surprises me.

In silence, we shuffle to my cabin.

Now and again, I pause to suck in huge mouthfuls of air, swallowing against the nausea building up in the back of my throat.

When we reach my cabin, Adrian takes the keycard out of my pocket and swipes the door open. Then he ducks inside and hoists me up, pausing to kick the door shut behind him.

My head is cradled against his strong chest as he carries me into the room. He sets me down on the bed, pulls the cover up to my chin, and disappears.

I sit up and am about to throw the covers off when I hear him in the kitchen.

He comes back with a glass of water and sets it down on the nightstand. "You should try and get some rest."

I sink further against the mattress. "Why can't we just have something normal?"

I know I've made a complete fool of myself tonight. So at this point, I don't even care how desperate or sad I look.

Adrian perches on the edge of the bed and takes both of my hands in his.

"Danielle, you're drunk now. I'm not going to have this conversation with you."

I huff and frown. That's not why. It's because he's embarrassed to be seen with me. I'm not good enough for him. That's why he keep changing his mind. Not to mention his psychological issues....

Adrian scooches closer and holds my gaze. "Get some rest, Danielle. And remember, you're the most amazing woman I've ever met."

I blink. He's so full of it. He's lying through his teeth.

"Sometimes you don't even recognize me."

Adrian leans forward and presses a kiss to my forehead. "I think you're confused. Try and get some sleep, okay?"

I shake my head and sit up. "No, I don't want to sleep."

Adrian frowns and takes a step back. "I don't know what you want me to say, Danielle. I can't talk to you right now. You still have alcohol in your system. I'm a bit too familiar with over drinking and what it can do to a person. Rest for now and I'll see you for a late lunch."

I release a deep, shaky breath. I can't even tell him how I feel. My eyes are heavy and my mouth is dry.

My butt hurts from the fall. My tongue is tied when it comes to expressing my thoughts of him.

Adrian frowns and steps closer to the bed, plants another kiss on my forehead, and holds my head for a second.

My heart melts at his touch and kiss, my eyes never leaving his face. Our gazes are locked.

I feel a wave of pleasure running through me just from the way he looks at me. I'm not even drunk anymore.

At first, I hold myself rigid, not wanting to give into him. Eventually, when he puts his arms around my waist, something in me snaps and breaks and I launch myself at him.

He makes a startled sound in the back of his throat, and we fall backward onto the mattress. He cups my face in his hands as I run my fingers over his back.

My head is spinning. The voice of reason in my head is screaming at me, but I ignore it. Ignore it as I lift Adrian's shirt up over his head and toss it to the floor.

I ignore it as I run my fingers down the length of his back, pausing at the waistband of his shorts.

And when Adrian lifts my shirt up over my head and unhooks my bra, the voice goes completely quiet.

And I'm all his again.

He wrenches his lips away and presses hot, open-mouthed kisses down the sides of my face and over my neck.

It feels like I'm on fire, and he's the only one who can save me.

We can burn away together, for all I care.

So long as he doesn't stop.

Because if he does, I'm afraid I'll have to shove him away again, and I don't want to do that.

He kisses a path down the slope of my chest, and I lift my hips up off the mattress. He helps me wriggle out of my shorts and then throws them over his shoulders.

Then he is kissing me again, nibbling on my lower lip. I gasp, allowing his tongue to dart in and begin a sensual battle with my own.

I'm moaning and panting when Adrian cups his hand over my thin panties.

His touch is sizzling, like he's claiming me for himself.

I arch my back, and Adrian pulls away again.

When I link my fingers over his back, his mouth traces a path down until he reaches my stomach. Using his hands, he rips my panties apart and throws them away.

Then he presses kisses along the inside of my thighs. He pushes one finger inside me and then another.

My vision goes white.

Each touch, each stroke, each kiss drives my insecurities further and further away.

With only the two of us together, nothing else seems to matter.

Especially when his tongue darts into my center, and I throw my head back.

I'm moaning his name, rivulets of sweat pouring down my back and the sides of my face while he swings his head back and forth.

Wave after wave of desire builds within me until my chest tightens. I race closer and closer to the edge, and when Adrian sinks his nails into my waist, I cry out for him.

I'm writhing and spasming as I ride out my high.

Adrian's hands move down to my legs, and he tightens them around his waist. In one quick move, he eases into me and groans.

My vision sharpens into focus, and I realize Adrian is hovering over me, a strained expression on his face.

I wriggle, and he sinks his teeth into my neck, sending dual waves of pain and pleasure through me.

I whimper as he eases out and then slams back into me. Over and over, he brings me closer and closer to the edge.

I rake my fingers over his back and squeeze his gorgeous ass.

Adrian drops his head and takes one nipple between his teeth. When he switches to the other one, his name is both a chant and a prayer on my lips.

My hands fall to my sides. I raise my chest, clutch a handful of sheets, and grind against him. He places his hands on either side of the pillow and quickens his pace.

We are moving with wild and animal-like abandon when another orgasm rips through me.

I'm still shaking and struggling to breathe when Adrian's own release comes, his entire body jerking.

Warmth seeps between my legs as I bury my face against his shoulders. Slowly, he eases out of me and collapses on the bed, next to me.

I can barely hear anything but the pounding of my heart.

When Adrian tucks me into his side, and I inhale the sweet scent of him, every part of me is still tingling. My eyelids grow heavy.

My last thoughts before I succumb to sleep are about how right this feels and about how much I wish it could last.

Chapter Twenty-Two: Danielle

Bright sunlight dances on my closed eyelids.

I yawn and bring a hand up to my face, pressing two fingers to my temples. I rub in slow, circular motions, a feeble attempt to ward off the splitting headache.

Then I pry one eye open and the other, wincing when my vision goes white. A pair of hands settles on my shoulders and squeezes.

I pry my tongue away from the roof of my mouth and mumble something incoherent.

Slowly, I open my eyes again and breathe a sigh of relief when I realize the room is actually dark.

Adrian shifts into focus, a smile hovering on the edge of his lips. Wordlessly, he hands me a mug of steaming hot coffee, a glass of water, and an aspirin.

With a sigh, I place the pill on my tongue and wash it down with the water.

Then I take a sip of the coffee. It trickles down my throat and settles in the pit of my stomach.

Smiling, I prop myself up against the pillow and set the mug down on my nightstand. "I wasn't expecting you to still be here."

"You slept for a few hours, and I thought we could have dinner together later tonight. I went out to take care of some business and I just got back in a little while ago." Adrian perches on the edge of the bed and takes my hands in his. "Unless you still want me to go."

I frown. "Dinner sounds good, but when did I say that I wanted you to leave?"

"In your sleep," Adrian replies, his eyes moving steadily over my face. "Danielle, I don't want to make you do anything you don't want to do. And I had no idea keeping us a secret was weighing so heavily on you."

I swallow. "It isn't."

Adrian gives me a pointed look.

"It doesn't, most of the time," I clarify, with a sheepish smile. "Look, I understand that you have a ranch to run. And that you have some difficult stuff to worry about, like your relatives for example. And I know why we need to keep things low key. But sometimes you take it too far."

Adrian shifts closer and squeezes my hand. "What do you mean?"

"Like when we're in public and you pretend like you don't know me." I say it with hesitation. It's not the most comfortable thing to admit. And I don't want to cross any lines with him, not yet at least.

Adrian lifts my hands up to his mouth for a kiss. "I'm sorry if I did that, Danielle. I didn't mean to. It was never my intention. This is new for me too, and I'm trying to navigate all of this as well."

I squeeze his hand back. "I guess we both need to work on it. You know you can tell me anything and you know we can overcome problems together, right?"

Adrian nods and crawls into bed with me. He tucks me into his side and strokes my hair. "I want you to know that you can come to me with anything, Danielle. You don't have to hide things from me. And you don't have to get drunk at the bar to get my attention either."

I twist to look at him, and my heart misses a beat. "I want to believe you, Adrian. But between your behavior and my past experiences, I'm having a hard time."

I'm opening my heart to him, and I don't want to regret it.

But I can't live with so much fear and uncertainty.

And being kept in the closet like some dirty little secret isn't easy on me either. The longer we keep hiding our relationship, the harder it's going to be to come clean about his behavior.

A part of me wants to continue to respect Adrian's decisions and his desire to protect his business.

But another part of me feels stupid for agreeing to the arrangement in the first place.

Would you really have said no if you knew what you know now? Who are you kidding, Danielle? You were a goner the second you laid eyes on Adrian.

He squeezes my shoulders. "Okay, how about this? We'll both talk about these things together. Whenever you're having doubts, or you feel like I'm not being honest with you, just tell me."

I search his face. "Are you being completely honest with me?"

Adrian pauses and glances away. "I'm being as honest as I can be."

I lean back and swing my legs over the side of the bed. When I stand up and place my hands on my hips, Adrian has risen to his feet too. "I don't know if that's enough for me. I can't have lies and secrets in my life. Not again."

Adrian runs a hand through his hair. "I understand, but there are some things I can't share with you yet. It's not because I don't want to. It's just complicated."

I frown. "You said the same thing the other night. You told me that you wanted to be honest with me."

"I do."

I make a vague hand gesture, and my stomach clenches. "Is this because you don't see this going anywhere?"

Adrian shakes his head. "No, that's not it at all, Danielle. I just think that—"

The rest of his sentence is cut off by the ringing of his phone. He fishes it out of his pocket, presses a button, and frowns. "Look, I just think that—"

His phone buzzes again, louder this time, cutting him off.

I take a few steps back and clear my throat. "You should probably get that."

"I'll take care of it later." He takes a few steps in my direction. "This is important."

I step into the kitchen and turn my back on him. "It's probably better if we talk later once we've had a chance to process everything that has happened so far."

Silence stretches between us.

I spin around, and Adrian has both hands in his pockets. A guilty look plays out across his features. "Are you sure?"

I force a smile to my face. "I'm positive. We can find each other later."

Adrian exhales. "For what it's worth, I do see a future with you, Danielle. It's all I've been able to see. Ever since I first set eyes on you."

Without waiting for my response, Adrian spins on his heels and leaves the cabin. In a daze, I grab the sandwich Adrian brought me and eat it over my sink.

Then I take a shower and spend the entire time turning Adrian's words over and over in my head. When I come out, I'm no closer to understanding him.

With a sigh, I change into my clothes and make my way to Doctor Sheridan's office.

She's sitting in her usual spot in the armchair by the window, and she gets up to shake my hand when I walk in.

The door clicks shut behind me, and I lower myself onto the couch, tossing my hair over my shoulders. I link my fingers together and stare at a spot on the wall.

"You seem agitated. How have you been feeling since we last spoke?"

"Confused," I reply without looking at her. "Adr—, er, Mr. X came to apologize, and he told me that he was falling in love with me. But it didn't make me feel the way it should've."

Doctor Sheridan wrote something down. "Why not?"

"Because it feels like I'm waiting for the other shoe to drop."

"Have there been any other incidents since the hike and the pool?"

I swing my gaze over to the doctor's and sink back against the couch. "No, but, I got drunk at the bar yesterday. And I fell on my ass by the pool and made a fool of myself."

"What happened after that?"

I clear my throat and look away. "He took me back to my room, and we spent some time together. He says he is being as honest with me as he can, but there are things he can't share with me yet. That doesn't make me feel very good about our relationship at all."

Doctor Sheridan studies the clipboard in front of her. "Do you think Mr. X makes excuses to get away from serious conversations? You've mentioned quite a few times that he leaves abruptly because he has stuff to take care of."

I shake my head. "No, that's the only thing I know he isn't lying about."

Doctor Sheridan pushes her glasses up her nose. "Do you still feel like he has issues he's not telling you about?"

I nod. "Now more than ever. What if he's got a split personality or something? It would explain a lot..."

Doctor Sheridan's expression doesn't change. "Whether or not he has issues isn't the problem here."

"How is that not the problem?"

"Because Mr. X isn't my patient. You are. So, unless he walks in here and asks for treatment himself, I can't help him."

I sit up straighter and my pulse quickens. "What if I could get him here? What if I convince him to come and see you?"

Doctor Sheridan sets down her clipboard and leans forward. "If he came, I wouldn't turn him away. But I think you're trying to avoid the bigger issue here, Danielle."

"What are you talking about?"

"You're fixating on his issues to avoid dealing with your own. You told me that you wanted a nice and normal guy to date. If Mr. X does indeed have issues, are you going to be able to deal with them?"

I pause, and my mind goes blank. "I...I guess so."

Doctor Sheridan gives me a sympathetic smile. "No one can force you to put up with something like this, Danielle. I need you to understand what you'll be agreeing to."

I stiffen. "I'm not shallow, doc. Everyone has issues."

Doctor Sheridan shakes her head. "Of course they do. I didn't mean to upset you, Danielle. And I don't think you're shallow. But you did come out of what sounds like a toxic and serious relationship. I'm not sure that throwing yourself into another one is the solution."

I frown. "What? You're the one who told me I needed to try new experiences. Now, you're telling me not to?"

"New experiences don't include repeating old habits," Doctor Sheridan offers. "You can't keep doing the same thing over and over and expect different results. Am I making any sense?"

I deflate and run a hand over my face. "So, you don't think I should stick around?"

Doctor Sheridan sits up straighter and picks up the clipboard. "I can't tell you what to do, Danielle. That's not why I'm here. I'm here to help you figure out what you want to do. And to help you decide what the best decision is for you."

"If he got help, things would be better."

"In theory, yes, but some psychological problems can last a lifetime. People don't just snap out of them. It can be an emotional roller coaster. And that could become your normal if you decide to continue pursuing a relationship with him."

A lump rises in the back of my throat. "I see."

"Why don't you take things slow, like I suggested? You don't need to have everything figured out right now, especially with so much change happening in your life."

I nod.

"How's work going? Have you had any news from your boss?"

"No, but I'm supposed to check in soon. I'm hoping that she's softened a little bit by then. So that I can talk to her about the changes I want to make."

Doctor Sheridan smiles. "Good. It's important to try and focus on the things you can control. Everything else, you take it as it comes."

For the rest of the session, Doctor Sheridan gives me sage advice and techniques to help combat anxiety and overthinking.

But I'm still pondering what she said about Adrian, about whether or not I can handle being with him.

Being with him properly. And without boundaries between us.

As I walk out of the session an hour later, I realize I have no idea.

I've been so busy trying to make sense of his mood swings and behavior shifts that I haven't stopped to wonder what happens when I do have my answers.

What happens when my month here is up? And we no longer have to hide? And I have to choose between accepting every part of Adrian or walking away from him for good?

Chapter Twenty-Three: Adrian

"I was wondering where you were." I step out of the forest and into the clearing.

Danielle has her neck craned over her shoulders, her hazel eyes tight with worry.

She is sitting on a blanket on the ground. Her knees are drawn up to her chest, and her face is half-bathed in moonlight.

When I step closer, a flicker of uncertainty flashes across her face. She stamps it out and swings her gaze forward.

In the distance, I hear the sound of rushing water.

Almost loud enough to drown out the unsteady pounding of my heart in my ears.

Slowly, I cross over to Danielle and sit down next to her. She leaves a few inches of space between us and hugs her knees. I swallow.

"Do you feel like you're ready to talk now?"

Danielle sucks in a harsh breath. "I thought I was, but after that therapy session, I'm not so sure."

My stomach clenches. "You didn't tell your therapist about us, did you?"

Danielle frowns and stretches her legs out in front of her. "I didn't use your name."

I blow out a breath. "Okay, good because that would complicate things for no reason."

Danielle's frown deepens. "Is that all you care about? You don't even want to know what she said?"

I twist to face her. A furrow has formed between her brows. "Do you want to tell me?"

Danielle makes a low noise in the back of her throat but won't meet my gaze. I'm facing her completely. I try to take her hand, but she moves it away.

I have no idea what's happening. Only that Danielle feels further away than she did this morning, and I don't like it.

I don't like it one bit.

"I don't know if I should tell you," Danielle says, in a voice so low that I strain to hear her. "On the one hand, I am working on being more honest and keeping lines of communication open between us."

I pause. "And on the other hand?"

Danielle swings her gaze to mine, her hazel eyes moving steadily over my face. "I don't know if it's going to do any good. Actually, I'm pretty sure it's just going to make things worse. And I don't think I'm ready for that."

I search her face. "Why would it make things worse?"

Unless she's ready to end things between us, I can't imagine anything tearing us apart. Or being big enough to justify her worry.

Except for Brian.

But she doesn't know about him yet.

Danielle makes a vague hand gesture. "Because we haven't exactly started off on the right foot. We're lying to everyone around us. And I know you explained the reasons to me. But it doesn't really give us a solid foundation, does it?"

I shake my head. "We know the truth, Danielle. Isn't that what matters?"

She stands up and runs a hand through her hair. "Yes, but I feel like there's a lot that we still don't know about each other."

I rise to my feet. "Like what?"

Danielle abruptly spins, so she's looking at me directly. "I don't know. That's the thing. You told me that you can see a future with me. But how does that work when there's so much we don't know about each other?"

I shrug. "Sometimes these things happen. Sometimes you meet someone. And you know that they're meant to be in your life. It's not unusual."

Danielle purses her lips. "It's not, but I don't know if I'm at a point in my life where a leap of faith is enough."

I take a step toward her and stop. "What are you saying?"

"There's too much I don't know." Danielle glances away and shifts from one foot to the other. "And without knowing all of the variables, I don't know if I can take that kind of risk."

"Variables?"

"Yes, variables," Danielle replies, pausing to move away from me. She begins to pace, leaves and twigs crunching against her feet. "You know how I feel about you, Adrian, but love isn't always enough."

I exhale. "Yes, I know that."

"And I came here to find myself again and pick up the pieces after the divorce. I didn't come here looking for this... Looking for you. It's all just a lot, and I need to think."

Silence stretches between us.

"I wasn't trying to put pressure on you earlier," Danielle continues in a whisper-soft voice. "I know what it looks like now, but I honestly thought it was what I needed to hear from you."

"And I am not going to pressure you either." I stand up straighter and ball my hands into fists at my sides. "You can take as long as you want to think about things."

Danielle stops pacing and looks over at me. "You're not mad?"

"Why would I be? This is a big step. In less than a month, we've admitted our feelings to each other. And here we are talking about whether or not we have a future together.... It can be a lot to process."

And no matter how sure I am of my feelings for her, that are not enough to sustain us.

I can see that she's allowing the impact of her previous relationships to get in the way of our relationship. She's trying to fix an issue that I don't even have.

Danielle needs to feel the same as I feel about her. And she has to want this as badly as I do. Otherwise, we are just going to end up hurting each other.

While a part of me hates this conversation, another part of me knows how important it is.

I'm holding my breath.

Considering her past, it's perfectly normal for her to be the one to have doubts. With a sigh, I give Danielle a small smile and wait.

She doesn't smile back.

Instead, she draws herself up to her full height and clasps her hands behind her back. "Thank you."

Without waiting for a response, she gives me a quick hug. Then she turns her back on me and disappears. I stare at the spot she occupied, wondering if I'm going to try to win her back.

Eventually, when I'm sure she's far enough away, I sink to the ground and take up her position on the blanket. Frowning, I stretch my legs out on either side of me and tilt my head back.

A half-moon hangs low against the backdrop of inky black sky and smattering of stars.

In the distance a wolf howls, but it's not enough to make me stir from my spot. Even concern for my own safety can't make me head back to the retreat.

Not yet at least.

Sometime later, I'm still lost in my own thoughts when my phone buzzes. I fish it out of my pocket, half-hoping it's Danielle and half-dreading it.

When my eyes settle on my phone, and I see Brian's message, my stomach gives an odd little lurch.

Hastily, I stagger to my feet, pausing to brush dirt and dust off of my jeans. Then I snatch the blanket up and sprint back in the direction of the ranch.

My heart is jumping around uneasily as I duck into the main cabin, through the backdoor. I rush down the hallways, taking a series of twists and turns until I reach Brian's room.

Without knocking, I burst in.

"What the hell happened? Are you okay?"

He's standing in the middle of the room, his back turned to me, his gaze fixed on something outside.

My eyes dart all over the room, taking in the clothes strewn everywhere, and the drawers hanging off their hinges.

Clothes, sheets, pillows, dishes, and more are strewn all over the room. I step further into the room and let the door click shut behind me.

Brian spins around, his eyes tight around the edges. He pushes his glasses further up his nose and exhales.

"It's over."

"What's over?"

"Vanessa and I," Brian responds, with a shake of his head. "She just posted pictures of their engagement. Can you fucking believe it?"

I blow out a breath. "Brian, I'm so sorry."

Brian lowers his head and presses two fingers to his temples. He begins to rub in slow, circular motions. "I don't know why I thought she'd wait for me again. I knew this time was different. Because she's never looked at me like that before."

I sit on the edge of his bed and pat the spot next to me. "You are doing the work to get better, Brian. Don't let her stop you. You've come too far."

Brian sits down next to me and stares straight ahead, a muscle ticking in his jaw. "I was doing this for her. All of this was to give us a chance to get better."

I frown. "I think it's beautiful, that you were willing to do this for her. But it's time you started doing it for yourself."

Brian's eyebrows furrow together. "I am doing this for myself."

"I meant that you need to start applying yourself more and taking all of this more seriously. I know that you're not a fan of therapy or medication, but they're meant to help you."

Brian tilts his head in my direction and snaps at me. "I know."

I exhale. "I need to know that you can take care of yourself because I don't know if I'm always going to be around. Do you understand what I'm trying to say?"

Brian swings his gaze over to me. "I do, and you also deserve to have a life, Adrian. God knows you've been dealing with my shit for too long."

I clear my throat. "You're my brother. There's nowhere else I'd rather be than standing in support of you."

Brian stands up. "I appreciate that, but you're right. I'm sorry I've been screwing up. From now on, no more distractions."

I rise to my feet and shove both hands into the pocket of my jeans. "Are you sure? That's a big commitment."

Brian nods and offers me a half-smile. "I'm sure. I don't want you to put your life on hold for me. Nothing lasts forever. Even the best feelings and relationships come to an end without our control. I'm tired, Adrian. I'm tired of me. I want to be normal."

In one quick move, Brian draws me in for a hug. I stiffen at first then slowly relax. A low unfurling begins in the center of my chest and spreads.

Finally, Brian releases me and turns away, so I don't see the tears in his eyes. I swallow past the lump in my throat and walk over to the door.

In the doorway, I pause to glance back at him, and for the first time in a long time, there's no tightness in my chest.

I feel lighter when I walk out into the hallway.

The feeling stays with me until I walk into my room, strip off my clothes, and crawl into bed. It smells like Danielle's floral perfume, and it makes my chest ache.

I bury my face in the pillow and squeeze my eyes shut. But as I toss and turn, I realize I'm not going to get any sleep tonight.

Not until I figure out what to do with Danielle.

With a sigh, I pull on a shirt over my boxers and step out onto the patio. I lean over the railing and glance out at the horizon.

Below, I see a flicker of movement. And when I turn to it, I recognize Danielle. She has a hoodie on her head. She jogs past, and I stare after her.

During her second lap, she glances up and sees me.

For the longest time, neither of us looks away.

She's the first to break our gaze. Then she wipe her hands on the back of her pants. Then she spins on her heels and leaves, her back ramrod straight.

I follow her until she turns into a speck and disappears into her cabin.

After that, I sag and go back into my room. I pause in front of the mini fridge and frown. Then I rummage until I find a small bottle of vodka.

I down it in one gulp then crawl back into bed and close my eyes.

I drift off when the first patches of gray light are on the horizon.

In the morning, someone raps on my door, rousing me from my stupor. I rub my hands over my eyes.

Slowly, I swing my eyes over the side of the bed and stumble in the direction of the door. My body is still heavy with sleep as I wrench the door open and peer out into the empty hallway.

I take a step forward and something crinkles.

When I see the note, my heart misses a beat.

I bend down to pick it up and step back into the room.

I miss you. I'm thinking of you. Let's have dinner in town. I'll be outside your door at seven o'clock sharp.

Danielle's note is cryptic and doesn't tell me much about her state of mind.

Still, a small kernel of hope takes root inside of my stomach and chest and soon blossoms. I leave the note on the dresser and step into the bathroom.

In the shower, she's all I can think about. How much I want to be with her openly and take her into my arms.

During breakfast at the dining hall, Danielle is nowhere to be found.

In the afternoon, I see her in the riding arena.

By the time evening rolls around, my stomach is in knots. I've convinced myself that I imagined the note.

As soon as I rounded the corner to my room and see her waiting outside my door, relief pounds through me.

Wordlessly, I duck into the room to change out of my sweat-stained shirt.

Danielle lingers in the doorway, a vision in her knee-length dress and sandals.

She follows me back down the hallway and out the backdoor. In silence, we get into my car, and I start the ignition.

The car purrs to life, and I settle back against the leather seat, trying not to sneak glances at her. When the ranch is far away in the rearview mirror, Danielle's hand darts out, and she laces her fingers through mine.

"Are you sure you don't want to pick a restaurant?"

Danielle shakes her head. "I'm sure. I want to go on an actual date with you and see how that turns out."

I rub my thumb along the inside of her wrist. "What made you change your mind?"

"I don't know if I have yet," Danielle admits, using her free hand to tuck her hair behind her ear. "But I'm trying to keep an open mind."

The town looms in the distance, hundreds of buildings glistening underneath the pale light of the moon. Trees and cars blur past me in either direction.

I pull up into a crowded parking lot, outside of a restaurant with a cursive sign out front. After killing the ignition, I race over to Danielle's door and hold it open.

She offers me a grateful smile and places her hand in the crook of my elbow.

I'm nervous as I lead her across the street and up a set of stairs.

Inside, there is soft music playing and rows of tables on either side of us. Red tablecloths and candles. Waiters in black and white uniforms. The smell of cheese and garlic linger in the air.

A waiter motions to us to the back side. He gestures to an empty table, with a single candle in the center, and I wait for Danielle to sit down.

She is studying the menu when I look up at the waiter. "We'll have a bottle of your best wine to start with, thank you."

"There you go again, trying to impress me."

"It is our first date." I link my fingers together and look directly at her. "Order whatever you want off the menu. It's my treat."

Danielle lowers the menu and holds my gaze. "I don't need you to spend too much money on me, Adrian."

I smile. "I want to."

Danielle tries to hide her blush. "Okay, fair enough."

"Don't tell me you're giving up so easily."

Danielle rolls her eyes and reaches for her glass. She takes a few sips, and some of the tension in her shoulders melts. "I'm not. I'm just picking and choosing my battles."

"A wise decision. It'll make you better prepared to handle failure."

Danielle sets her glass down and raises an eyebrow. "Don't tell me you're one of those sore winners."

I take a sip of my own drink, the fruity aftertaste trickling down my throat. "I'm not."

Danielle's eyebrow climbs higher. "I guess we'll have to see about that."

A bowl of steaming hot pasta with several meatballs on top is set in front of her.

I pick up my fork to dig into my risotto. We keep up a steady stream of conversation throughout dinner.

Danielle is growing more and more relaxed by the minute. I think that I've finally broken through her defenses, until that is I spot someone I know.

Cursing, I sink lower into my seat and hide my face behind a menu.

Once he brush past, I sit up straighter and breathe a sigh of relief.

It lasts until I look over at Danielle, who has her lips pursed, a guarded expression on her face.

The ride back to the ranch is quiet and filled with tension.

"You've given me a lot to think about," Danielle says, as she rummages through her purse. "Thanks for dinner."

My stomach tightens. "Look, about that man at dinner—"

Danielle finds her keycard and holds a hand out. "I get it. The ranch's reputation has to come first. I've had a long night, Adrian. I'm going to sleep now."

I lean forward, but she turns her back on me.

Moments later, the door is being slammed shut in my face.

Chapter Twenty-Four: Danielle

"I've been trying to get in touch with you all day."

I shift the phone from one ear to the other and drift closer to the window in the main cabin.

Through the glass, I see Adrian astride his horse, shirtless, his skin glistening with sweat. I try to convince myself to look away, but I don't want to.

He looks carefree and vulnerable.

And it's making me want to go outside and run straight into his arms.

It's taking every ounce of self-control I have not to do that.

Instead, I continue to stand there, in the air-conditioned room, searching for something to fill the time.

With Savannah in a parent's meeting, and the heat outside, I know there's little for me to do.

Not unless I want to end up in a pool of my own sweat.

And I'm not ready to face Adrian, not yet.

"Yeah, I did tell you in my email that there's a technology detox here. I'm only allowed access to my phone and socials for an hour each day." I stop to run a hand over my face. "It's why I've been communicating via email."

Gina, my boss, doesn't sound pleased when she speaks again. "I read the proposal you sent over, about the ranch, but it's missing something."

I hold my breath and pulled the phone away from my ear.

Gina Tate is the kind of woman who knows exactly what she wants. Having risen through the ranks shortly after her promotion, I know she's not used to being told no.

She's left no stone unturned, no party unattended, and it's all part of her carefully crafted image.

My boss likes staying ahead of the game, and she's got killer instincts.

"I read up about the ranch," Gina continues, a strange hissing sound in the background. "I think a piece about it is a good idea. But I feel like you need to include a few paragraphs about the owner and founder."

I swallow. "Adrian Steele?"

"There has to be some good juicy facts about him. The tabloids would love that," Gina adds, her voice rising toward the end. "I'm thinking this could be an expose."

I let the curtain fall back into place and take a step back. "That's not what I'm trying to do here."

"You should. Anyone who's that rich surely has lots of family drama to unpack."

I frown. "Gina, I'm really not comfortable writing the article from this angle. We're not some trashy gossip magazine."

"Scandal sells," Gina reminds me, after a brief pause. "It sucks, but it's the truth, and if you don't write about it, someone else will."

A flicker of unease races up my spine. "Adrian Steele is a person. I've met him. And I've gotten to know him. He really cares about this place and his family."

"Good, so you can use all of that in your article."

"I don't want to write about him, or his family problems."

Because that's a line I'm not willing to cross.

Adrian and I might not be on the same page sometimes, but I'm not going to use whatever information I've gleaned to get my fifteen minutes of fame.

It isn't worth destroying what we have.

Or what we could have.

Gina sighs, and I hear the disappointment in her voice. "I thought you were ready for the big leagues, Danielle. You've been discussing the possibility of a promotion for a month. This is your chance to prove yourself."

I exhale. "So, you're telling me I have to do this story?"

"I'm telling you that doing this story is going to open up a lot of doors for you," she responds, cheerfully. "Think about it. You'll have complete creative control, and it'll be your first foray into the world of serious journalism."

"Gina, I—"

"Before you say no, I want you to take some time to think about it. Think about what this could do for your career. We both know you need a win right now."

"Not like this. I'm not using Adrian Steele to get ahead."

"I'll expect your answer by the time you get back."

I open my mouth to protest, and the line goes dead.

With a shake of my head, I glance up. I do a double take when I realize Adrian is standing a few feet away, a surprised look on his face. He slams his mouth shut and wanders over to me.

"What was that about?"

"I pitched the idea of writing about the ranch to my boss." I tilt my head back to look up at him. "She thinks it doesn't have enough spice."

Adrian's eyes move over my face. "She wants you to write about me?"

"And your family drama," I add, without breaking our gaze.

Adrian's mouth tightens. "And, What do you think about what she asked you to do?"

I shake my head.

Adrian takes a step back and shoves both hands into the pocket of his shorts. "So, that's it then? You're going to write about us?"

"What? No, I wouldn't do that, Adrian. I already told you that I'm not one of those journalists."

Adrian studies me. "Not even to get ahead?"

"Especially not then. When I get a promotion, it's going to be the right way," I reply, with a quick look around. "And no matter what happens between us, I'm not going to use any of that to write a story."

A long and tense moment passes.

Adrian presses his lips together and doesn't say anything.

I shift from one foot to the other and fold my arms over my chest. "Stop looking at me like that."

Adrian's eyes dart around the empty lobby. Then he drifts closer. "I don't know what you're talking about."

I make a vague hand gesture. "Yes, you do."

Adrian frowns and opens his mouth to respond. Maureen appears in front of him, a clipboard held to her chest.

She glances over at me and then back at him. While I wait for them to finish their whispered conversation, I turn the idea over and over in my head.

Am I an idiot?

Am I making this personal?

Writing a story about the ranch and featuring Adrian doesn't have to be an expose. Not if I don't use anything personal.

A part of me can imagine my words already, the painstaking detail I'll use to describe the ranch, and all of its wonder.

The other part of me shirks away from the idea, knowing full well how Adrian is going to take it.

If his reaction is anything to go by, Adrian isn't going to accept anything I write about him, flattering or otherwise.

With a slight shake of my head, I move to step away from Adrian, but his hand darts out to close around my wrist. He says something else to Maureen then his eyes settle on my face.

"Ms. Clark, can you step into my office? I'd like to discuss this issue further, so we can come up with a solution."

I stare between his hand on my wrist and his face.

Finally, Adrian releases me, and I take an uncertain step back. Slowly, I nod and unfold my arms. Adrian spins on his heels and leads the way down a series of twists and turns.

My feet are light and soundless against the carpeted floor, and I try not to gawk at the paintings hung up on either side of me.

Many of them are done with broad brush strokes and bright colors.

At the end of one hallway, Adrian stops and takes a key out of his pocket. He swipes, and the door clicks open. Then he glances over at me and pushes it open all the way.

I duck underneath his arm on the way past, the scent of pinewood hitting me first.

Inside, there is a small rectangular-shaped desk, with rows of bookshelves, and a small window partially overlooking the riding arena.

An AC whirs in the background, and the smell of lavender and pinewood lingers in the air. The door clicks shut behind me, and Adrian brushes past.

He steps behind his desk and rummages through his drawers till he pulls out a decanter of whiskey. After pouring a generous amount into two glasses, he circles back to me.

Adrian leans his hip against the desk and continues to stare at me.

There is a low buzzing in the back of my head. I take the glass from him and swallow the whole drink in one gulp.

Then I exhale and place the glass on the desk. "I don't appreciate you treating me like I've done something wrong. It's not like you found out that I'm writing a story about you."

"Would you have told me if I hadn't overheard you?"

"Considering I have no intention of writing it, what good would it have done?"

Adrian frowns. "Because a story like this could get you the promotion you've been wanting. Your boss already brought that up, didn't she?"

I let my hands curl into fists at my side. "Even if she did, you should know me well enough by now to know that I wouldn't take a story like that."

"I think I know you. But you keep insisting that you don't know me," Adrian protests, his eyes blazing with emotion. "This is never going to work if you keep doubting me, Danielle."

"I wouldn't have to if you were honest with me."

Adrian's expression darkens. "I already told you that I don't like to talk about my relatives, not yet. There are still issues to work on. I've had too many people try and cozy up to me for a story. I'm not going to let it happen again."

I throw my hands up in the air. "Oh, is that where we are now? You actually think I've been lying to you this whole time?"

Adrian pushes himself off the desk. "Don't put words in my mouth."

"I don't, but you're the one who's acting like I've committed some sort of crime. I pitched an idea to my boss, and she had suggestions. Of course she would suggest that I include you in the piece. She'd be crazy not to!"

Adrian holds himself very still. "So, you are going to write the piece?"

"Oh, for fuck's sake, Adrian. I'm not the problem here. You are. You're the one who's been playing games for the past couple of weeks. You tell me that you're falling in love and that you want future. But then you act like I don't exist and are embarrassed to be seen with me."

Adrian's eyes flash with anger. "When have I ever done that?"

"At the restaurant the other day," I retort, with a shake of my head. "I saw you hide your face behind the menu. We were supposed to go out, so we could give us ourselves a chance in the real world. And you behave like that."

"The man we saw at the restaurant owns the local newspaper. He loves to write things without checking facts, and I didn't want him writing about us."

"And yet you felt the need to keep this from me. Do you see why I'm having a hard time trusting you? Because it feels like you don't even trust me."

Adrian makes a low noise in the back of his throat. "Let's not kid ourselves here, Danielle. You don't trust me because you don't want to."

I suck in my breath harshly. "What the hell is that supposed to mean?"

Don't say it, Adrian. Don't say it. Don't—

Adrian folds his arms over his chest. "Since we've met, it's like you're waiting for me to screw up. For the other shoe to drop. And it doesn't matter what I say or what I do. You're never going to trust me. And you're not willing to wait until I'm ready before I share certain things with you. You're kind of forcing me."

My ears are ringing now. "That's not true. I've worked hard on my issues, and I've been trying to open myself up to you. You're the one who keeps pushing me away."

"I'm pushing you away? What the fuck are you talking about?"

I point a finger at him and bridge the gap between us, so there's only a few inches of space. "You tell me you're in love with me then you ignore me. You're affectionate and sweet in private. But when we're in public, you can't get away from me fast enough. And don't tell me you're being discreet or whatever bullshit excuse you're going to give me. Not after how you acted in the woods, by the pool."

"I'm not sure what you're talking about. All I've done is be attentive to you and show you love."

I take a few steps back and shake my head. "Here we go again. No, you know what? I'm done being nice, Adrian. You've got a serious problem, and you need help. I don't know how you've managed for so long without treatment, but you can't—"

Adrian's eyes flash, and he let outs a low, humorless laugh. "Hold on. What are you saying?"

I wince. "I'm trying to avoid using terms that are offensive, but you do have issues. Serious ones by the looks of it, and it's okay to get help."

Adrian runs a hand over his face, his face is red. "Okay, we need to stop talking right now before this goes any further. Or we're both going to say more things we'll regret."

I snap my mouth shut and stare at him.

Part of me wants to cover the distance between us and take him into my arms.

Another part of me wants to run out of the room and keep running till I make it back to the city and the comfort and familiarity of Savannah.

I do neither.

Instead, I continue to stand there and stare at the man whose face I've come to know, wondering what I should do next.

What we should do next.

Doctor Sheridan was right. You aren't equipped to handle this and there's nothing wrong with that.

A few long moments pass, during which a clock ticks in the background.

Adrian pours himself a drink, and I move in the direction of the door. "You're right. We shouldn't talk about this. I think it's best if I go."

Adrian eyes me over the rim of his glass. "I think that's for the best too."

Tears prick the back of my eyes as I wrench the door open and hurry outside.

It takes me a few tries to find my way back to the main part of the cabin and by then I've pulled my glasses down low.

Hot tears are sliding down my cheeks as I step out into the sweltering heat. I make a beeline for my own cabin, weaving in and out of the throngs of people on my way past.

Once I've made it there, I slam the door shut, lean against it, and bury my face in my hands.

I don't realize I've sunk to my knees until I draw them up to my chest and bring my head to rest against them.

For the longest time, I stare into space, a headache pounding in the back of my skull.

When my phone rings, I'm startled out of my stupor. I realize that I've been sitting there for two hours. Gingerly, I push myself up to my feet and stumble toward the bedroom.

I snatch my phone off of the dresser and press it to my ear without checking the screen. Thank goodness for the signal.

Savanna's warm and exuberant face makes me burst into a fresh wave of tears. Thank goodness for the signal.

"What the hell happened? What did he do? Do you want me to come down there and chop his balls off?"

I wipe my face. "No, I don't think that'll make me feel better."

"But it'll make me feel better," Savannah reasons. "And then I'll help you feel better too."

I swallow and clutch the phone to my ear. "I think coming here was a mistake, Sav. It was meant to be a fresh start for me, but it's just turned into a mess."

Savannah sighs. "Babe, I am so sorry that asshole ruined the ranch for you. I still don't think you should let him drive you away. You deserve to rest and relax. But maybe you should leave. But it's your decision. At the end of the day, you have to choose what's best for you."

I perch on the edge of my bed and run my fingers through my hair. "If I come back, you're not going to fuss over me, right?"

"I make no promises," Savannah replies, after a brief pause. "But I'll also binge watch trashy TV with you.

And I'll bring you all the ice cream and pizza you can eat."

I sniff. "You're the best, Sav. I don't know how I'd survive any of this without you."

"Not to toot my own horn or anything, but you wouldn't. I take full credit for this."

I choke back a laugh. "You should."

"Skittles and I are here, whatever you decide to do," Savannah adds in a softer voice. "Why don't you sleep for an hour or two and see how you feel when you wake up?"

I nod. "Yeah, I'll do that. Hey, Sav?"

"Hmm?"

"Thanks for being my friend," I whisper through my tears. "I'll fill you in when I've made my decision."

Chapter Twenty-Five: Adrian

I knock and clasp my hands behind my neck.

A long moment passes. I don't get a response.

With a frown, I press my ear to her cabin door and listen. When I don't hear anything, I knock again, louder this time. "Danielle, it's me. Open the door, please. I think we've both had some time to think about things, so let's talk about this."

Silence meets my statement.

My frown deepens as I reach into my pocket for the master key. After glancing around to make sure none of the other guests are watching, I swipe and push the door open.

The cabin is dark, with all of the curtains pulled shut, and a stillness in the air. On the tips of my toes, I creep over to the nearest window and fling the curtains open.

I repeat the process till bright sunlight floods the room.

Slowly, I spin around and tiptoe to the room.

The bed is made and doesn't look like it's been slept in. And the doors to the closet are open. Unease settles in the pit of my stomach as I cross over and peer into the closet.

My heart hammers uneasily when I get to the bathroom and see that all of Danielle's things are gone.

Her fluffy bathrobe. Her hair and skin products.

All of it is gone, like she was never there to begin with.

I'm muttering to myself as I step out of her cabin and into the morning air. The sun is hot on the back of my neck, and I'm sweating by the time I make it to the main cabin.

Maureen is bent over a map with a guest, a look of fierce concentration etched onto her features. I dig my nails into my palms and shift from one foot to the other.

As soon as she's done, I stride over to her and place both hands on the desk.

"Have you seen Ms. Clark? She asked for a private riding lesson. I stopped by her cabin but no one was there."

Maureen's brows furrow together as she turns to the computer. Her fingers move quickly and deftly. "Ms. Clark checked out this morning."

My stomach clenches. "What?"

Maureen types in something else and peers at the screen. "Yeah, Maurice checked her out this morning. She said something about a personal issue. Oh and that it was okay if we couldn't refund the money for the remaining few days."

I frown and link my fingers together. "Did she say anything else?"

Maureen shakes her head. "I'm sorry, sir."

I take a step back and exhale. "Okay. Thank you, Maureen."

On my way to the office, I run into Doctor Sheridan who is muttering to herself and flipping through her files.

After apologizing, she beckons me into her office, where she shuts the door and leans against it.

"I know I'm breaking confidentiality here, but I'm worried about Ms. Clark."

I blink. "Why? What did she say?"

"She was really distraught when I saw her this morning, and she kept talking about how tired she is of everything. As you know, it's the protocol for me to reach out to her emergency contact if I believe a patient is a danger to herself or others."

My heart misses a beat. "Have you been able to reach that person?"

Doctor Sheridan pushes herself off the wall and gives me a peculiar look. "No, she isn't answering her phone. Mr. Steele, I'm sorry to ask you this, but are you Mr. X?"

"Mr. X?"

"You can't be." Doctor Sheridan shakes her head and steps behind her desk. She pulls out another folder and flips it open. "It's not possible."

I cross over to Doctor Sheridan and lean over the desk. "Who is Mr. X? What has Danielle said about me? This is really important."

"She didn't mention you at all," Doctor Sheridan replies, without looking at me. "She was seeing this other guest at the ranch, a Mr. X, a man who she believed had serious psychological problems."

I taste bile in the back of my throat. "Treating her? Did she say anything else?"

Doctor Sheridan looks up and pauses. "She was confused and hurt by his behavior. A lot of it doesn't make sense to me either. I couldn't figure out this Mr. X guy. It seems to me he was playing with her. I don't know. That's what I got from it."

I push myself off the desk and ran a hand over my face. "Doctor Sheridan, can you tell me about one of the incidents?"

"I really shouldn't—"

"You said yourself you were worried about her and that if you're worried about a patient, you're allowed to break confidentiality. I can help her."

She gives me a dubious look.

"I can at least try," I add, giving her a pleading look. "Where's the harm in trying, right? You don't have to tell me all of the specifics."

Doctor Sheridan sits behind her desk and takes off her glasses. "She mentioned the hike she went on. Mr. X showed up in a very strange outfit all covered up, trying to hide from others including her. He even saw her but totally acted as if he didn't know her. She also mentioned a very similar incident at the pool. He was there again, and in another strange outfit. He was hiding behind chairs and totally ignored her. She's many moments like that the past few weeks. He's hot one minute and cold the next."

A throbbing feeling begins in the back of my skull. I sit still for what seems to be a very long time. I can't believe this is happening.

I sink into the nearest chair, my mind racing with possibilities. "Did she tell you about an incident where she snuck into his room at night, and he screamed?"

Doctor Sheridan's expression turns to surprise. "As a matter of fact, she did. I forgot about that. It led me to the conclusion that this Mr. X of hers has serious commitment issues."

Nervous laughter bubbles up within me.

Was Danielle Brian's mysterious naked lady that night? That can't be it. It just can't. Why didn't she just say something about it?

I sit back against the chair and look directly at the doctor. "During all of those incidents, she was sure she was dealing with Mr. X?"

Doctor Sheridan sat back down behind her desk. "Yes, she was sure. I have no reason to believe she's lying. She got to know the guy and thinks he might have a multiple personality disorder."

"Not lying, just unintentionally duped," I mutter, pausing to scrub a hand over my face. I lean back over the desk and hold the doctor's gaze. "What if I told you that Mr. X doesn't have issues?"

Doctor Sheridan raises an eyebrow. "I would have to ask what you're basing this on, Mr. Steele. I can't base a diagnosis on one person's interpretation of events. It takes sessions and months of close monitoring to be able to determine if someone has a problem."

I nod, slowly then faster. "Yes, I understand all of that. But I need to tell you something, doc. I know I'm not your patient, but indulge me for a second. I think that what Danielle perceived as a split personality was actually a completely different person."

"Multiple personalities?"

I shake my head. "No, it's two different people. Mr. X has a twin brother."

Comprehension dawned on Doctor Sheridan's face. She sat back against her chair, folded her hands in her lap, and blew out a breath. "Well, that certainly explains things."

"I'm Mr. X, and my twin brother is staying at the ranch for treatment," I tell her, the words pouring out of me in a rush. "I've asked a few of the staff members who are aware to be discreet and as private as possible. I didn't want him to get the wrong kind of attention or let the fact that he's my brother to interfere with the healing journey. Dr. Masterson is seeing him."

Doctor Sheridan picks up her glasses and sets them down. "And why didn't you tell Danielle all of this?"

"Honestly, it never occurred to me that they would cross paths, He wasn't supposed to leave his room. I think he went out once without my knowledge and he came right back, being uncomfortable outside. I didn't know he'd been going out on disguise." I admit, with a wince. "And I wasn't ready to tell her about Brian because it's a lot of shit to put on a person. And I didn't want that to overshadow our relationship."

"You were afraid she was going to reject you."

"I've had that happen before. I knew Danielle was special and different from the moment I set eyes on her. I wanted to give us a fighting chance before bringing the real world into our bubble."

Doctor Sheridan exhales. "I understand why you didn't feel ready..."

"I was an idiot. I should've told her about Brian anyway." I stand up and begin to pace. "Now I've driven away the only women I've ever felt anything for."

And I have no way to make any of it better.

I can't believe the things I told her during our last encounter. I was so mean and cold to her, accusing her. An apology isn't good enough. And because she's now gone, I can't show her how I really feel.

And what a fucking idiot I've been for not confiding in her.

Way to go, Adrian. You've done it again. You've screwed up another relationship by not being honest.

Doctor Sheridan pushes her chair back with a screech. "Look, this might be none of my business, but for what it's worth, I don't think it's too late."

I stop pacing and wheel around to face the doctor. Then I shove both hands into my pockets and blow out a deep, shaky breath. "I appreciate the sentiment doc, but we both know this is my fault."

"You wanted to protect your brother, and your heart," Doctor Sheridan continues, as if she hasn't heard me. "You might not have gone about it in the right way, but that doesn't mean your heart wasn't in the right place."

I offer her a rueful smile. "Yeah, but it didn't do me any good either."

Doctor Sheridan stops and gives me a kind smile. "If I were you, I would go to her. Explain everything and tell her the truth. And then let Danielle decide if this is too much for her or not. It should've been her choice from the beginning."

"You're right, but what if it's too late?"

"Then you'll have your answer once and for all. You can't just make a decision based on an assumption of an outcome. You have to do the act and see what comes up and then deal with it," Doctor Sheridan replies, pausing to take off her glasses.

She looks directly at me and gives me an encouraging smile. "I think you're going to be okay."

I'm halfway out the door when I stop and glance over my shoulder. "I need her emergency contact's number."

Doctor Sheridan writes it down on a piece of paper and rips it out. Wordlessly, she hands it to me and gives me a slight smile.

I offer her a grateful look and rush out of her office and into my own. There, I open and close drawers, searching furiously.

When Maureen comes in, I've upended half the file cabinet.

I'm rifling through my jacket pockets when I address her. "I need you to book the private jet to New York."

"Sir?"

"I've got business to attend to, and I can't find my passport."

Maureen blinks. "It's in your safe, sir. You asked me to remind you in case you forgot."

I stand up and dust myself off. "Do you think you can handle everything while I'm away?"

Maureen stands up straighter. "Of course, sir. There's absolutely nothing to worry about."

"Can you have the car ready to take me to the airport? I'm going upstairs to pack my things."

Without waiting for a response, I brush past her.

In my room, I stuff a few random articles of clothing into a small carry-on and zip it shut.

When I'm done, I call Maureen. I smile when she tells me everything is ready.

I'm coming for you, Danielle. Don't give up on us.

Chapter Twenty-Six: Danielle

I throw the ball up in the air and catch it again. I do this a few more times, focusing on the smooth and rhythmic motions of the gesture until some of the tightness in my chest unfurls.

Once it does, I close my fingers around the ball and squeeze my eyes shut.

I'm counting backward from ten when someone raps on the door. I call out in a hoarse voice and Savannah pokes her head in, carrying a tray of food.

She pushes the door open the rest of the way and steps in.

Slowly, she creeps forward and sets the tray down on the dresser. Then she rips the curtain open, allowing bright sunlight to pour in.

I wince as spots dance in and out of my field of vision.

"You can't stay in your room forever," she says, pausing to sit on the empty side of the bed. "I know you're angry, and I know you're hurt, but you've got to come out at some point."

"It's only been a day and a half."

"A long ass day and a half," Savannah replies, pausing to squeeze my shoulders. "Skittles and I miss you. Watching trashy TV isn't the same without your running commentary."

"You hate my running commentary. You always complain that you can't hear what they're saying because of me."

"That was old me."

"That was three and a half weeks ago." I sit up straighter and prop myself up on the pillow. "What's changed since then?"

"I've seen the light," Savannah jokes. "And I realize the shows are actually a lot more interesting this way."

I raise an eyebrow. "Uh-huh, and what about my feet on the coffee table?"

Savannah's eye twitches. "Endearing."

"Cheeto dust all over the couch and my clothes?"

Savannah's other eye twitches. "All part of your quirky personality. Who doesn't have flaws? I'm sure I do some things that drive you crazy."

I let the ball fall onto the bed and fold my arms over my chest. "Okay, who are you and what have you done with my best friend?"

A part of me appreciates what Savannah is trying to do. But the other part of me can't stand the pity. Or the silence.

She's been walking on eggshells since I arrived yesterday afternoon, when her hands were deep in a bowl of popcorn, and she had half a bottle of wine on the coffee table.

Savannah had been so pleased to see me that she nearly dropped the popcorn bowl when she opened the door for me, but that didn't matter.

Being in Savannah's airy and sun-filled apartment felt right. Or it was going to once I pulled myself out of my funk.

It's not forever anyway. Just until you get back on your feet and then you can move out again.

Until then, I'm going to keep my head down and put in the work.

How are you going to do that if you haven't left the room? You've barely eaten. You need to shower, and you need to wash your dirty clothes from the trip. Come on, Danielle. Get up.

Sitting around and pining over Adrian isn't going to help.

Nor is staring at pictures of him on my phone and holding my breath whenever I see a weird number flash across the screen.

So far, I've received several calls from the ranch, but I'm not ready to answer. While I don't know if this is Adrian's attempt at reaching me, I do know one thing.

Having plucked up the courage to leave the ranch, the last thing I want is to be dragged back into a vicious cycle with Adrian.

Not only is it not going to do either of us any good, but it's also going to keep us from moving on.

"....are you even listening to me?" Savannah waves a hand in front of my face and frowns. "Were you thinking about Adrian again?"

I nod and sink lower against the mattress. "I don't want to. I know we weren't together for long, and I should just get over it, but I can't."

Because I don't think I'm ever going to feel this way again.

About anyone.

In three short weeks, Adrian found his way into my heart and my soul, and I can't get him out of it. No amount of wishing, pleading, or bargaining is going to change that.

And the sooner I can accept it, the easier it's going to be for me to move on.

Someday.

"Time isn't a measurement when it comes to these sorts of things," Savannah offers, with a smile. "Knowing someone for years doesn't mean that they really know you. Or that they really have your back.

On the contrary, I've had people who had a major impact on me in a short amount of time."

I blink. "Why are you being sympathetic? You hate him."

"I don't hate him, but I hate what he's done to you," Savannah says, with a frown. "And I still think you fell too hard, too fast. But who am I to argue with love?"

I swing my legs over the side of the bed and duck into the bathroom. There, I splash cold water on my face and pause to pat my face dry. "You're starting to freak me out a little."

Savannah materializes in the doorway and crosses one arm over the other. "Has Gina gotten back to you yet?"

I finish patting my face and avoid my reflection in the mirror. "No, and I don't think she's going to. I think I really blew it, Sav. She's probably not going to give me any serious jobs, and I'm going to be stuck writing fluff piece for the rest of my career."

Savannah steps to the side and allows me to pass. "Come on, I'm sure that's not true. You'll make your case when you see her and see how that goes."

"I don't know if I'm ready to go back to work."

Savannah stands behind me as I rifle through the closet. "I think you should at least try."

I stop rifling and glance at her over my shoulders. "Will it get you off of my back?"

She pauses and folds her arms over her chest. "It will help, but I won't be completely off your back. Someone has to make sure you're alive and clean."

I offer her a raised eyebrow. "Thanks."

The door creaks open, and Skittles darts in, black tail swishing back and forth. He jumps onto the bed, curls up in a ball and purrs.

With a smile, I stride over to him, scoop him into my arms and give him a big, noisy kiss.

Skittles purrs even more and snuggles into me. I bury my face against his fur and try to ignore the knots in my stomach.

But even a shower doesn't wash Adrian away.

And when I pull on a skirt and blouse and see the slew of missed calls from the resort, it doesn't make me feel better.

As I slide into my shoes and grab my purse, I think of my time with Adrian.

I see us together sitting by the light of the moon snuggling against each other.

And I remember how it felt to wake up to him, to finally feel safe and loved in his arms. But that doesn't ease the ache in my chest.

> Savannah pours me a cup of coffee, and I sip it in silence.
>
> She hovers while I nibble on a bagel but doesn't say anything.

In my mind, I see Adrian making me breakfast, his muscled back turned in my direction. When I blink, Savannah is rummaging through the fridge for more food.

She looks at me over her shoulders, and her expression softens.

I give her a grim smile. Savannah walks me to the door and hands me an apple, a bottle of water, and a paper bag with a sandwich in.

During the bus ride to work, my knees are bouncing up and down, and I can't stop glancing out the window. I'm suddenly glad I decided not to drive.

I lean my head against the glass, the world outside rushing past in either direction. I see Adrian's face everywhere I go, and I can almost swear I hear his laugh in the whistling of the wind.

The longing in me grows stronger as I get off the bus and stand outside the tall metal building.

Men and women in business suits rush past me in either direction.

I take a deep breath and push my way through the revolving doors. A blast of cold air hits me in the face when I emerge on the other side.

I walk past two large tables and a row of plush leather chairs into the lobby.

In the elevator, I tap my feet impatiently.

The doors finally ping open, and I step outside.

As soon as I do, the cacophony of voices hits me first, followed quickly by the scent of berries air freshener.

I take a step forward and see Gina, who is power walking the floor, heels clicking behind her, a phone pressed to her ear. She does a double-take when she sees me then motions for me to follow her.

My stomach drops as I fall into step behind her.

Her name is engraved into the glass outside her office, and she takes her shoes off by the door, gesturing for me to do the same. Reluctantly, I step out of my heels and link my fingers together.

Although I know that Gina likes everything in her office to be kept in pristine and immaculate condition, being in my stockings feels weird.

Slowly, I walk across the carpet and wait for Gina to sit down and tuck a lock of blonde hair behind her ear, still on the phone.

She says something in a hushed voice, hangs up, and sets the phone, face down, on her desk.

"Don't you still have a few days of paid leave left?"

"I came back early," I reply, pausing to shift from one foot to the other. "I thought I might as well make myself useful."

Gina studies my face, her catlike blue eyes giving nothing away. "I see."

"About the ranch piece, I'm sorry that you feel it isn't spicy enough—"

Gina holds a hand up and leans back in her chair. "It's fine. It's interesting enough to stand on its own two legs. But there is going to have to be a profile on Adrian Steele included. His accomplishments, a picture, all the works."

My heart misses a beat. "Without any of the salacious stuff?"

Gina sighs. "Yes, fine. Just make sure it's good. Your ass is on the line."

My eyes widen. "Me?"

Gina raises an eyebrow. "You wanted something more serious, right? You've been asking for a while. I have to admit I had no idea how committed you were until recently. So, this is your chance to prove yourself."

I'm still struggling to process her words when Gina rises to her feet. "You're not going to change your mind, are you? This is your first big piece, Danielle. Don't blow it."

I clear my throat. "Thank you so much, Gina. I won't let you down."

Gina takes a bottle of water out of her mini-fridge. "Good. Now, get out of my office and get back to work."

With one last grateful smile in her direction, I scurry off to my desk.

Once I sit down at my cubicle, I glance at everyone else over the edge, a strange thrum of excitement pulsing through me.

When I pull my chair closer and wait for the laptop to start up, I can't deny how hopeful I feel.

For the first time in weeks.

I place my earpiece in, turn up the music, and try to drown out the voices in my head.

All my doubt and insecurity and fear is washed away as I begin the first draft of my article, moving back and forth between different versions of my writing.

Then I connect my phone to the laptop and scroll through some of the pictures I took.

It's all beautiful and scenic.

But seeing the ranch makes something deep and unfamiliar stir within me. A sadness takes over me, a longing for the ranch and for Adrian.

I want to be back there, riding my horse through the open air or standing atop the cliff overlooking the waterfall.

And in both scenarios, I see Adrian by my side, holding my hand and smiling.

With a sigh, I save my draft and look it up from my screen. Only then do I realize that the light outside has begun to wane.

Slowly, I stand up, take my earpiece out. My eyes dart around the mostly empty office.

Then I stretch my arms up over my head and yawn.

When I'm done, I power down the laptop and leave it on the desk. I slip my feet back into my shoes, reach for my purse, and walk to the elevator.

Downstairs, I'm standing on the sidewalk, inhaling the crisp evening air when a long black limo pulls up next to the curb. I glance on either side of me, but no one comes up.

A uniformed driver in a black suit and hat comes out and holds the back door open.

He looks directly at me and smiles.

I press my phone to the ear to dial Savannah. I'm brushing past the limo when the sound of his voice makes me freeze in my tracks.

In a daze, I hang up, look inside the limo and see Adrian leaning sideways, dressed in a pair of jeans, and a dark button-down shirt. He offers me a winning smile and pats the seat next to him.

"I've been trying to call you, but you won't answer."

I startle and I stiffen. "I didn't want to."

"You left without saying goodbye." Adrian's easy expression doesn't falter as he shifts closer. "Why did you do that?"

"Because I don't want to do this anymore." I make a vague hand gesture and sigh. "Look, Adrian, I'm sorry you wasted your time by flying all the way out here. But I have to go back to my life now. I belong in the city at my job."

Adrian's brows furrow together. "What about us?"

I swallow. "I don't think there can be an us."

Before I start to walk away.

"Before you make a decision, I think you're going to want to hear what I have to say. I have a twin brother," he blurts out when I open my mouth to protest.

Say what? He turns the phone his phone around to show me a video call in progress.

Adrian's brother is wearing a baseball hat and large sunglasses. He takes off the glasses and offers me an awkward wave.

"We haven't officially met. I'm Brian Steele. I'm Adrian's twin."

I make a low startled noise in the back of my throat. No way, that can't be, what is he saying? I feel heat rising up to my head.

"I think we met a few times when you were on the ranch," Brian continues, in an upbeat voice. His half-smile doesn't leave his face. "I'm sorry about all the times I blew you off or made you feel bad. I'm sure you can understand why it was very confusing for me."

I stand up straighter and swing my gaze back to Adrian. "You're a twin?"

Adrian nods, relief flooding his features. "That's why we had issues, and why you thought I was blowing you off. It wasn't me. It was Brian. I didn't put two and two together until you left. Brian confessed that he had been leaving his room in disguise—it's a long story—and I spoke to your therapist—"

"You spoke to my therapist?"

Adrian nods, sheepishly. "She was worried about you because you left so abruptly, and I couldn't get a hold of Savannah. Anyway, I flew out once I realized the truth. But I got here late, so I waited to get in touch with Savannah myself."

I blink, and my heart misses a beat. "You've been in touch with Savanah?"

Adrian nods and pats the seat next to him again, more earnestly this time. "Now, can you please come inside? We need to talk properly."

My feet move of their own accord, before I realize what I'm doing.

I duck and get into the limo. The door clicks shut behind me. The car starts moving as I slide the seat belt over my stomach, and it clicks into place.

Then I fold my hands into my lap and twist to face Adrian.

His entire body is twisted, so he's looking at me directly. I release a deep breath and something unfurls in the center of my chest.

"Why didn't you tell me you had a brother?"

"He's at the ranch because he's trying to get away from the world. And he's been having some personal and psychological issues that he needs to work on. I wanted and still want to respect his privacy. I cannot talk about his issues openly to anyone else. It's not my place. And I didn't want whatever was happening with him to overshadow us."

"Oh."

Adrian takes my hands in his. "I've known you were special from the moment I laid eyes on you, Danielle. But I was scared, and I was stupid, and I told myself I was protecting you. I'm sorry that I let you down, and I'm sorry that I wasn't honest."

The warm feeling in my stomach grows.

"I should've told you the truth. I should've had more faith in you and us," Adrian continues, his voice growing softer and softer. He holds my gaze as his lips lift into a half smile. "Will you come back to the ranch with me?"

My breath hitches in my throat. "I...I want to, but I can't. I just got back to work, and my boss is finally giving me something I want to work on—"

"I've already spoken to your boss, and I told her I'd sit down for an exclusive with you at the ranch," Adrian interrupts, with a smile. "Savannah already packed your bag, and it's already in the trunk."

I offer him a weak smile. "You really have thought of everything, haven't you?"

Adrian nods and brushes his thumb along the inside of my wrist. "I tried, so what do you say? I've got a surprise planned for you."

Chapter Twenty-Seven: Adrian

I pull her onto my lap and bury my face in her neck. "You smell amazing."

Danielle squirms and sighs. "No, I don't. You didn't even let me go home and shower."

I press a kiss underneath her ear. "Because I didn't want to waste any more moments without you."

Danielle stirs and leans back to look at me directly. "You do realize I wasn't going to change my mind right? About coming back with you, I mean?"

I wrap my arms around her waist and smile. "I know."

Because I saw the look on her face.

Flying out to her was the right thing to do and my honest explanation was exactly what Danielle needed to hear.

Over the past few weeks, she and I have been dancing around each other, getting close but never close enough.

Now that I've finally come clean about Brian, nothing is going to get in our way.

Not if I can help it.

Danielle offers me a tentative smile. "What about the other guests? I'm still technically a guest."

"Not anymore. The minute you checked out, you stopped being a paid guest. But I don't give a shit either way."

Danielle's smile grows bigger. "You don't? What about that pesky journalist from the restaurant?"

"The only pesky journalist I want in my life is the one on my lap," I tease, before I tuck her hair behind her ears. "All joking aside though, I mean it, Danielle.

I want us to have a real shot this time. No more secrets or lies."

Danielle's expression softens. "I'd like that."

I press a kiss to her forehead. "I'm going to make a quick phone call. I'll be right back."

She blows out a breath and slides off of my laptop and onto the seat next to me.

Then she glances out the window, at the private runway, awe and surprise written across her face.

With a smile, she presses two fingers to the glass and traces it. Then she takes her phone out of her pocket, and I hear her murmuring to her friend.

I move further down to the private plane and fish out my phone.

Maureen answers on the fourth ring. "Mr. Steele, I trust all of the travel arrangements were to your liking."

"Everything was perfect, Maureen. Thank you. How's everything at the ranch?"

"Everything's fine, sir, and ready for your return."

I glance over my shoulders and lower my voice. "Everything's ready for our arrival?"

"All of the details have been taken care of, sir. I've recruited all of the staff, and they were excited and pleased to help."

I nod and look out the window, at the clear blue skies. "Good. We'll be there in a few hours. Please keep this as discreet as possible. I don't want anyone disturbing us or Brian."

"You have nothing to worry about, sir. I hope you have a pleasant flight."

"See you soon." With that, I hang up and push the phone back into my pocket. When I turn back around, Danielle has her feet propped up and is sipping on a drink through a straw.

I drop a kiss on top of her head, lift her feet up, and sit down opposite her and press two fingers against the soles of her feet.

She lets out a low whimpering noise. "That feels good."

"Your feet are so pretty." I switch back and forth between feet, smiling when Danielle sinks lower and lower into her seat. "I'll do whatever it takes to earn back your trust."

She sets down her drink and makes a low unintelligible sound.

The plane purrs to life underneath us and begins to move. She sits up straighter, pushes her hair out of her eyes, and tightens her seatbelt.

I smile, fold my hands in my lap, and wait. A blonde uniformed stewardess in a navy and white ensemble appears, offering us a view of her pearly white teeth.

Once the plane settles in the sky, she returns with two glasses of champagne.

I touch my glass to hers and smile. "What should we toast to?"

Danielle's expression turns thoughtful. "To new beginnings?"

"Who's being cheesy and corny now?"

Danielle rolls her eyes. "How about second chances?"

"And fate," I add, before taking a sip of my drink. Danielle eyes me over the rim then sets her glass down. She links her fingers together and sighs.

I finish half of my drink and give her a confused look.

"Are you okay? Do you want me to get you something else to drink?"

Danielle drapes an arm over her stomach and shakes her head. "No, I'm okay. I'm feeling a little nauseous. I guess private air travel doesn't agree with me."

I unbuckle my seat belt and wait for her to do the same. "There's a bed in the back. We can both go and lay down."

In silence, we make our way down the aisle. I pause to slide the door open and wait for her to duck inside.

After she kicks her shoes off and leaves them by the door, I wait for her to climb onto the bed and make herself comfortable.

Slowly, I take off my shirt and kick off my shoes, and join her.

I pull her to me, and she curls up against me, her familiar floral smell wafting over me.

A day and a half without her was excruciating. I don't ever want to do it again.

As I hold her to me and breathe in the scent of her, Danielle's body begins to go slack. Her breathing evens, and she murmurs something in her sleep.

I press a kiss to the back of her neck and bury my face in her hair. Then I squeeze my eyes shut and try to sleep.

Except I can't stop thinking about how it must've felt for her.

To have carried this around for three weeks and not be able to confront me.

Why hadn't I seen it earlier?

Why had it taken Danielle leaving for me to see the truth about us?

Slowly, I pull myself away from her. She shifts and curls up against a pillow. Then I swing my legs over the side of the bed and creep forward.

In the main part of the plane, I select a chair closer to the back and gesture to the stewardess. She ambles over with a small tray and holds it out to me.

I offer her a small smile as I reach for the glass of whiskey.

On my fourth sip, the door to the bedroom slides open, and Danielle comes out. She is barefoot, and her hair is in loose waves around her shoulders, but she's got a strange glint in her eyes.

Wordlessly, she takes the glass from me and sets it down. Then she pulls me to my feet and drags me back inside. As soon as the door shuts, her mouth descends upon mine.

She always taste like blueberry muffins.

I feel like I've been starving for air.

I cup the back of her neck, and she makes a low noise in the back of her throat. She presses herself against me, with only the clothes on our backs as barriers.

Then she hoists herself up and wraps her legs around my waist.

One hand stays on the back of her neck, and the other cups her ass. After giving it a firm squeeze, I stumble forward in the semi-darkness until my knees hit the edge of the bed.

With a smirk, I lower Danielle onto the mattress and pause to pull my shirt up over my head. After it falls to the floor with a flutter, I reach for the buttons on my jeans.

Danielle sits up, and in one quick move, she pushes the jeans down to my knees.

My heart is hammering unsteadily the entire time, and the sound of her heavy breathing is like music to my ears.

I fumble for her shirt and manage to pull it up over her head.

Her skin is glistening as she stands up and kicks her skirt away. In her white bra and panties, she is the most beautiful thing I've ever seen.

We reach for each other at the same time and fall backwards onto the mattress. I touch her, and she sighs into my mouth.

She runs her fingers down my back, pausing at my behind.

With a growl, I unhook her bra and let her breasts spill forward.

I take one nipple between my teeth, sucking and biting as I do. When I move to the other one, Danielle arches her back and begins to moan.

Groaning, I place a hand over her mouth and bury my head in the crook of her neck. The floral smell of her makes the knots in my stomach tighten.

She links her fingers over my waist and draws me closer. One hand drops between us. She touches me through my boxers, sending a jolt straight through me.

When she pushes herself against me, all of the blood rushes to my groin.

Using one hand, I pin her arms up over her head, and with the other, I tug down my boxers. Abruptly, I stand up and push them off.

Danielle is pulling her panties off but I stop her. I can't make out her full expression but in the dim light of the moon, I catch glimpses of her hunger.

Her yearning for me.

I use my mouth to pull her panties down over her legs, pausing when I reach her ankles. Then I throw them over my shoulder and pull her to me.

My mouth descends on hers, hot, searing, and demanding.

She melts against me. She threads her fingers through my hair and tugs, sending dual waves of pain and pleasure ricocheting through me.

I'm breathing heavily as I push one finger inside her.

She sinks her teeth into my shoulders and twists her head to the side. "Oh, Adrian. Oh, fuck."

I insert another finger and watch her face carefully.

It's glorious and unfiltered, and it makes me want to bury myself in her.

As I begin to move my fingers back and forth, Danielle's breathing grows louder. She bites down on her bottom lip. Beads of sweat form on her forehead and the sides of her face.

Then she twists her head to the side, a whimper falling from her lips. I sink my teeth into her neck and rub myself against her.

Danielle grinds against my fingers, moving slowly, sensually, as if we have all of the time in the world.

My heart is pounding so loudly now that I can barely make out anything else.

Her breath catches in her throat as she writhes and spasms, coming undone underneath me. I draw back, wait for her to catch her breath, and kiss her again.

Then I position myself at her entrance and thrust.

"I'm never letting you go, Danielle," I whisper. "You and I belong together."

Danielle releases a deep, shaky breath. "Yes, we do."

I ease out and slam back into her. "No one else is ever going to make you feel the way I do."

Danielle meets each thrust with one of her own. "No."

I pin her arms over her head and stare at her until she looks at me. "I want to hear you say it."

Danielle blinks and looks up at me. She holds my gaze, licks her lips, and clears her throat. "No one can make me feel as good as you do."

I growl and ram into her. "Say it again."

Danielle's pupils dilate, and she groans. "I'm yours, Adrian."

I ease out and slam back into her, filling her to the hilt. Then I release her hands and bring my arms to rest against the headboard.

Danielle rakes her fingers over my back, making me hiss in response. Every touch, every sound, every kiss drives me closer and closer to the edge of oblivion.

She's all I can see or hear or taste.

And I wouldn't have it any other way.

I push myself off of the headboard, and look down at her. Danielle is playing with her own nipples.

She is pinching and pushing them together and something about the sight makes something in me snap.

I give her a quick kiss then hoist her legs up over my shoulders.

As soon as I do, I sink further into her and growl. Her arms fall on either side of her, and she is grabbing fistfuls of the sheet.

Over and over, I thrust in and out of her.

Each tantalizing whisper, each breathy moan turns my blood molten.

I press my head against the headboard, and my chest is tight. "You drive me crazy, Danielle. Can't you see how you make me feel?"

Danielle makes a low unintelligible sound.

I squeeze my eyes shut and surrender.

We move against each other with wild and animal-like abandon, hurtling closer and closer to the edge. The sound of her moans reverberates inside of my head, and I can't get enough.

In long, practiced strokes, I drive her crazy.

Danielle has to feel what I feel. This undeniable pull between us.

Her breath quickens, and she is falling again, the force of her orgasm ripping through her. I slow my pace and draw back to look at her.

Her face is covered in a thin sheen of sweat, her chest rising and falling unevenly. With a smile, I lower my head to kiss her, and she is soft and yielding.

When her hands flutter at her sides and then wind themselves through my hair, the swell of emotion in my chest tightens.

It unfurls and runs through my veins. Danielle sinks back against the mattress and releases a breath. Slowly, she sits up and presses her forehead to mine.

I give a few more quick thrusts, my own release overpowering me. When my vision clears, and I can see again, Danielle is looking at me with so much love and trust that it makes my heart burst.

Exhaling, I ease out of her and collapse against the mattress.

She tucks herself into my side and drapes an arm over me. I press a kiss to the side of her head and draw her closer.

Then I bring one arm up behind my head and drape the other over her shoulders.

I'm tracing idle circles down her back when I feel her eyes on me. I twist to face her, and she presses a sweet kiss to my lips.

"What was that for?"

"I didn't thank you for coming for me," Danielle whispers, her voice catching. "I'm really glad you did. In case it wasn't obvious."

My hand falls down to her ass, and I give it a firm pat. "Oh, I know how thankful you are. Yes, it was obvious."

Color creeps up her neck and cheeks. "Oh, is that so?"

I nod, giving her a slow and wicked grin. "Oh, absolutely. You've been waiting for it since we got into the limo, haven't you?"

Danielle huffs back a laugh. "I didn't hear you complaining."

I press another kiss to her forehead. "Oh, I'm definitely not complaining. In fact, if you wanted to do it again, I wouldn't mind."

Danielle slaps my arm. "We can't do it again. It's bad enough that the whole plane knows what we did."

I shrug. "It's not as bad as you think. There is too much noise in the plane anyways. They can't hear anything."

Danielle is raising an eyebrow when my gaze flicks down to hers. "How many times have you done this?"

I remove my arm from around her shoulders and sit up. Then I throw one leg over her, so I'm straddling her.

A myriad of emotions dances across Danielle's face as she stares up at me in confusion.

"You're not asking the right question," I whisper, into her ear.

"I'm not?"

I shake my head and pepper her neck with kisses. "The right question is how many times do I plan on doing it from here until we get to Montana."

Danielle releases a deep, shaky breath. "How many times?"

I draw back to look at her. My eyes move over her face and down the slope of her chest. "I'm thinking that if we get some food in you, and I let you have a quick break in the middle, there's no reason it can't be a few times."

Danielle's face turns bright red. "A few times?"

I release her hands and grip her waist. "At the very least. We have a lot to make up for."

Danielle stares at me through hooded lashes. "We do?"

"Oh, absolutely." I lower my head, take one nipple between my teeth, and tug. When I move onto the other one, I don't stop sucking and biting until they're both as hard as pebbles.

Danielle whimpers when I lean back to look at her.

When she smiles, she takes my breath away, and it takes me a minute to remember how to breathe again. Then she writhes underneath me, and there's a low whistling sound in my ears.

I grin, lower my head, and take her bottom lip between my teeth.

"I'm going to have you begging me for more," I say, in a deep and throaty voice. Danielle's sharp intake of breath echoes in my head as I ease into her again.

· ♥ · ♥ · ♥ · ♥ · ♥ ·

I press a kiss to the side of her head. "Wake up."

Danielle mutters something incoherent under her breath. She sighs when I begin to pepper her neck with kisses. Still, she murmurs sleepily.

I brush my fingers against her nipples, but she doesn't react. I trace a path down her back, pausing at the curve.

Then I sink my teeth into her flesh and wait. She shifts and scooches closer to me.

One hand stays on the back of her neck, and the other trails down until I'm between her legs. I stroke the inside of her thighs, pausing to splay my fingers over her.

Abruptly, she jerks and is jolted awake. Her eyes are wild and unfocused and thick with sleep when she twists to face me.

"What are you doing?" Her voice is hoarse and scratchy. "What's happening?"

"I'm trying to wake you up," I tell her, with a smile. "We're half an hour away."

Danielle sinks back against the mattress and flips onto her back. She brings a hand up to her forehead and rubs in slow, circular motions. "How long have I been out?"

"A while," I reply, with a quick kiss. "Did I wear you out?"

Danielle gives me a wry smile. "What do you think?"

"I think it's not enough. We've still got a lot to make up for."

Danielle stifles a yawn. "We've got time. What's your hurry?"

I prop myself up on my elbow and study her. "No hurry. I'm just nuts about you."

Danielle gives me a sleepy smile. "I'm nuts about you too. But I still need food, water, the basic necessities."

"If you must."

She props herself up against a pillow and pushes her hair out of her face. "You look like you haven't slept."

I give her a slow smile. "Thank you."

"You're probably going to have work when you get back. Don't you at least want to close your eyes for a few minutes?"

I shake my head. "I'm fine. By the way, Brian will be waiting for us when we get there. He's really excited to meet you."

Danielle's smile lights up her whole face. "I'm looking forward to meeting him properly."

Slowly, she sits up, and the sheet pools around her waist. She leans between us, gives me a quick peck on the lips, and sighs.

Then she swings her legs over the side of the bed and wraps the sheet around her waist.

Barefoot and tousled, she sticks her head into the adjoining bathroom, a furrow appearing between her brows.

"This is a lot more spacious than I thought it would be," Danielle says, mostly to herself. "How do you even make that work?"

"I'll let you know if I ever find out," I respond, before standing up and stretching my arms over my head.

Without responding, Danielle steps into the bathroom, and I hear the water running.

When I step into the bathroom, she's already behind the shower stall, lathering up with the soap and humming to herself.

In the mirror, I watch her run her fingers through her hair.

I brush my teeth and examine them in the mirror, allowing myself a full view of her gorgeous curves. She spins around, pushes her hair out of her eyes, and her eyes fly open.

She has the most beautiful eyes.

She gives me a long look and cocks a finger at me, beckoning me forward. In a daze, I step behind the glass door.

When I take her into my arms, I realize what she's planning. She's got a devious smirk playing on the edge of her lips.

Danielle lowers herself to her knees and looks up at me.

· ♥ · ♥ · ♥ · ♥ · ♥ ·

"Again, I'm so sorry about the incident in the bedroom," Danielle says, her eyes swinging back and forth between the two of us. "This is going to take a lot of getting used to."

Brian waves her comment away. "I'm sorry that I freaked out. It wasn't you by the way. From what little I could see—"

I slap Brian on the back of his head. "Do not finish that sentence."

Brian scowls and rubs his neck. "I was going to give her a compliment. Don't worry. I can keep it classy."

Danielle hides her giggle behind her glass.

The three of us have been sitting in the outdoor section of the restaurant, underneath a blanket of stars for the past few hours.

With all of the curtains closed, and no other guests around, I can almost believe my plan is going to work.

Except for the part where Brian and Danielle hit it off.

Not only are the two of them getting along well, but I'm realizing what an idiot I was to keep the two of them apart.

On the surface, the two of them have nothing in common, but neither of them seems to care.

Getting past the initial awkwardness was the hard part, now that everything is out in the open, Danielle and I are finally free.

We have an actual fighting chance, and I couldn't be more grateful.

I signal to one of the waiters, and I'm only half-listening to their conversation when he comes in.

I whisper something into his ear, and the waiter gives me a quick nod.

When I turn my attention back to Danielle, she is giving me an amused look.

"What? Do I have sauce on my face?"

Danielle shakes her head. "Do you have something you need to do?"

"Actually." I push my chair back with a screech and stand up. "I do. Come with me."

I give Brian a meaningful look, and he lingers behind. In silence, I lead Danielle through the double doors of the restaurant, with my hands over her eyes.

After offering the waiter a quick look, the lights flick on.

I remove my hands from around Danielle's eyes and watch as she takes in the scene.

The overhead lighting is dim and intimate and soft music is playing in the background.

The dining room is empty except for us.

There is a single table in the center of the room. A crystal vase and a red rose adorns it. A crisp white envelope is propped against it.

Danielle twists to face me, a vision in her knee-length black dress and matching heels. She laces her fingers through mine, tugging me forward.

"What's all of this?"

I nod in the direction of the envelope. "Open it."

With trembling hands, she reaches for it and runs her fingers along the edge. Then she turns it over, a myriad of emotions playing out across her features.

When she rips it open, I withdraw my hand and get down on my knees. Danielle glances from the envelope to the ring that fell to the floor with a clatter.

Wordlessly, I pick it up and hold it out to her. "I know we haven't known each other long, but deep down in my heart, I know you're the one for me."

Danielle snaps her mouth shut, and the empty envelope falls to the floor with a flutter. "I...are you asking what I think you're asking?"

I hold the ring up and the tiny diamonds sprinkled along the outer edge of the band glisten and sparkle. "I love you, Danielle Clark. All my life, I've been used to women throwing themselves at me. Always wanting something from me but never bothering to get to know the man behind the money, behind the name."

Danielle's eyes fill with tears.

"You're the first woman to ever look at me and not care about any of that. When I'm with you, you make me feel invincible. Like I'm the only man in the world and like nothing could ever be that bad as long as I have you by my side."

Tears spill down her cheeks. "I love you too, Adrian."

"I know you've been hurt before. I know you've been let down, but if you give me a chance, I am going to do everything within my power to make you happy. I am going to do everything I can to make sure you feel loved and cherished and respected. Every single part of you."

Danielle takes both of my hands in hers. "My answer is yes."

"I haven't even asked the question yet," I tease, my eyes never leaving her face. "How do you know what I'm going to ask you?"

Danielle chokes back a laugh. "Because I know you."

I take her hand in mine and slide the ring onto her finger. "Will you do me the honor of becoming my wife?"

A slight tremor goes through Danielle as she nods.

"We can't hear you!"

Danielle's head snaps up, and she glances over her shoulders at Brian and Savannah, who are standing in the back of the room, smiling at us.

I help her to her feet, and she's laughing through her tears.

"What are you doing here?"

"Well, I didn't fly here on a private jet, but Adrian was nice enough to fly Skittles and I out," Savannah says. "Don't let me interrupt your nice moment. We just couldn't hear you from over there."

Danielle cups her hands over her mouth. "I said yes."

Savannah and Brian let out a whoop.

I take Danielle into my arms, dip her back, and kiss her thoroughly. We are both breathless when we come up for air, and the rest of the wait staff comes out, clapping steadily as they do.

Danielle is tucked into my side, a dazed look on her face. She pulls Savannah in for a hug.

Later, when the two of us are in my room, Danielle perches on the edge of the bed and pats the spot next to her. I pause to kick my shoes off and sit down. "Why do you look so serious?"

"There's something I need to tell you, and I don't know where to begin."

"You're not still married, are you?"

Danielle blows out a breath and twists, so she's facing me directly. "No, I'm not still married. I've been trying to figure out how to tell you this... I thought we had more time."

I take both of her hands in mine and frown. "Okay, you're scaring me a little bit. Are you okay?"

"I'm okay—we're okay."

I kiss her. "Good."

Danielle shakes her head and drapes a hand over her stomach. "No, I mean we're okay or at least I hope we are. I'm not sure yet."

I look down at her stomach and back up at her face. "You—we... What?"

"I missed my period," Danielle explains, the words pouring out of her in a rush. "I realized after I got back, and I was going to get a pregnancy test, but I was too depressed and miserable. Then you showed up and everything else was a whirlwind, and here we are."

I search her face. "So, you don't know yet?"

Holy shit.

Am I going to be a dad?

Danielle withdraws her hands and stands up. She begins to pace. "No, I have no idea. I could be wrong by the way. But Savannah brought a few pregnancy tests with her because she knew I'd want to know. I know this wasn't part of the plan. And I'm sorry if you feel like I tricked you."

I stand up and cross over to Danielle. "Why didn't you tell me sooner? Danielle, you don't have to face these things alone. Not anymore."

She lifts her eyes up to my face. "So, you're not mad?"

I wrap my arms around her waist. "Why would I be? Whatever happens next, we're going to face it together. A baby is a blessing."

Chapter Twenty-Eight: Danielle

I set the laptop down on the dresser and spin around to face Adrian. He's been on the patio for the past hour, looking out at the mountains in the distance, a mug of coffee in his hand.

Not wanting to disturb him, I've showered, changed out of my clothes, and gone over some of the notes for my article.

But I can't help but want to push it all away.

It's not a can of worms I want to open back up. Especially now that Adrian and I are finally on the same page.

Given everything we've had to go through to get here, I'm more than a little reluctant to risk it all, and for an article, no less.

A part of me is excited about the prospect of a future with Adrian. But the other part of me can't deny the pull of having the article published.

In big, bold headlines.

Gina has even dangled the possibility of it being on the front page.

A tactic to get me to write something juicy no doubt. Still, I trust that Gina is going to give me some wiggle room.

Since this is the first exclusive Adrian has ever agreed to, I know my boss doesn't want to take any chances.

Neither do I.

I have a week to write an article that paints Adrian in the best possible light while also giving the story an extra kick to keep it interesting.

After a quick email exchange with Gina this morning, I've made it clear to her that I have no intention of using Brian.

Now that I know about his existence, I can't bear the thought of Adrian's brother being used for clout or any kind of leverage.

Brian is a human being, with plenty of demons to battle, and I don't want to add to his problems. With a sigh, I turn my attention back to the laptop and pull a chair out.

As my fingers hover over the keyboard, my mind drifts to the pregnancy test at the bottom of my purse. I fish it out of my bag and place it on the desk close to the laptop.

Stop stalling. Just get it over with, so you and Adrian can move on.

Like planning a wedding.

I type up a few things, my eyes constantly flicking over to the ring. Half an hour passes. I hold the ring up to the light and admire the little diamonds along the outer edge of the band.

Then I hold it up higher and find myself picturing Adrian in a white suit on the beach, underneath a flower arch with crystal blue waters crashing in the background.

When I blink, I see myself walking toward Adrian in a floor-length strapless dress with a plunging V-neck, a tiara on top of my updo.

I'm so enamored with the scene that I don't realize Adrian has come back into the room. He draws me to him and wraps his arms around me from behind.

With a smile, he presses a kiss to the back of my neck and exhales.

"Penny for your thoughts?"

"I was just picturing us getting married," I reply, with a dreamy sigh. "How would you feel about a beach wedding?"

"I don't care if we get married in a junkyard in our sweatpants. As long as I get to marry you."

I spin around in his arms and link my fingers through his hair. "I would marry you in paper bags if I had to."

Adrian bridges the distance between us and kisses me. "Good, because you look amazing in everything, even a paper bags. Is that the article?"

"Yeah, I thought we could work on it a little bit if you're okay with that."

Adrian kisses me again, lingering a little longer this time. "You don't want to do the pregnancy test first?"

I shake my head and step out of his arms. "I'm still trying to work up the courage to take it."

Adrian's eyes move over my face. "You do know that you have nothing to worry about, right? I'm not going anywhere."

I clear my throat. "Yeah, I know."

But I'm more worried about my own reaction.

In the span of a few weeks, my entire life has been turned upside down and inside out. And I'm not sure how I feel about all of this happening at once.

As happy as I am to marry Adrian and start a life with him, I can't help but wonder if throwing a baby into the mix is going to be too much.

You know everything you need to know about Adrian, including that he's going to be a great father. Look at how much he cares about his brother. If that's not an indication of the kind of heart he has, I don't know what is.

When I sit down on the chair and gesture to Adrian to make himself comfortable, I realize it's not Adrian I'm worried about. I'm the one who came here in search of healing and a brand new start.

Out of the all scenarios I imagined, getting married to the owner of the ranch and having a baby with him, isn't one of them.

I tap my pen against the notepad. "Are you sure you're okay with me writing this? We don't have to do it, you know. I can tell Gina you changed your mind. She'll get over it."

"I've never given an exclusive before. I've never accepted an offer for one before." Adrian sat down in the middle of the bed and linked his fingers together. "It's not a secret that I'm not a fan of the press."

I chew on the tip of my pencil. "Why?"

"Because I feel like media is biased. And as much as we'd like to believe in freedom of the press, it's just a construct."

I let out a low whistle. "That's a pretty heavy accusation to make. You don't pull any punches, do you?"

Adrian offers me a small smile. "Are you asking as my fiancée or as a journalist?"

I hold his gaze. "Both."

Adrian leans forward, the smile lighting up his face and highlighting the stubble peppered across his jaw. "You can ask me anything you want, Danielle. But I reserve the right not to answer."

I scribble something down. "Fair enough. I'm assuming Brian is off-limits."

Adrian shifts from one side to the other. "I've spoken to Brian about the article, and he agreed that I can discuss him briefly."

I raise an eyebrow. "What does that mean?"

"It means I can acknowledge that he's had trouble in the past but that he's working on changing and redeeming himself," Adrian replies, without breaking our gaze. "Beyond that, I can't go into detail."

I underline something in my notepad. "Are you willing to discuss your aversion to the press?"

Adrian chuckles. "Now who's the one who's going all in?"

I set the notepad down with a thud. "I really need this article to be good. I need it to be fun and engaging, and I'm worried I don't know how to do that."

"You've written puff pieces before. How is this any different?"

"Puff pieces are heavy on the emotion and corniness. A piece like the one I'm working on is meant to balance humor, levity, heart, and logic. It's a tricky and fine line to navigate."

Adrian nods. "I can imagine. I have a suggestion."

"I'm all ears."

Adrian stands up in one fluid movement and holds his hand out to me. After a quick look at his face, I allow him to pull me to my feet.

He spins me out and then back into his arms with a grin that makes the butterflies in my stomach explode.

"Your suggestion is for us to dance?"

Adrian smiles and spins me out again. "It helps relax the body."

In one smooth move, he dips me back. The breath leaves my body in a whoosh.

I link my fingers over his neck and pull him down for a deep kiss.

He smiles against my mouth and pulls me back up.

In silence, we sway to our own beat, with his arms around my waist, and my head buried in the crook of his neck.

I inhale the familiar scent of him, sigh, and allow it to wash over me.

When he draws back a short while later, the sound of his phone slices through the air. With a frown, he fished it out of his pocket and pressed the device to his ear.

He says something, but I don't pay attention.

I am running my fingers through his ash brown hair and admiring the hard feel of his body pressed against mine when he hangs up.

I bring my head to rest against his chest, over the pounding of his heart. Adrian steps back, picks my purse off the dresser, and hands it to me.

"It's time."

I search his face. "Okay."

He leads me into the bathroom. I rip the box open and unfold the instructions.

After placing the stick under me, I squeeze my eyes shut. Then I put it on the bathroom sink. When I'm finished, I lather up some soap and wash my hands.

In silence, I press my head against Adrian's back. "It's going to be ready in ten minutes."

Adrian sets a timer on his phone. Then he carries me into the room and places me on the bed.

With a sigh, he climbs onto the bed and stretches out opposite me. I link my fingers under the pillow and drink in his features.

"We're going to be great parents," Adrian says, his voice barely above a whisper. "And don't worry about getting married before you start showing because I don't care."

I snort. "Thanks, but I kind of want to fit into a nice dress."

Adrian's lips lift into a half smile. "Fair enough. How do you feel about Tyrion as a name?"

I pull a face. "We are not naming our baby after a character in an R rated fantasy show on TV."

"Tyrion was a great character."

"Yeah and unless you want our baby to be bullied, the answer is still no."

"What about Arya?"

I pause. "I like that name. We can keep that one."

We spend the next few minutes discussing all of the names we can think of.

When the timer on Adrian's phone goes off, I stand up. I take a few deep breaths and march to the bathroom.

In the doorway, I pause and glance at Adrian over my shoulders. He gives me a reassuring smile and rises to his feet.

In the bathroom, I reach for the test with my heart pounding in my ears.

A slight tremor moves through me as I turn it over and hold it up to the light. Adrian steps into the bathroom, and I catch a glimpse of his reflection in the mirror.

When I see the two lines, I turn around and swallow past the lump in my throat.

"I'm pregnant."

Adrian's face breaks out into a grin. He draws me to him, places a hand over my stomach, and glances down at it. "I can't wait to meet you."

I laugh when Adrian scoops me into his arms and carries me back into the room.

We lie in bed. His head is on my stomach, and my hand is in his hair. I realize that I'm not as scared as I thought I was.

Although I know nothing about being a mom, and I have no idea what the future holds, I know that it can't be bad.

Not with Adrian by my side.

Together, the two of us can face anything.

Including parenthood.

"I can't wait to meet you either," I whisper, looking down at my stomach. "I love you, Adrian."

Adrian lifts his gaze up to mine, and his answering smile makes my stomach dip. "I love you too, Danielle."

I look into his eyes and an intense feeling of gratitude takes me over.

Tears well up in the back of my eyes, and a flash of my memories, from the moment I stepped out of the car when I first arrived at the ranch to right now.

Nothing matters anymore, I have what I dreamed of. What Adrian and I deserve to have together. Pure love.

Chapter Twenty-Nine: Danielle

Epilogue

Several months later

"Adrian Steel, a self-made millionaire, rose through the ranks of the business world with a few smart investments before striking off on his own and creating several successful projects, including his privately owned ranch in Montana, the Four Elements Ranch. On a quiet and warm July weekend, he wed Danielle

Clark in a private beach ceremony a few months ago. Ms. Clark, who works for a small newspaper, looked put together in a store-bought Vera Wang gown—"

I hold a hand up and pull a face. "I don't think I want to hear the end of that sentence."

Savannah sits down next to me and tucks her legs under her. "Don't you want to hear all about how handsome Adrian looked?"

I giggle and bring my arms up over my head. "I already know how handsome he looked. I was there, remember?"

Savannah held the magazine up and pointed to a picture of Adrian and I, standing beneath an arch of wildflowers, the crystal blue waters of the ocean behind us.

There are a few cropped faces in the picture, but there's no denying the bright smiles on our faces, or the familiar gleam in Adrian's eyes.

Between several in-person meetings with Gina to finalize the feature piece on Adrian and getting my entire life boxed up and moved out to Montana, I've had a lot on my plate.

It took two months just to get my life in the city sorted and settle into a routine at the ranch. Adrian was an absolute saint the entire time, but I knew he was getting impatient.

We've both been eager to start our lives together.

One month after asking me to marry him, Adrian and I finally held an intimate but tasteful beach wedding.

Due to the help of a wedding planner, the two of us were free to wander around and enjoy a stress-free period.

The planner took care of everything from the flower arrangements to the guest list.

Both Savannah and Brian took it upon themselves to supervise the entire thing. They get along really well.

Having already walked down the aisle once, I was relieved to have one less thing on my plate.

Now, months after the wedding, and a week-long trip to Morocco for the honeymoon, it's a relief to be back home on the ranch and starting my real life together with Adrian.

And with Savannah in between teaching jobs, it makes all the sense in the world for her to stay here with us.

Especially after that unforgettable moment when my doctor first placed the stethoscope on my stomach, and the rhythmic melody of the baby's heartbeat filled the room.

A few moments later, a hint of concern and confusion crossed her face, and with a furrowed brow, she looked up directly at us and delivered the surprising news: "I think you're having twins—I hear two heartbeats."

With a move of the device over my stomach, suddenly the sounds of two heart beat filled our ears and our heart.

The look on Adrian's face was priceless. His grin spread from ear to ear and his eye brows arched.

I didn't know if I should cry or laugh and a feeling of worry settled in my stomach. But Adrian assured me that it was going to be just fine.

We didn't expect to have twins. It was a heartwarming and nerve wracking experience.

I'm going to need all the help I can get, since the twins are coming in one short month. We decided against knowing the gender of our babies.

Although we picked two boys names and two girls names, we welcome any combination.

"....the pictures aren't very good. You'd think with the effort they go to in order to get their information, they'd at least manage to get a few decent pictures."

I blink and give a slight shake of my head. "I think they were a little more focused on sneaking the pictures in."

Savannah tosses the magazine next to her and crosses one ankle over the other. "How did they get in anyway? Didn't you have really tight security at the wedding?"

"My guess? Catering staff."

Savannah sighs. "They really are obsessed with Adrian."

I drape an arm over my stomach. "And the unborn babies."

Savannah twists to face me, but I can't make out her expression from behind her sunglasses. "You're going to be a mom soon."

"I still have one month to go, which is a good thing. Gives Adrian and I more time to get things ready."

"I thought the cabin was ready?"

I smile and shrug. "It is, but you know how Adrian is. He's a perfectionist, so he's still trying to get it just right. And it's twice as much work as if it was only one baby."

Savannah leans sideways and fishes her phone out of her purse. "I still can't believe you get to live out here. Doesn't it feel weird not to live in the city anymore?"

I study the pool in front of me, where Brian is currently doing laps on his back and soaking up the afternoon sun. "A little, but I think that'll go away. I love it here, and I think it's a great place to raise our babies."

"What about—"

My hand darts out, and I grab Savannah's arm a little too forcefully. "I'm sorry. I've been having these Braxton-Hicks contractions all day."

Savannah covers my hand with hers. "Do you want me to take you to the hospital?"

I shake my hand as another wave of pain shoots through my stomach. "No, it should be fine."

Savannah swings her legs over the side and places her glasses over her head. "Maybe I should take you back to the cabin. You could lie down, and we can watch a movie or something."

"No, really, I—" I stop mid-sentence and lower my head. Another sharp wave of pain hits me, making me clutch my stomach with both hands.

When I glance up, Brian is standing in front of me, dripping water all over our lounge chairs. I still can't tell which one is which. They even sound alike.

Their only difference is their clothes. I know what Adrian wears every day.

Brian shakes his head, sending droplets of water in every direction. Then he crouches in front of me, his eyes wide and unflinching.

"What's happening?"

I let out a low moan.

"She's having Braxton-Hicks contractions, or at least that's what she said. I think you need to find Adrian. We should take her to the hospital."

Brian shoves his feet into his flip flops and races out of the private pool area. When the gates creak shut behind him, Savannah drapes an arm over my shoulders and squeezes.

She uses her free hand to take out her phone and scrolls through it.

"Okay, you need to breathe deeply. I'm not getting the best signal right now, so I can't really look anything up." Savannah tosses the phone onto her own lounge chair and pushes me back.

I'm lying on my back with pillows under my upper body, staring up at the clear blue skies.

Savannah is stroking my arm and muttering to herself when her phone rings. Her fingers are slippery, and she drops it a few times. "What?"

Savannah pauses and gives me a confused look. "What do you mean you can't find Adrian? He has to be on the ranch."

"Check the stables," I say, in between heavy panting. "Or maybe the cabin. He said he was doing some manual labor round the ranch today."

Whatever that meant.

Another wave of pain washes over me, and I cry out.

Savannah hangs up and dials emergency services. Then she helps me to my feet, and we hobble out of the private pool area, and in the direction of the main cabin.

There, Savannah helps me sink into the nearest chair and hurries over to Maureen.

Moments later, Savannah helps me change and Maureen grabs the duffel bag I prepared for when I went into labor.

My eyes widen. "I don't think I'll need that yet."

Savannah takes the duffel bag from Maureen and sets it on the floor beneath my feet. "Better safe than sorry."

"We're still trying to reach, Mr. Steele, but he's not answering." Maureen glances from Savannah to me and then back again. "Is there anything I can do to help?"

"Make sure the security team knows that an ambulance is on the way," Savannah says. "With any luck, it won't be much longer."

In the distance, the familiar siren sound slices through the air.

Savannah and Maureen each take one arm and help me hobble outside, into the summer air. A warm breeze drifts past as we wait on the porch.

The ambulance is heading towards us, kicking up dust and gravel as it does. On the last step, I stop, bend over, and squeeze Savannah and Maureen's hands.

There's a low gushing sound, and I feel something trickle down the inside of my thighs seconds as my water breaks. Savannah says something, but I can't make out what it is.

Suddenly, I'm being helped onto a gurney, and Savannah doesn't let go of my hand until they hoist me up. I wave at Maureen as Savannah climbs into the back of the ambulance with me.

The doors slam shut, and it drives off.

A dark haired man in a black and blue uniform is standing opposite Savannah and holding my wrist. "Ma'am, how far along are you?"

"Eight months," I wheeze, in between heavy breaths. "I'm having twins."

"Your pulse is thready. I'm going to need you to put on an oxygen mask." He opens a cupboard and helps me secure the mask.

Then he sits down and takes out a pressure cuff. I fix my gaze on Savannah who is holding one of my hands and using her other hand to send messages on her phone.

Once we reach the hospital, they put me in a wheelchair and wheel me through a set of double doors. The smell of disinfectant hits me first, followed quickly by the smell of sweat.

Then I'm being wheeled down a blue hallway, and a group of doctors and nurses in scrubs descends upon me.

Savannah is struggling to answer with their questions when I hear Adrian's familiar voice.

I prop myself up and see him racing toward us, his wet hair matted to his forehead. Brian is struggling to match his stride.

As soon as he reaches me, Adrian brushes my hair out of my eyes and kisses my forehead.

"You didn't think I'd miss the birth, did you?"

I let out a shaky laugh. "I was beginning to worry."

Adrian takes my hand in his and kisses it. "Not a chance. I'm going to be one of the first people to look at Diana and Nyla."

"Or Miles and Jacob," Savannah adds, breathlessly. "We'll be outside when you're ready."

I twist to watch as I'm wheeled away from Savannah and Brian, who are standing side by side.

Brian peels off his sweater and hands it to Savannah, who is still in her one-piece swimsuit with a robe over it.

She offers me a smile and a wave before the doors slam shut behind her. Then it's a flurry of activity as I'm taken through another set of doors, and my robe is pulled off.

I'm cold and anxious as a petite blonde-haired nurse helps me into a paper thin hospital gown in my private room.

Through the glass window, I see Adrian pulling on scrubs and a mask. Wordlessly, he helps the nurse prop me up on the bed and takes one of my hands in his.

The medical staff that surrounded me has dwindled to four, a total of two nurses and two doctors.

One of the nurses, the petite brunette who helped me out of my clothes, is setting up some kind of drip.

The other nurse is adjusting a tray of medical tools.

My contractions are getting closer and closer, and with the water broken they can't take any risks. The babies have to come out now.

Something pinches my arm, and I grip Adrian's hand tighter. "We were supposed to have a couple of more weeks to month."

Adrian squeezes my hand. "I guess they were too excited to be here."

I throw myself back against the mattress. "Where were you anyway?"

"At the waterfall," Adrian replies, his voice a little muffled. He pulls down the mask and gives me a smile. "I must have been out of sight when Brian came looking for me. It's a good thing I had other things to do, or I wouldn't have cut it short."

I release a shaky breath. "Yeah, true."

One of the nurses props my legs up, and I set them down on either side of the bed. The Doctor Pierce comes in, dressed in scrubs.

Her eyes are bright and kind.

"Are you ready?"

Sweat breaks out across my forehead. "No."

She pats my knees. "That's okay. We're all here for you, Danielle. In a little bit, I'm going to need you to start pushing."

I shake my head and more sweat breaks out across my forehead. "I can't. I can't do it. It's too painful."

The doctor, whose face is half obscured by the mask looks over at the petite nurse. She steps forward and adjusts something in my IV drip.

Then she steps back and gives the doctor a nod. Doctor Pierce holds her gloved hands up and smiles.

"How do you feel now? Do you feel better?"

I pause and give her a quick nod. "Yes."

"Good. We need you to push, when I tell you."

My eyes widen and dart over to Adrian. "What if I end up being a horrible mom?"

Adrian comes to stand next to me and takes my hand in his. He brings it up to his lips for a kiss and lowers the mask.

After pressing a kiss on each one of my knuckles, he gives me a blindingly white smile, the same one that made me fall in love with him.

My stomach gives an odd little dip. "That's not an answer."

"I thought it was pretty obvious." Adrian chuckles and squeezes my hand. "You're going to be an amazing mom. And you're not going to do it alone."

I grip his hand tighter as a wave of pain washes over me. "You better not leave me."

"I won't," Adrian promises, before pressing another kiss to the center of my hand. He smiles and stands up straighter. "Are you ready?"

Another wave of contractions wash over me, and I falter. "I don't know."

Doctor Pierce's head disappears, and I feel her cold fingers between my legs. I release a sharp hiss of pain and try to inch away from her. "Doc, what are you doing?"

"You're fully dilated." Doctor Pierce looks back up at me, and her brows are furrowed together. "On the count of three, I'm going to need you to push."

I prop myself up on my elbow and square my shoulders. "On three or after three?"

"After." Doctor Pierce glances at Adrian and then at me. "One, two, three. Push."

I release a deep breath and use every ounce of energy at my disposal. My entire body hurts, my muscles aching and screaming in protest.

I'm panting heavily now, and sweating like crazy. Still, I'm dimly aware of Doctor Pierce's voice in the background, urging me on.

Adrian still has my hand in his, and he drapes his free arm over my shoulders. Now he is whispering something into my ear, but I can't make out what he's saying.

My body is folding in on itself.

It feels like I've run a mile.

At Doctor Pierce's behest, I give another strong push and heave a shaky breath. "Is it over? Can I stop now?"

Doctor Pierce shakes her head. "Not yet, but you're almost there. Come on, just a few more pushes."

I collapse against the pillow and shake my head, slowly at first then faster and faster. "I can't. I can't. Just get them out of me some other way."

"Breathe," Adrian whispers, into my ear. He squeezes my hand tighter. "You can do it, D. Just focus on me."

I twist my head to look at him and study his handsome face.

It calms the erratic racing of my heart, but the discomfort is still there. I refused epidural at first but at one point I couldn't take the pain anymore.

Doctor Pierce's hands are on my knees now, cold and urgent. I swallow, keep my gaze on Adrian, and inhale through my nose then out through my mouth.

I do this a few more times until spots dance in my field of vision, and I can barely hold myself up.

Before I collapse against the pillow again, a sharp cry fills the room.

Through my blurry vision, I struggle to sit up. Doctor Pierce's head emerges again, and even through her mask, I can tell she's beaming.

"It's a girl," Doctor Pierce says, a smile in her voice. "She's a beautiful and healthy baby girl."

Out of the corner of my eye, I see a flash of movement. The nurse put the baby on my chest for a few seconds, and then whisks her away.

Adrian laughs. "Nyla is here. Now let's welcome Diana now."

Then Adrian releases my hand and bends down to kiss my forehead. He tilts my head back and gives me a kiss on the lips, leaving me even more light-headed.

I link my fingers over his neck and sigh, allowing the smell of him to wash over me. When Adrian pulls back, he brings his forehead to rest against mine.

I'm trying not to breathe too loudly as I listen for my baby.

She is fussing and whimpering while the nurse, who is standing on the other side of the room, cleans and examines her.

Adrian shifts away and wanders over to the baby to check on her.

I see him peer down at her, and my heart swells to twice its size. Doctor Pierce's voice pierces through the fog, and I find myself looking back at her.

Doctor Pierce pats the knee closest to her. "Are you ready to push again?"

I suck in my breath. "No, but I don't have a choice, do I?"

Doctor Pierce pats my knee again. "You've got this, Danielle. Take a deep breath and remember to keep taking them."

Adrian returns to my side and fluffs up the pillows. After propping them up on either side of me, he takes my hand in his. "Here we go. You can do this, babe."

I square my shoulders and tilt my head back to look up at the ceiling. "Okay."

"One, two, three and push."

I use whatever energy I have left to do as the doctor says. When I'm done, I push again and again, and the last of my energy is seeping away, leaving me dizzy and light-headed.

Adrian drifts in and out of my field of vision, but he's still by my side and refusing to let go of my hand no matter how hard I squeeze.

It feels like I'm going to break his bones, but he doesn't falter.

I focus on him until I can't focus on anything.

Then I switch my gaze to Doctor Pierce, who is alert and eager.

She offers one encouraging word after the next, the smile never leaving her face. Another baby's scream fills the air.

Doctor Pierce emerges with a bundle in her arms and looks up at us. She lowers her mask, and there's a furrow between her brows.

"You're never going to believe this."

Adrian drops my hand and takes a step in the doctor's direction. "What is it? What's wrong?"

My arms are shaking as I try to sit up. "What happened? What's wrong with my baby?"

"There's nothing wrong with your baby. Diana is a boy," she says with a big smile on her face.

I frown. "Oh! I thought we were having identical twins. How is this possible?"

Doctor Pierce hands the second bundle over to the nearest nurse, the one with wisps of blonde hair peeking out from under the cap.

She puts the second baby on my chest for a second before taking him away.

"It's not unheard of. Sometimes these things happen," Dr. Pierce confirms.

Adrian looks back at me, a dazed expression on his face. "We have a boy and a girl."

I nod and sink back against the bed. "It's unbelievable, isn't it? I wasn't expecting that at all."

Doctor Pierce strides over to where the babies are being taken care of. Both of them are still crying and fussing, and they have been put side by side in their beds.

She listens to their heartbeats with her stethoscope while the nurses watch her intently.

As soon as she's done, she turns to both of us with another smile. After untying the straps of the mask from around her mouth, she tucks it away.

"We're going to take the babies away for a little bit. When we're done, we'll run a few tests but everything looks good."

I'm fighting to keep my eyes open by now. "We don't have any pairs of names ready for one of each."

"We have two girl names and two boy names," Adrian adds. "Obviously, we didn't expect this"

I stifle a yawn, my eyes watering. "Do we have to name them right away?"

"We can call them the Steele babies for now," Doctor Pierce suggests, her expression still calm and patient. "As soon as you settle on the names, you can let us know."

Adrian's expression lights up. "Wait, let me go tell Savannah and Brian."

He darts out before I can stop him, and Doctor Pierce stands next to me. She is fussing over me and checking my vitals when Brian and Savannah appear behind the door, sneaking a look inside.

The two of them look reluctant as Adrian gestures to me and then makes a sweeping hand gesture to indicate the babies.

Once he's done, he moves closer to them, and I can see their lips moving.

I look over at my babies, and my heart swells to twice its size. "Are they going to be okay? Since they were born early?"

"It was only a couple of weeks early, so it's fine. They seem better than fine," Doctor Pierce says, her fingers cool and steady against my wrist. "Would you like me to get you anything?"

I yawn. "No, I think I'm okay."

Doctor Pierce pats my hand. "You did great. Deliveries can be hard, and you had to bring two babies into the world. That's no easy feat."

I pull the covers up to my chin. "I feel like I've run a marathon."

Doctor Pierce chuckles. "That sounds about right. I remember how painful it was to have my twins. Just make sure you take it easy over the next few weeks."

Adrian bursts back into the room, his eyes bright with excitement. "Savannah and Brian suggested names, but I didn't like them."

I giggle. "So, why do you look so happy?"

"Because when I rejected all of their suggestions, Savannah told me to just—"

I yawn again, louder this time, and it drowns out the rest of his sentence.

"Can you tell me what you decided on later? I'm exhausted."

Before I drift off, I insist on holding the twins in my arms. Gently, one is placed on either side, and they nuzzle against me. I press them closer and squeeze my eyes shut.

Adrian drapes an arm over my shoulders and kneels down next to me. I listen for the sound of their light breathing.

Then the nurses take them away and place them in their beds, side by side.

I watch with a heavy heart as they're wheeled away. "Do you think they'll be okay?"

Adrian kisses each of my hands. "Do you want me to go with the nurses?"

I nod, a little too eagerly. "Please."

"Okay, let me just bring Savannah in here." Adrian drops a kiss to my forehead and hurries out. He comes back in with Savannah hot on his heels.

She drags a chair across the floor, takes my hand in hers, and smiles.

I manage to muster a half-smile before exhaustion takes over, and my eyes fall shut.

It doesn't take me long to fall asleep.

All my dreams are of my babies.

·♥·♥·♥·♥·♥·

I stare down at my daughter's beautiful face and touch my pinkie to her tiny nose. "I still can't believe they're here."

Adrian is standing next to the bed, rocking our son back and forth. "Me either."

"What are the chances of us having fraternal twins?"

Adrian glances up and blows out a breath. "It is possible. I have identical twins genes from both of my parents, but we got fraternal twins."

I frown. "Interesting."

Adrian is still rocking our son back and forth. "They are just perfect, just like their mom."

I smile and look back down. "They are perfect! Just like their dad."

It was a surprise to hear the doctor announce the arrival of our son, shortly after our daughter.

My mind is still reeling, and my entire body feels like I've been run over by a truck. But it is all worth it.

When Adrian hands over our sleeping son, I pass him our daughter, and my smile grows wider.

Adrian sits down in the chair next to the bed. "So, I guess we should choose their names."

"I like Miles for our son," I whisper, before tucking him against my chest. "He looks like a Miles, don't you think?"

Adrian leans forward. "And I like Nyla. Miles and Nyla. It has a nice ring to it."

Slowly, he hands me our daughter. Both babies nestle against me, breathing quietly. Adrian climbs onto the bed, as carefully as possible, and drapes an arm over my shoulders.

"Welcome to the world, my precious little babies."

"We're your Mommy and Daddy," Adrian adds, in an equally soft voice. "And we love you so much already."

I press my head against his side and smile. "I love our little family, Adrian."

"Me too."

THE END

Chapter Thirty: Sneak Peek

I hope you enjoyed "Surprise Babies For My Billionaire Rancher".

Here is a sneak peek of the next book:

"My Secret Baby With The Billionaire: An Age Gap Second Chance Romance"

I have read ALL of Olivia's books, and I have to say I haven't come across any of her books that I didn't like or enjoy. This is another great story of love and lies and hate that just draws you in. Jared's character is so much fun, and he seems like such an ideal man. I love how they treat each other—so playfully despite their age difference. Really sexy. Love that in this one his wealth is not the focus of the story and she's such an independent woman. I get lost in her stories, and once again, I enjoyed this one very much!!!! (review on Amazon)

This is a wonderful story that I loved from start to finish. The plot is too good, it has everything I love, age-gap, secret romance and secret baby. Sophie and Jared met when the two of them boarded the same taxi, then they met at a wedding, then the two started a relationship, but they had many things against them and what led to their separation was that they wanted different things for their futures. Years later they met again and after fixing more complications they achieved their happiness forever. (review on Amazon)

To start things off with this book the cover is HOT. The second-best thing is how Sophie meets Jared and they have some of the best toe-curling sex you could imagine. It made me want to be in Sophie's shoes. :)

I was really glad that the book ended in a HEA and that things between her and Jared worked out. I am not giving any details away from this book, but wow it is going to give you one heck of a ride. This book is a 10-star read in my opinion. (review on Amazon)

When I came to town for my sister's wedding, I never expected to meet a gorgeous silver fox, let alone get pregnant.

At first he made my blood boil. I thought I'd never see him again.

Until I got to the wedding.

Turns out he's more than just another wedding guest.

Jared Fox is my baby sister's father-in-law.

He wants me, and I'm powerless to resist him.

His gaze on me triggers butterflies in my stomach.

Despite our age difference, the heat between us is wild and delicious.

His touch on my skin leaves a trail of fireworks that keeps burning hotter and hotter.

When he whispers in my ear, the whole world disappears.

All I see are his hungry eyes and his thirsty lips for me.

He showers me with his affection, and our relationship feels like it couldn't be more perfect.

Until my heart breaks into pieces, and I also find out I'm carrying his baby.

Content Warning: This book includes spicy content. Reader discretion is advised.

My Secret Baby With The Billionaire: An Age Gap Second Chance Romance

Chapter One: Sophie

"What do you mean you can't find Cameron? You guys are supposed to be getting married in four hours."

With a sigh, I wince and pull the phone away from my ear. "Okay, Mel. I'm going to need you to calm down because I only got about half of that."

"He was supposed to stop by the apartment to pick up a few things, including an extra shirt in case he sweats. You know he sweats a lot."

I frown and wheel my suitcase behind me. "No, I really didn't know that. I could've lived without that piece of information."

"How can you joke at a time like this?"

I push through the glass doors and am met with a blast of hot air, raising the hairs on the back of my neck. With one hand, I cradle the phone between my neck and shoulder, and with the other, I move the suitcase.

I come to a stop on the edge of the sidewalk and glance down both sides of the street, eager for a glimpse of a taxi.

Heat rises from the asphalt and shimmers. The afternoon sun is high in the sky, and I've already sweated through my shirt. But none of those matters.

Not when my little sister's wedding is in a few hours, and she's having a meltdown. When I find

Cameron, I'm the one who's going to give him a piece of my mind.

"....do you think he could be having cold feet?"

I squint into the distance and spot a cab, crawling forward at a snail's pace. "I honestly don't know, Mel. I thought the two of you were doing well. Did it seem like he was having second thoughts?"

Out of the corner of my eye, I see a flash of movement. An older man in a suit with some salt and pepper hair steps forward and blocks the cab door.

His phone is pressed to his ear, and his back turned to me as he yanks on the knob. With a scowl, I slide in after him, set my suitcase on my lap, and slam the door shut with a thud.

"Mel, I'm going to have to call you back." I end the call and twist my body to face him. "You can't steal my cab."

He turns to face me, a furrow appearing between his brows. "It doesn't have your name on it. This cab is fair game."

"I don't think so. I have a wedding to get to."

"So do I. And you were on the phone."

"So were you."

He puts his phone into his jacket and faces me completely. Suddenly, I notice two things at the same time.

One, he's incredibly attractive with an angular jaw, almond shaped eyes and dark hair with some white hair, that made him look even more attractive.

Two, his custom-made suit costs more than I'll ever make in this life. It does little to hide the broad shoulders, and the lean, muscular body underneath.

Holy hell. He is the most attractive man I've ever seen. And I can't decide if I want to chew him out for trying to steal my ride right from under my nose, or if I want to lean forward and kiss him squarely on the lips.

Before I can decide on either of these options, he reaches into his pocket and pulls out a wad of bills. "Why don't I give you something for your trouble?"

I glare at him. "I'm not interested in your money. I need to get to the hotel, so I can find my sister afterward. And if you have that much money, why are you even taking a cab? You can have your own private ride."

He sighs. "Well, I like taking a cab sometimes. Life is not always about choosing the most comfortable way, annnd...mmmm....mmmy driver is stuck in traffic. Why don't we share the cab then? I'm going to the Westin Piedmont hotel."

"So am I."

"Fine."

"Great."

The driver, a bald-headed man in a Hawaiian shirt with pit stains and a protruding stomach, shrugs and eases away from the curb.

Through the glass, I see cars whiz past in either direction, tall and gleaming buildings glistening in the distance.

It feels strange to be back after all this time. Leave it to Melanie to bring the family back together out of the blue.

I shift and squirm underneath the suitcase. I pick my phone up and send Melanie a quick message. Once she responds, I sigh and press my face against the cool glass.

"We could ask the driver to pull over, so you can put your bag in the trunk."

"So, you can tell him to drive off? I don't think so."

"You really have trust issues, don't you?"

I swing my gaze back to his and raise an eyebrow. "So, you're telling me you haven't thought about it?"

"The thought did cross my mind." His lips twitch in amusement, a strange glint in the depth of his hazel eyes. "But you've gone through all of this trouble…you must really love your sister."

"I do."

He flashes me a smile and holds his hand out. "I'm Jared."

I hesitate, then hold my own hand out. A jolt of electricity immediately courses up my arm. "Sophie."

"It's nice to meet you, Sophie."

"I would say the same, but I'd be lying."

Jared chuckles and continues to hold my hand. "I like a woman who isn't afraid to speak her mind."

"I like a man who doesn't steal cabs."

Jared releases my hand and sits up straighter. "It looks like we both have strong opinions."

"I guess so."

My skin is still tingling where he touched me, and I can't get over it. *Get a grip, Soph. I know it's been a while since you've been with a man, but you can't throw yourself at the first man you see. No matter how good looking he is.*

Because I didn't have time to be distracted. I have a groom to locate.

We spend the rest of the ride in silence, my fingers moving furiously over my keyboard. Once we pull up outside the hotel, I get out of the cab first, the suitcase falling onto the pavement with a clattering sound.

I scowl and bend down to pick it up. When I wheel around to pay the driver, he's already driven off, joining a slew of other cars headed in the opposite direction.

Jared has a small bag at his feet and is messaging someone.

"How much do I owe you?"

Without glancing up, Jared brushes past me and up the stairs to the hotel. "Don't worry about it. I owe you for trying to steal your cab."

I scowl at his back. "So, you do admit it."

At the top of the stairs, Jared pauses to flash me another smile over his shoulders. I try to ignore the butterflies in my stomach as I race past him and into the carpeted lobby.

I wheel my suitcase over hardwood floors in the direction of the main desk, where a group of uniformed men and women are sitting.

As soon as I'm done checking in, I take my bag and hurry to the elevator. Before the doors ping shut, I catch a fleeting glimpse of Jared.

He's leaning casually over the counter, a small but a playful smile on his lips, while a uniformed woman stands across the counter from him, clearly captivated by his presence.

I roll my eyes, and the elevator door pings shut. On the fourth floor, I get out and hurry down a carpeted hallway with doors on either side.

Once I reach my room, I swipe the key card and grope for the switch. Yellow florescent lights blind me as I kick the door shut and dial Melanie's number.

"Okay, I'm at the hotel, and I'm on my way to you now. Are you at Mom and Dad's?"

"I called his friends. They're searching everywhere for him."

"Have you tried his mom? You mentioned that he likes to go there sometimes."

"I didn't think of that. Soph, you're the best."

"I'll be there soon."

With that, I hang up and change my clothes. An hour later, I am driving Melanie around in her wedding dress, the windows of Mom's Prius rolled down and soft country music playing in the background.

We are circling back to our parents' house when Melanie receives a call and breathes a sigh of relief. "Okay, they found him at his mom's. Apparently, he fell asleep, and his phone ran out of juice."

"At least it wasn't cold feet."

Melanie adjusts the folds of her dress around her. "Oh, I'm still going to give him a piece of my mind. After the wedding."

I reach between us and squeeze her hand. "Atta girl."

Melanie sighs and stares out the window. "Do you think I'm doing the right thing?"

With a frown, I pull to a stop outside our parents' house and kill the engine. I twist to look at her and raise an eyebrow. "You're asking me for marriage advice?"

Melanie turns, so she's facing me completely. "Well, yeah. Who else am I supposed to ask?"

"You could ask mom or dad. I don't think I'm the best person to ask about this, but yeah. You and Cameron are a good match."

And he did strike me as the kind of man who is going to stick around through thick and thin.

Melanie and I might want different things out of life, but I want her to be happy.

I push the car door open and spill out. After a brief pause, Melanie does the same and stands in the middle of the sidewalk in her wedding dress and lifts her gaze up to the sun.

The door to the house bursts open, and our parents emerge in the doorway, in a suit and lilac dress, respectively, wearing identical anxious expressions.

Once they see us, they wave us over, and I steer Melanie in their direction.

As soon as we step in through the door, everyone breathes a sigh of relief. Suddenly, we are surrounded by family and friends on all side, many stopping to greet me and pull me into hugs.

I keep an eye on Melanie who is swept upstairs and into her old room where her friends are already waiting. I stay downstairs for a few more minutes, making small talk until my sister calls out for me.

When I go upstairs and see her sitting in a chair facing her dresser, I wrap my arms around her for a hug. "You're going to be fine, sis. This is going to be a great wedding."

Melanie nods and smiles. "I'd steer clear of Aunt Josephine if I were you. She's been talking about setting you up with her accountant."

I chuckle and release Melanie. "Maybe he won't be so bad. You know I have awful taste in men."

"He's like three times your age," Melanie whispers, pausing to glance over her shoulders. "I've seen him. Trust me, you'll thank me for this later."

Before I can respond, our cousin sweeps in, with her hair piled high on top of her head and reeking of a pungent smelling perfume.

Melanie and I exchange a quick look in the mirror and smile.

As soon as she leaves, I wave my hand in front of my face and close the door to her bedroom.

"It's time for more important stuff."

Melanie stands up and smooths out her dress. "Like what?"

"Please tell me you've reconsidered the edible lingerie Aunt Christine got you."

Melanie throws her head back and laughs. "Don't even remind me. I'm going to be thinking of that every time I see any edible lingering set."

I giggle. "I think that's the point."

We both laugh out loud.

Read more for FREE on Kindle Unlimited:
https://www.amazon.com/dp/B0CKX6P8N4
Stand-Alone Book Link

Visit Author Page for more books by Olivia;

https://www.amazon.com/author/oliviamack

· ♥ · ♥ · ♥ · ♥ · ♥ ·

Get your FREE copy of my book:
"Off Limits NAVY SEAL: An Age Gap Best Friend's Brother Romance"

https://dl.bookfunnel.com/p5b9qs6g5b

That night when I slammed into a wall with a heartbeat and a pair of green eyes, my life took a sudden turn.

Soon after, I found myself in the back seat of his car, losing my V-Card.

To my surprise, the man with whom I had fogged the car windows with that night, was my best friend's estranged brother.

And when I agreed to vacation with my friend's family, I didn't think he would be sleeping in the room next to mine.

This bad boy and ex- NAVY SEAL definitely adds an exciting twist to this family getaway.

Every time he enters the premises, I'm hit with a rush of sensations, his scent alone sends shivers down my spine.

His sister warned me that he was cold-hearted and prone to breaking hearts, but I'm unable to resist him.

I find myself sneaking into his bed late at night, wrinkling his sheets.

Now, I question whether it's love or just a temporary game.

My heart aches with uncertainty, yet this secret relationship ignites a passion I can hardly control.

· ♥ · ♥ · ♥ · ♥ · ♥ ·

If you enjoyed my books above, you will also enjoy my next book.

Here is a sneak peek of:
"Damaged Forbidden Billionaire: A Bad Boy Surprise Pregnancy Boss' Daughter Romance"

This has a deep and emotional storyline that captures your heart and won't let go. Luke and Sasha met at a club. He has the dangerous bad boy look with all his tattoos, earring, gold chain necklace, long hair hair hanging in his eyes, t-shirt and stressed jeans. He also rides a motorcycle. Sasha, the attorney is the put together career woman who seems out of his league. They spend the night together. The next day, she and her 2 partners, start as the new legal counsel for Constellation Properties. They are introduced to the board and CFO, Luke Maddox — her one night stand. It's a roller coaster ride from that moment on. The characters were well developed and I loved Luke, his past left him with many scars and you can't help rooting for them both. Awesome story! (review on Amazon)

Forbidden Billionaire is absolutely stunning. A dynamic, heart-wrenching, inspiring, beautiful story of love, loss, and togetherness. So much more than I ever expected it to be, I could not put this book down. Luke and Sasha have phenomenal chemistry and a love for the ages. The supporting characters blend the different storylines together magnificently, and the world building is incredible. I found myself swept away and unwilling to come back until the end of the story. I did not want this book to end! It has touched me in profound ways...it is unlike any other love story I have ever read and shot straight to the top of my favorites. After I read the last sentence of this novel, I sat in silence absorbing it for quite a while. This is such an amazing book. We should all be so lucky as to share a connection as deep and beautiful as Luke and Sasha. (review on Amazon)

loved this story much more than I thought I would. It was more in-depth and more to it then I expected. It drew me in right from the start and I could not put it down till I was done. (review on Amazon)

My night out with friends turned into a whirlwind romantic adventure with a stranger, Mr. Tattoo Muscle.

Riding on the back of his motorcycle was exhilarating and completely out of my element.

His enigmatic nature is intriguing, leaving me wanting him more and more.

His deep, soulful eyes hold secrets, and I feel inexplicably connected to him.

None of that was planned and neither was the positive pregnancy test.

Shockingly, my baby daddy turned out to be one of my dad's most trusted employees, and he has the worst reputation when it comes to women.

His rough exterior hints at a complicated past, and I want to know everything about him.

My dad forbade him from even looking at me and disappointing him would lead to consequences.

I've seen his passion and his pain, I know all his secrets, but I can't stay away.

I want him to claim me and the baby.

But I'm uncertain of our future, I wonder if he would stay or run away and hide.

Content Warning: This book includes spicy content and the emotional experience of pregnancy loss. Reader discretion is advised.

Damaged Forbidden Billionaire: A Bad Boy Surprise Pregnancy Boss' Daughter Romance,

Chapter one: Sasha

"What will it be tonight—blonde or brunette?"

I snort and my best friend Emilia Finlay aims her mojito glass across the club. "I think I'll have the black tonight."

I grab her wrist and pull her glass down on the bar. "Don't you know it's rude to point? You'll tip him off!"

"I think he likes it!"

Emilia waggles her eyebrows at the strapping, muscular black guy standing against the opposite wall.

Ten other guys stand around over there. Emilia and my other best friend, Ivy Judd, can't put their eyeballs back in their sockets from ogling the specimens on display.

Emilia is right about the guy liking her attention. I can't deny that. The black guy sees her making eyes at him and he grins back at her. He crooks his finger to call her over to him and she laughs.

"I'm going for blonde." Ivy gives a very tiny wave to a guy in the center of the pack. He has the most obviously peroxide bleached hair I've ever seen and his eyebrows and eyelashes are the darkest brown ever. "Yum! Come to Mama, baby!"

She squirms in her sequined dress and the guy smirks back at her.

I roll my eyes and turn away on my stool to face the bar. "You guys are shameless! Is this any way for future millionaires to act?"

"You bet it is!" Emilia gives her big black stud a suggestive wink and finally suffers to turn around on the stool next to me. "Oh, come on, Sasha! Let your hair down! We earned this."

Ivy slides onto a stool on my other side. "She's right, Sasha. Tonight, is probably our last chance to have some fun before we get sent up to life imprisonment under the worst tyrant in corporate history."

"Shut up!" I yell back. "My dad is not a tyrant!"

"A couple hundred ex-employees say otherwise," Emilia replies. "Your dad's reputation is notorious. I don't know what we were thinking applying for the legal contract for Constellation Properties. He's known as one of the toughest bosses in the industry."

"We were thinking this is the biggest, most lucrative contract we've ever even heard of," Ivy chimes in. "We were thinking we stood to make a boatload of money as Constellation Properties' legal team and this contract would put us on the map. That's what we were thinking."

"My dad is not a tyrant," I insist. "He's tough, but fair. He won't mistreat us."

Emilia sighs. "I guess it doesn't make much difference. We've been slaving away ever since we graduated from law school. We've worked harder for ourselves than we ever did for any boss. Carter London can't possibly be any harder on us than we've been on ourselves."

"Exactly," I reply. "Besides, we earned this contract by being the best there is. He knows that. He won't treat us as anything less than the professionals we are."

"He won't have a choice," Ivy remarks. "His corporate board hired us. Being his daughter had nothing to do with it."

"He dissuaded them from hiring me if he did anything," I tell them. "He wouldn't want anyone even to suspect that he gave me special treatment."

"Wow!" Emilia breathes. "He sounds really tough! I'm sorry, baby. What a rotten childhood you must have had."

Ivy bursts out laughing and I have to join in. "Yeah, right!" Ivy fires back. "He worships the ground she walks on. She's Daddy's little girl."

I turn bright red and try to focus on my drink, but this talk about our upcoming contract with Constellation Properties has ruined my appetite for relaxation.

I want to get back to the office and get to work. We have way too much to do to get ready for our upcoming contract.

A strange mix of excitement, terror, and something like stone-cold determination floods me when I think about what a massive step up this contract is for our firm.

Emilia, Ivy, and I have been keeping our noses to the grindstone ever since law school—and even before.

We've built London Partners Group from nothing and our hard work is finally paying off.

Now we just have to ride the wave and enjoy our hard-earned success. What could possibly go wrong? Nothing better go wrong and none of the three of us will let anything go wrong.

We worked too hard for this and we're all committed to the same goal.

The other two must be thinking the same thing because now it's Ivy's turn to sigh. "Well, I guess none of us are cut out for having any fun, anyway. Let's just finish our drinks and get out of here. This girls' night out was a terrible idea."

"No way!" Emilia springs off her stool. "We aren't leaving until we make fools of ourselves. Come on, Ivy! We have too hot studs waiting for us over there."

"You know what? You're right!" Ivy stands up, downs her drink, and squares her shoulders. "Let's go."

Emilia grabs her hand and elbows me. "You better wrangle yourself a stud for the night, Sasha. If we find out you went home alone tonight, you'll have egg on your face."

She shoots me one last wicked smirk and turns away. Ivy lets out a high, extra-loud laugh and they sashay out across the dance floor to go lasso their chosen studs.

I don't turn around. I don't want to watch the mayhem ensue.

If their plan is to make fools of themselves tonight, I'd rather have egg on my face from going home alone than to be anywhere within a hundred miles of the fallout.

I take another sip of my drink and decide to watch people instead.

Maybe inspiration will strike, or on the other hand, I might just go back to my apartment and go over the documents from Constellation Properties.

I can't think of anything I'd rather do than put myself in the best possible position to ensure our firm successfully executes this contract.

I raise my glass to finish my drink when I see him. The bar forms a big square in the center of the club.

At least a hundred people crowd around it on all sides so just one of them should blend in with the mass of bodies.

For some reason I can't explain, this guy stands out a mile from everyone around him. He isn't the biggest and he definitely isn't the best dressed.

He isn't wearing classy business casual like a lot of the other guys in the club. They're all trying to show off for the girls how studly they are, but this guy just naturally radiates studliness without even trying.

He wears a tight white t-shirt over nothing but muscle and tattoos. Ink runs down both arms in two full Japanese floral sleeves.

The V neck of his t-shirt reveals the two curved sides of his chest tats ending in a long, thing bare cleft where his kimono would fall.

A plain brown leather belt surrounds his narrow, chiseled waist and he sports faded blue jeans.

They aren't acid-distressed, either, which means he didn't buy them faded and worn to make himself look cool. They really are faded and frayed from years of wear and tear.

He wears a single gold chain around his ropy, muscular neck and a matching one around his left wrist, but these chains aren't heavy, ostentatious gangster-style bling.

They're just thick enough to look masculine, but not thick enough to draw anyone's attention to them—no one's attention but mine.

His straight brown hair hangs over his eyes and he turns away from talking to someone next to him to pay the bartender for his drink.

The strobe lights on the dance floor glint off the earring in one ear. He immediately catches my attention simply because he looks so different from everyone else here.

He looks wild and dangerous—like he might actually be the hardened motorcycle gangster criminal that every other wannabe wants to look like but isn't.

Now that might be the kind of guy I could take home, have a wild fling with, and then forget about the next morning. He looks dangerous enough to be exciting, and I would never have to see him again.

We obviously don't move in the same circles, and I could laugh about it later without worrying about him coming back to haunt me.

I sip my drink while I watch him. He talks to a few people on either side of him, but I can tell right away that he's here alone. He doesn't stay with anyone for very long, but he isn't working the room, either.

He isn't looking for a girl to hook up with. Most of the guys who didn't come with a date are all trying to hit on someone, and when they fail, they move on to their next target.

This guy talks to other guys at least as much as women. He laughs and smiles a lot, but it's obvious that his unusual appearance sets him apart from everyone else and they can't help but notice.

A few people actively shun him like they really think he might be dangerous. They probably think he's in the wrong club or maybe the wrong part of town, but I can't believe that.

He's too self-possessed, and when they ignore him or end the conversation, he doesn't seem too concerned about it.

In a little while, he migrates off into the crowd and I lose sight of him. Oh, well. He's the least of my worries. I take one more swig of my drink and glance over my shoulder.

Ivy and her stud are dancing way too close on the dance floor. Emilia is getting closer to hers against the wall. Neither of them will notice me making my escape.

I polish off my drink, bend down to pick up my handbag, and nearly give myself a concussion against a solid wall of muscle sliding into the stool next to me.

I rear back in surprise and my eyes fall out of my sockets when I see the motorcycle gangster from earlier sitting down right next to me.

Read more for free on Kindle unlimited:

https://www.amazon.com/dp/B0C5B52Y7G

Visit my Author page on Amazon for more books with great stories,

https://www.amazon.com/author/oliviamack

Printed in Great Britain
by Amazon